This book should be returned to any Lancashire
County Council Library on or before the date shown

Lancashire County Council Library Service,
County Hall Complex,
2nd floor Christ Church Precinct,
Preston, PR1 0LD

www.lancashire.gov.uk/libraries

D1343666

Natalie Daniels is the pseudonym for screenwriter, author and actress Clara Salaman who you may recognise as DS Claire Stanton from The Bill. She lives in London and in Northern Spain.

TOO CLOSE

NATALIE DANIELS

CORGI BOOKS

TRANSWORLD PUBLISHERS
Penguin Random House, One Embassy Gardens,
8 Viaduct Gardens, London SW11 7BW
www.penguin.co.uk

Transworld is part of the Penguin Random House group of companies
whose addresses can be found at global.penguinrandomhouse.com

First published in Great Britain in 2018 by Transworld Digital
an imprint of Transworld Publishers
Corgi edition published 2019
Corgi edition reissued 2021

A CIP catalogue record for this book
is available from the British Library.

ISBN
9780552178624

Typeset in 12/14 pt Dante MT Std by Jouve (UK), Milton Keynes
Printed and bound in Italy by Grafica Veneta S.p.A.

The authorized representative in the EEA is Penguin Random House Ireland,
Morrison Chambers, 32 Nassau Street, Dublin D02 YH68.

Penguin Random House is committed to a sustainable
future for our business, our readers and our planet. This book
is made from Forest Stewardship Council® certified paper.

For Chus, with all my love

Who can stop grief's avalanche once it starts to roll?

Euripides, *Medea*

It's odd because everyone always calls her beautiful. Her beauty has become a fact; it has been said enough times for any doubt to have been forgotten. But the first time I saw her in the park all those years ago, I have to say she didn't strike me that way; her beauty took a while to floor me. She was small with wispy blonde hair and pale blue veins that ran down her temples. She had dark bags under her dark eyes – which I know is just called parenting – and from a certain angle her freckled nose looked like someone had given her a good punch. She had a peculiar way of looking at you from the corners of those big dark brown eyes. And she blinked too much. All in all, she struck me as an anxious sort of person. No, I wouldn't have called her beautiful at all. Not then.

I'd been late picking Annie up from nursery and had found my daughter sitting alone on the bench under-neath the empty coat hooks, holding a wooden lollipop stick with a scrunched-up piece of red tissue bodged on to the end.

'Darling, sorry I'm late,' I said sitting down next to her, glad to get my breath back. 'What have you made?' I asked, looking at the lolly stick in her hand. Karl was bet-ter at this sort of thing than me; every shite offering they brought home from school he marvelled at as if the kids were little Leonardos. Left to his own devices, the house would look like one of those hoarder's places you see on TV, full of clay rubbish and splodges of paint on crinkled paper.

'It's a poppy.'

Of course it was. Remembrance Day was coming up and Annie's nursery never missed a chance to get creative. 'That's lovely! Do you know why you've made it? Who is it for?' I might be late, forget carol concerts and barbecue days, but my God, I do a bit of educating when I can.

She looked up at me and passed me the lolly stick. 'For you?'

'No,' I said, 'I mean, *why* have you made it? Who is it *for*?'

'It's for *remembering*,' she said.

'That's right.' She was a genius, my child. 'Remembering who?'

She had no idea. She shook her head, her cherubic curls bouncing this way and that. Not for the first time I marvelled that such a sweet being came from me.

'It's for all the soldiers who died in the *war*,' I said, sounding incongruously cheerful about it. She looked up at me, eyes wide with wonder, lips opening in surprise as the mini cogs in her brain whirred. She frowned and turned slowly to examine the wall behind her, reaching out her little fingers to gingerly touch the bumps of roughly applied plaster beneath the clothes pegs.

'In *this* wall?' she asked.

Sometimes she was so adorable I could eat her. 'Let's get some sweeties and go to the park!' I said.

So Annie had scooted ahead, cheeks full of Smarties. She was a kamikaze kind of child. By the time I caught up she was at the top of the slide, bottom lip out, face brimming with misery, staring down at the brightly coloured trail of Smarties bouncing off the ladder and on to the spongy tarmac. Another little girl was standing at the bottom of the ladder picking up the Smarties and popping them into her mouth as fast as she could.

'No! No! No!' Annie cried, furious at the nasty little opportunist below her.

The mother was oblivious to the scene; she was busy making something on the bench with an older girl. I started picking up the Smarties and was shortly joined by the mother, who was looking down at her fat-cheeked child and making the right remonstrating noises. *'Naughty*, Polly. They are *not* yours.'

I'll tell you something peculiar: I remember there was something about her voice that put me on alert; it wasn't her tone, which was low and calm, or what she said, which was nothing unusual. It was a more intangible feeling: there was something about it that I found deeply comforting yet deeply disturbing at the same time. Church bells do that for me too. I'm not making any sense, am I?

For many years, I would remember that day as a fine example of how we must *not* trust our first impressions, how foxing they are. Because the truth was, just at the very beginning of it all, I felt an inexplicable and powerful aversion to her, like a tug from the wings, as if I were receiving a warning signal from the great puppet master.

We made polite child-soothing conversation for a while and were then forced to sit together on the bench as the three girls struck up an immediate kinship and went off to look for snails, dropping their grievances with that enviable childhood ease.

'Do you live nearby?' I asked.

'Just beyond the swimming pool,' she said, nodding vaguely in the direction. 'We've just moved in.'

'Oh! Which street?'

'Buxton Road.'

'Really? Which end?'

And so we discovered that we were neighbours. She lived just around the corner from us – only four doors away. In fact, I could see her house from the back windows of my own. Our conversation shifted then, as it became evident our lives would be impacting on each other's – screaming children, rows in the garden, perhaps noisy once-in-a-blue-moon lovemaking on a hot summer night. Why do we women feel impelled to forge intimacies? Two men probably wouldn't have struck up a conversation at all.

I'd opened Annie's snack box by now and was picking at some soggy strawberries as our talk moved smoothly from our surroundings and our progeny to ourselves.

'What do you do?' she asked me.

'I write,' I said.

And without a pause or a further question she said, 'I write too!' Something about the way she said it, so rapid a response, seemed rather competitive – I got that tug again.

'What do you write?' I asked, offering her a sweating strawberry which she declined.

'Poetry.' I looked at her afresh. That was interesting;

4

no one *admits* to writing poetry. 'When inspiration strikes,' she added.

Well, excuse me for being a snob but that is *not* a writer. That is a *dabbler*. A writer doesn't have the luxury of waiting for inspiration; a writer plods on regardless, a writer takes the gamble, lives in penury, gives everything up to be a slave to her art. I didn't let my feelings show, but I suppose in my own way I went straight for the jugular.

'Do you make a living from it?'

'No, no.'

Precisely my point: she was *not* a writer. (We writers have to do any writing we *can* to fund the writing we *want* – I ghost-write, I interview, I copy-edit, in order to afford the time to write books that no one wants to publish.)

'I'm—Or rather, I *used* to run galleries. You've got some . . .' She gestured that I had some strawberry juice on my chin. I wiped it. She shook her head and gestured again so I wiped it again.

And then – perhaps you'll disagree, perhaps you'll think this is what any mother does – she did something that seemed strangely intimate to me: she licked her finger and gently started to rub my chin with it. And as she did so – it was a stubborn stain – I couldn't help but take her in: the freckles, the contrast of the blonde hair with those dark eyes. I was just going to ask her about this gallery business when she said, 'You smell really good. What perfume are you wearing?'

Again, oddly intimate, no? But I'm a sucker for a compliment and I must have visibly brightened.

'Thank you! It's Jo Malone: Lime Basil and Mandarin.'

She smiled. She had good teeth, neat and white, like an advert mouth. 'It's gorgeous.'

I thought so too but it was very nice to have it pointed out. Looking back, it was probably the compliments that blinkered me to those palpable warning signs. How pathetic is that?

'What does your partner do?' she asked me.

'He's a consultant in communications,' I said, which never fails to shut people up. 'What about your husband?' I asked, after the pause.

'Wife, actually. She works in TV.'

Well, that shut *me* up. She was a lesbian. How refreshing. This neighbourhood needed a bit of diversity wherever it could find it; the school had got whiter and blonder with each passing year, the parents more homogeneous – a growing number of men in salmon cords with hearty laughs and women with salon-shiny hair being walked by dogs that didn't moult. I immediately wanted to ask her about the girls: who was the biological mother? Who was the father? What do they call you? All those obvious questions that no one likes to ask but everyone wants to know. Then all the unobvious questions I wanted to ask, like how she *knew* she was gay. I was intrigued. I'd always been straight as a die. The idea of making love to a woman had never held any allure for me. I *loved* men. I loved their bodies, I loved their differences, I loved their masculinity. But I didn't ask her anything, of course; I tried to give the impression of being cool.

'I like your hair . . . your fringe,' she said. 'You'll have to tell me where a good hairdresser's is around here . . .

I don't know the area at all.' She was patting her wispy locks, looking at me in that sideways way. I have to say, I'd only just had my hair cut and was feeling rather self-conscious about it. Potentially I looked a bit 1974 – and not in a good way. The hairdresser had been somewhat gung-ho and on leaving the salon, I'd caught a glimpse of myself from the side with what looked like a well-groomed guinea pig perching on my forehead.

'Sure! There's a good place up by the library,' I said, leaning over to get a better view of Annie, who was roaming about in a way that made me suspicious – she had been known to squat down for a crap in the bushes. She's too feral, that child of mine.

'I'm Ness, by the way!' she said, holding out her hand.

'I'm Connie,' I replied, shaking hers.

And so the bond was made.

This all seems a very long time ago now. Six long years ago; like a different lifetime, back in the days when I would pass homeless people in the street curled up in urine-drenched corners and carelessly think *how on earth did your life go so wrong?* Well, now I know. The answer is: quite easily, as it turns out. You'd think it might be a slow process of deterioration but the truth is it can turn in a moment, maybe even on a stranger's whim – with a neighbour accepting an offer on a house in Buxton Road, for example.

Chapter 1

I am looking out of the window at the naked, groaning tree and am taken by surprise, once again, by the state I find myself in. It is as if I have been misplaced; I've no idea where I've gone. Even my body is unrecognizable; I have deep open wounds on my left wrist beneath the creamy bandages. Every now and then they wink up at me, a wet pinky-red. My right arm, torso and right thigh are an angry bumpy mass of redness, scabbed in places; my thigh is vermilion-raw in the shape of a huge pear, my shin shiny and taut, my foot itchy and peeling. And yet these walls are becoming familiar. I know it is eleven o'clock because I can hear the Squeak coming down the corridor; I am in the last room. She's very punctual. I don't think I've been here very long but I might be wrong. Perhaps a week or so but there is little variety to the days so it's hard to tell. This place is even worse than the other place; here they have bars on the windows. The Squeak is under the impression that I do nothing in the mornings. She is wrong. It is a blustery day out there; a day when the weather can't focus, keeps changing its mind. My attention, however, is acutely focused. In the mornings, I study this one particular leaf. I have done ever since I got here. It sits right at the top of the tree, which is in my sightline. The gardens slope downwards towards a stream, so I'm told. I say a stream – it's probably more of a litter-filled brook; we are in London after all. This single leaf flutters furiously in the wind; for some reason it is clinging on to life. I have the greatest admiration for its bravado.

Squeak squeak, rattle rattle, here she comes. I can't take my eyes off the leaf. I worry that it is waiting for me to do so before it will let go. Sometimes I find myself worrying so much in the night that I get out of bed and lift the blind to check on it in the orange glow of the streetlight from the other side of the wall.

The Squeak unlocks the door, gives a perfunctory knock and enters regardless. I don't care. There is nothing I would not do in front of her. I listen to her cross the room. Her shoes are sensible, crêpe-soled; she sacrificed style for comfort a long time ago. It is in fact her trolley that squeaks. She stops in front of me and I'm forced to drag my eyes away from my leaf. She is looking particularly unattractive today; her forehead is a mound of bumps and blotches and there is a cold sore at the corner of her downturned lip.

'Morning,' she says cheerlessly, handing me my medication, pouring me water from the institutional plastic jug that must have been transparent once but now is a filmy grey. The water is tepid and tastes of jug. I swallow the pills.

'It hurts to swallow,' I say. I don't even recognize my own voice. I'm all raspy.

'Well, it would, wouldn't it, Connie,' she says. She is standing, I am sitting, and my head comes up to her shoulders. She has dark circles under each armpit on the pale blue of her uniform. I myself am something of a sweater.

'Perspirex. It works. For problem perspiration,' I say. 'You should try it. You can get it in Boots.'

She is immune to pretty much anything I say. Besides, she is half reading her *Daily Mail*, which sits on the trolley. She's not meant to let me see newspapers. 'And why would I take any tips from you, Connie?'

She's such a cow.

'You shouldn't speak to the guests like that,' I say.

'You're not a *guest*,' she says, not unkindly, passing me another two blue pills, her attention still on her paper. She's reading the cover story, which is accompanied by a photograph of a bushy-bearded bomber. Or maybe he's a celebrity. I have to say I'm surprised how the fundamentalist look has really caught on. Since when did it become trendy to blow people up? Now I sound like my mother.

'Is anyone bringing my mother to visit?'

She pauses, looks up from her paper and stares at me. 'When are you going to stop playing dumb?' she says, which obviously reminds her of something because she bends over, her ample thighs stretching her polyester trousers to the max, and produces a flimsy old laptop from the lower shelf of the trolley. 'Dr Robinson wanted me to give you this – she wants you to write it all down,' she says, sighing with disapproval. She puts it on the little table beside me. 'It's fully charged.'

I look at the laptop and wonder if I can get online.

'You can't get online,' she says. She likes to remove breaths of wind from scraps of sails.

'No donkey porn then.' I notice that I am feeling in quite good spirits today.

The Squeak bares her teeth at me. She's not smiling; it's more of a snarl. Not for the first time I notice that she has rather pleasing teeth. They go slightly inwards, like a shark's. Then I remember that I'm in her bad books.

Yesterday, or was it another day, Mental Sita and I were watching telly in the telly room. The telly room contains nothing but a telly, which is screwed into the wall, a sofa and a plastic chair, both of which are screwed to the floor. Mental Sita is in love with that blond doctor on the reruns of *Embarrassing Bodies*. She's obsessed with him. She wants to be in an enclosed white space with him in some city centre, suggestively sharing her psoriasis. We both love that show. No one can be uncheered by other people's embarrassments. It is a winning formula.

That particular episode involved Blond Doc rummaging around Sharon-from-Hartlepool's folds of flesh in an elusive search for some vaginal warts. Sharon herself could barely reach her own nether region, let alone see it. Mental Sita and I, however, got an eyeful. And found it mesmerizing for different reasons. Sharon was a hirsute lady, a natural blonde. To me, her vagina resembled some sort of small sleeping creature, a dormouse perhaps, snugly curled up in the cranny of a haystack. Yet there was also something so neglected and lonesome about it that it made me feel a little sad. Not Mental Sita; she was sprawled out on the blue sofa, idly masturbating at the sight of the Doc near a vagina of any sort. I was perched on the plastic chair. I'd been desperate to pee since Sharon had weighed down the trailer, but I was so engrossed by what lay between those head-crushing thighs and Blond Doc's capable plunging hands, and somewhat lulled into a stupor by Mental Sita's rhythmic fingers working away, that I was unable to rise from my seat. In fact, I took a leaf out of Mental Sita's rule-less book – and realized that I no longer *had* to get up and go to the toilet; I no longer *had* to behave in any particular way at all. It felt so profoundly relaxing – I try to grab hold of positives wherever I can (my mother is a great advocate of this kind of thinking and I've tried to instil that in my own children) – that there on the plastic chair, I let those pelvic floor muscles go.

It sent me right back to childhood, to fond memories of bedwetting. It struck me then how much I have missed all those things you have to give up as a child: tantrums and bodily laxness, to name but a few. Perhaps it was time to reclaim them. The wonderful thing about losing everything, about having nothing left to dread, is that once your fear and reality have merged, there is only liberation; once that wardrobe of convention has been taken off your back, the relief is momentous. However, it was then that the Squeak had walked into the room to find two apparently unconnected events taking place: urine dripping from my chair and Mental Sita with her pants down. Mental Sita is truly mental; the Squeak barely gave her a glance. Me, she isn't so convinced about. She thinks I'm a fake. The others are nervous around me. They think I am a danger, that I am something to be monitored. Except possibly the policeman who arrested me. I heard him talking to a colleague while I was put in the cell. He could always *tell them apart,* he said. *The guilty ones, relieved at last of the burden of their own crimes, settle down and sleep like babies.*

I didn't sleep a wink.

The Squeak hands me the last of my pills. It really is agony to swallow them.

'My mother will be very worried about me. Is someone going to bring her to visit?'

She closes her paper and folds it up. 'I don't know anything about your mother,' she says, sounding bored.

'I don't remember when she said she'd come . . .'

'There's quite a lot you'd think you would remember,' she says, tapping the laptop with one hand and reaching for her trolley with the other.

The staff can be very rude here. But I don't get upset by it. And she does have a point: I don't quite remember how my wrist got so cut up but I presume *I* must have done it; it would seem most unlikely to get randomly stabbed in vertical stripes.

I go back to the leaf. The wind has dropped and it has ceased to tremble. I think about the old me. Sometimes I'm amused by her. When I think of the energy I used to expend getting hurt or offended. All those years I spent running the rat race, chasing my ratty tail, following the rat rules, being the right kind of mother, wife, daughter, breadwinner, keeping my home the right way, wearing the right clothes, holding the right opinions, drinking the right wine, eating the right food, bearing the right cynicism. For what? It all seems so utterly pointless. Is that what Dr Robinson wants me to write about? The darkness? Those nights I would wake up in a panic, my heart beating so fast, that ache in my body, like I was breaking?

I don't want to think of the pain. I am safe now. That was the old me, who felt too much.

Now I am free.

I glance down at the computer. It's an old Dell with no plug – in case I try to prong myself to death, I suppose. I can't remember when I last wrote anything.

'What am I meant to write?' I ask. The Squeak wipes a little spilt water off the tray and puts the serviette in her pocket. Before she goes she leans forward and looks me in the eye.

'Why don't you just do everyone a favour and write down what fucking happened?'

She's kind of impressive. She's straight to the point. I go back to watching my brave little leaf while she and her fat arse leave the room.

I won't let her upset me. I get up and go to the bathroom. It's not *that* great pissing your pants, to be honest. I use the loo and wash my unfamiliar hands in the mini basin. There's a sheet of shiny metal above the sink and I see myself again. Thank God it's blurry but I can tell I've had better days; I'm not looking my best. My hair is no longer lovely. It grows in strange red clumps like patches of coarse grass, my scalp visible. What the hell happened? I pat my head. I resemble a much-loved, worn-out child's soft toy, although I feel no love, only exhaustion. I peer closer. My eyes are bloodshot, the whites all red. My face is covered in broken veins, my neck a myriad of colours: purples and reds, greens and yellows. I bring my hand up to my throat to check I'm not wearing some kind of ghastly autumnal scarf my mother might have given me. But this is no place for the fashion-conscious. I rub soap over the sheet of metal until I start disappearing.

*

I hear Dr Robinson from a way off. She wears the shoes of a tap dancer. I haven't made up my mind about her yet. I have only seen her once. Dr Twat introduced her to me in an awed silence so I presume she must be a high-flyer in the world of Quackdom. I am not sure how much I like the idea of being *forensically examined*. That's her title: Forensic Psychiatrist, which sounds frightfully swanky – though she most definitely is not. In fact, there's something rather invisible about her. Dr Robinson has a soothing, knowing, professional voice that she has probably spent years perfecting; it's all a bit too perfect. She is spruce and clean-looking; her clothes are expensive but deathly dull, unlikely to attract attention of any sort. Only her shoes have an attitude; they let you know she's coming. Today, as she walks into the room, I notice a bit of bird shit or porridge on her right toe tip.

She is here *to help me*, so she said last time, *to get to the root of it all*. I did some forensic examining of my own and caught sight of her travel pass: she lives in north London where the rumour is that there are more therapists than nutjobs. So, really, if you look at it, I'm the one doing *her* a frigging favour with her slatted blinds and her kitchen island and her Pouilly-Fumé cooling in the fridge.

She smiles at me. Not a real smile, a professional smile. She has trained herself to enjoy eye contact. She thinks she's good at it, but no one can out-loony a loony. Besides, I have all the time in the world.

Everything about Dr Robinson is both intense and measured. She is a serious person. Nothing tumbles out by surprise. I appreciate that, having once been a tumbler myself. She has dark, glossy hair cut in a longish bob that slips out from behind her ear; the gesture with which she tries to correct this has become punctuation for her methodical thinking. *I see.* Hair back in place. *And what do you think* – hair back in place – *she meant by that?* Hair back in place.

As she takes off her jacket at that leisurely pace of hers, I get a waft of menthol cigarette, or it could be a mint trying to cover the smell of a normal cigarette.

It's a weakness, smoking.

I'd rather my forensic psychiatrist didn't have such obvious weaknesses.

I watch as she hangs her jacket over the back of the chair, which she then carefully pulls out from the table, before quietly sitting down in it and putting her hair back in place. Her phone beeps from the breast pocket of the jacket. She looks annoyed, slides it out of the pocket, bends over and glances at the screen. I can read it from where I am sitting because the text size is set to large. Yes, she's late forties, like me. It's a good age; our eyes might be fading but our powers are peaking. It's a WhatsApp message from *Si Hubby*. Another flicker of irritation crosses her face as she reads the message, which she's angled away from me now so I can't read it. She turns the phone off and looks back at me with that stretched professional smile.

'Sorry about that,' she says, not sounding sorry at all, putting her bag down on the floor. Dr Robinson very much lives in the land of rules and etiquette and she likes to pretend that I am with her there. She is very particular; she is not satisfied with the position of her bag and moves it to the other side of her chair. Then she gives me her full attention, cocking her head at that particular angle, a slightly alarmed expression on her face, as if she can hear the howl of a wolf some distance off. Her eyes bore into me. I fascinate her. I am like Sharon's vagina: captivating but repulsive.

'Right, Connie. Good to see you again. How are you settling in here at Tatchwell?'

I don't like this attitude of hers. So bloody superior. Well, two can play that game. I slowly pick a hair off my tracksuit bottoms.

'You remember what we were going to discuss today?' she says. 'We were going to talk about Ness . . .'

I yawn. I'm looking at the unostentatious ring around her wedding finger, next to the gold band. Everything she says is a question, which is rather draining. She is constantly trying to catch me out. Today I am going to try and answer all her questions with questions.

'Ness?'

'Yes. Vanessa Jones.'

'Is she coming to visit me?' I ask.

She pauses and shakes her head. 'No, Connie. She is not.'

I am momentarily hurt by this news. And Dr Robinson sees this; I see a little spark in her eye. Inside her head a crowd of idiots are whooping.

'And why do you think Ness won't be coming to visit

you?' she says, stretching the inch I accidentally gave her into a mile. She gives me the long stare and then takes a deep, changing-the-angle breath and puts her rebellious silky hair back in place. 'I thought we could start at the beginning,' she continues, as if the idea is stunningly original.

'I'd like one of your cigarettes.' I don't smoke, but it's nice to have things in here. I've started to collect bits and pieces where I can.

'You can't smoke in here.'

I stare at her. She's so wrapped up in what she's supposed to do, she could become tedious. She leans back decisively and stands up. She stretches and winces a little. She wanders over to the window, her back to me, to show me how she isn't intimidated by me, how we could just be friends having a catch-up. She stands there looking out. I don't want her to notice my brave little leaf manically waving at her; I feel rather possessive of it. She wanders slowly down the stretch of the unbreakable windowpane. I watch her. I like her body: it is strong and solid, fit, a body ready for hard physical labour, broad but languid – an unusual combination. She tries to open the window but it is locked, of course. Anything and everything in this place that can be opened is always locked: cupboards, windows, doors, minds. It is rather sweet that she seems annoyed. She tries a different window. Maybe she fancies herself as a bit of a maverick, an opener of windows.

Slowly she walks back across the room and sits down again. 'Are you going to use that computer we brought you?' she asks.

'I'd have preferred a MacBook Air,' I say.

She smiles. For the first time I think that if it wasn't for a hundred different things, I might quite like her.

'You're a writer – don't you miss writing?'

I'm free of all that crap in here.

'Sometimes we find that writing things down works as a memory trigger. It can unblock the amnesia.'

She really hasn't got it.

'You could try. See what you recall . . .'

'How old are your kids?' I ask.

She crosses her legs and smooths her skirt. 'Am I right in thinking this all started six years ago?'

'And you and Si Hubby, how long have you known each other?' I ask.

I'm starting to annoy her. 'This isn't about me, Connie.'

'But one-sided relationships are not conducive to inti-macies.' I smile at her. It's a genuine smile. I'm having fun. 'Go on,' I say. 'Where did you and Si Hubby meet?'

She squints her blue eyes, angles her head and listens to the howl of that wolf. This is a serious pose. She can come over a little headmistressy; she ought to be careful about that.

'You know, Connie, we all have to accept responsibil-ity for our choices and for our actions.' She seems impressed by her own profundity. 'You are not going to be able to use avoidance tactics for ever.'

I think about this while she changes her focus and looks out of the window. I think she's spotted my leaf. She turns to me decisively. 'I am here to help you,' she says. 'We can go about it any way you wish, Connie, we can take different roles if that is more helpful . . . ?' She lets that idea float about for a bit. I hope she can read my expression: she can ram her drama games where the sun don't shine. Talking of which, the sun has stopped shining and the room seems suddenly dark. She is still staring at me. She's got flecks of brown in those hard blue eyes.

'Would you say your life's pretty good?' I ask her, folding my arms, cocking my head, listening out for her wolf. 'You've got this interesting job, you must make decent money. You've got lovely Si Hubby . . . He's such a good loyal husband, isn't he? Maybe he's put the kids to bed by the time you get back tonight after your hard day of being so *helpful*. You get home, chat in the kitchen, open a bottle of wine, move through to the sitting room, maybe have dinner in front of a few episodes of the latest Scandi TV drama. Then eventually you'll go up to bed.

'Ah, here's the rub,' I add, sotto voce for maximum effect. 'It might turn out to be *that* night, the one you've been subtly avoiding: the once-a-month duty fuck. Or perhaps you can continue to avoid it, stall a bit, or go up before him and feign sleep. Don't get me wrong – you're a good wife, you love him and all that, and you know that sex is important in a relationship, blah blah blah, all the magazines tell you that; in fact *you* probably tell people that, troublemaker that you are. But still, you'll eke out your time in the bathroom in case, you know, he tries something on. You're *so* tired, you see, saving all these people, such exhausting work. And besides, sex is such an effort. But how long can you realistically avoid it when it's all part of the deal, the unspoken contract of a couple?

'You get into bed, hoping he won't . . . but, oh, he does, he makes a slight advance, just a touch, more of a nervous hand reaching out, nothing more, but you know where it's going, what he wants, although even he has almost given up these days. *Yes. Tonight is the night I really ought to make the effort*, you say to yourself. So you roll over to signify that he may continue and you let him do it. And it's not nearly so bad once you get started. *I should do this more often*, you think as you feel him inside you; it's even quite pleasurable (although you're ready for it to be over pretty soon) . . .'

I pause. She is staring at me; her facial muscles seem to have gone a little lax. I lean in a touch, whispering in my strange new rasping voice that I'm beginning to rather enjoy. 'But *fucking* is easy, isn't it, Doc? It's *kissing* that you can't fake; kissing is the real intimacy. It's kissing that's unbearable. When *did* you last kiss Si Hubby? Not a peck on the cheek kind of kiss, no – a real melt-in-the-mouth kiss. Think about it, that mouth of his: the disgusting way it eats, the stupid things it says, the idiotic expressions it pulls . . . that mouth you're stuck with for the next forty years. But you try not to think of it like that because . . . well, a lifetime without passion?'

I sit back and look into those steadfast unblinking eyes. Then I start to laugh – really laugh. She's not quite as cocky as she was half an hour ago. 'I think all of us use avoidance tactics, don't you, Dr Robinson?'

Chapter 2

Emma sat on the bus. It was a horrible evening. The clocks had fallen back an hour and winter had arrived like a smack in the face. She wiped a clear smear in the condensation of the window so that she could see out on to the slippery streets of Wood Green beyond, the lights of consumerism reflected on the glistening pavements, the uniform, disgruntled people piling out of the tube station with such purpose, an army of wet misery marching onwards in this hour when people rush. The bus stank of damp bodies and fusty clothes, like a charity shop. The rain had magnified the senses and Emma was bombarded by sounds: tyres through puddles, footsteps, engines, voices, tinny thumping headphone noise.

She tried to go back to her book, *Hotel du Lac*. She was only reading it because it had been on her shelf for years and she couldn't bring herself to throw away an unread book; it didn't seem right. Besides, it was short and light and fitted in her bag. But it was a futile exercise. She couldn't concentrate. She felt tired and irritable, her mind an endless tangle of disquiet. She hadn't practised meditation or yoga for months now. Always the same: as soon as she re-established her own calm, found a little peace, she forgot to continue with it. And her mind would crowd itself again. She really *should* try to prioritize it.

More people piled on board: city folk, inner-city folk, last of the schoolkids, a bus full of all colours and creeds, everyone equally tired and wet. Her eye was caught by a woman in a burka carrying two heavy bags full of shopping. The truth was that Emma found burkas scary. She stared at her, this formless shadow like death without the scythe; she had no idea whether the woman was staring back because her eyes were not visible. To Emma, who was feeling irked by everything today, she was a walking symbol of female oppression, a woman who had been both blinded and made invisible by men. It made her angry; *we, as women, have worked very hard in this country to be heard and seen.*

Immediately she felt guilty and shifted apologetically to make room for the woman, but the actual room she was making was nothing; she was merely demonstrating that she was a good person and that she wasn't Islamophobic. Or *was* she Islamophobic? No, misogyny was the problem and that was a cultural problem, not a religious one.

The woman sat down and put the bags between her legs, her thigh rubbing against Emma's. Emma instinctively responded in the trusty British way: 'Sorry,' she said, and shifted again. But instead of politely retreating, the woman's thigh quickly took up the new space Emma had provided. Emma felt annoyed then guilty again, hoping that the woman didn't think she'd moved her thigh away because she was a racist. The bus lurched forwards and the driver beeped. She was longing to get home, to get this day over and done with. Like a magic trick, the woman then produced a phone from within the folds of her garment. Emma watched the scrolling screen from the corners of her eyes; the woman's fingernails had little pictures of moons and stars on them. They stopped at the name *Mo*. The woman held the phone to her ear, which was almost equidistant from Emma's own ear, and Emma found herself waiting expectantly for Mo to pick up.

The woman's voice was loud and harsh. She spoke an unidentifiable language from which only one thing was for certain: she was not remotely oppressed. Emma listened in wonder and slight envy of this woman's confidence and unselfconsciousness, how little she cared about the impression she was making on her fellow travellers, what freedom she felt to be herself. The irony was not lost on her. She listened to Mo's tinny protests. She wondered vaguely where they were from, whether they were refugees or immigrants. She had felt ashamed to be British recently. She pretended to look around the bus, letting what she hoped was a friendly smile rest on her lips, itself an apology to the woman, an attempt to signify that she personally welcomed immigrants and refugees, all people in plight. But the woman took absolutely no notice of Emma at all. Perhaps she despised this country with its shameful binge-drinking city centres, its Magaluf youth, its lack of morals, its greedy landlords; its petty, vain concerns while children still drowned in the Mediterranean Sea.

A wave of sadness washed over her.

Emma turned her face away and looked out into the street again.

It had been a deeply unsettling day. Her head ached and she felt claustrophobic with this woman pressed up against her with her harsh language, the dank smells of wet human beings assaulting her nostrils, the roar of the engine beneath her vibrating seat, the heater blowing stinking used air on to her legs, the soles of her shoes sticking to the filthy floor, the man in the seat in front with dandruff speckled on his rain-splattered shoulders – she was repulsed by humanity, and she wanted to climb out of her own body and escape.

Off the bus, she put her brolly up and crossed the road, huddled up like everybody else. The rain had stopped by the time she got to her street and she hurriedly folded her brolly away, feeling faintly foolish for not having noticed sooner. She spotted old Clarence coming down the street towards her. She really hadn't got the energy for a conversation about recycling or the state of Royal Mail so got out her phone and pretended to chat, sternly admonishing an imaginary errant colleague. A black-and-white cat, taking refuge from the weather under a parked car, seemed unconvinced and stared accusingly at her as she passed by.

Once Clarence had passed her with a nod of his head, she was forced to continue the absurd charade all the way to her front door until she could see that he'd rounded the corner. She looked back at the cat guiltily, putting her phone away and shaking her brolly, fumbling for her keys, feeling ashamed of herself. She peered through the white slatted blinds; there was a light on in the sitting room.

'Si?' she called, but the house was quiet. She couldn't

help but feel relieved. Of course, he'd texted earlier – *that* text that had given her away. He was going out with the boys. She took off her coat and hung it up. It slipped off the hook and brought several other coats down with it. She paused as she picked them up, noticing for the first time in a long time the small hole in the wall where once had hung the stair-gate. She promptly hung up the fallen coats and neatly slipped out of her shoes, lining them up with the other pairs against the wall. How small they seemed next to Si's. She glanced at the post: only one interesting-looking envelope, addressed to Dr and Mrs Robinson. The usual gender assumption riled her; she headed down the hall to the kitchen, placing the post on the kitchen island. She opened the fridge door and pulled out an opened bottle of Sancerre. She poured herself an unjustifiably large glass. She opened the sliding doors to the garden and stood there looking out on to the drenched lawn. She patted her pockets for her cigarettes and lit up. She took a deep, yogic breath full of menthol and relief. She knew exactly why she was feeling so ill at ease.

She could resist it no longer. She stubbed out the barely smoked cigarette, closed the door, sat down at the table and turned on her MacBook Air. She was eager to see if Mrs Ibrahim had sent any documents of Connie's.

When Emma saw that she had a new document in her work inbox she felt strangely excited, as if she were opening a love letter. Connie had called the file 'The Beginning of It All'. Emma's heart skipped a beat or two as she nervously clicked on it. She read it fast the first time and carefully the second.

This was progress. She gave herself a metaphorical pat on the back. She was intrigued at this glimpse of the woman before the crime – the mother fresh from the hairdresser who picked her child up late from nursery and took her to the park. She was just the same as any other working mother: distracted but indulgent, doing her best. Emma could only see her as she was right now in that psychiatric wing, sitting in that chair covered in burns, bruises and wounds; her bald head, the fuzzy red clumps, her bloodshot eyes with no whites at all, only pinks and reds; every blood vessel on her face burst open, and those dreadful marks around her neck – purple, black and blue streaked across her throat like some ghastly necklace. Everything she said was delivered in that awful rasping voice like something from a horror movie. The police report said she'd wrapped the seatbelt around her neck, doubly determined in her search for oblivion. And in some way she had succeeded in her mission: was it surprising that she remembered nothing? Or was it the magic of the human brain, protecting her to the last with one sole objective: survival.

Emma went upstairs and began to run a bath; her attention was caught by the remnants of a bottle of Jo Malone bath oil, an old present from Simon's sister a few Christmases ago. She opened it, sniffed it and got a whiff of that other Connie Mortensen with her glossy red hair, nothing to do with that small, fierce figure sitting there in that desolate room with the harsh fluorescent light, staring out of the window.

Emma filled the Jo Malone bottle with water and shook it up and down before pouring it slowly underneath the tap. It smelt so good. She popped it into the bin, catching her body unawares in the mirror, before she had time to kid herself with the tummy-suck. It was depressing. She looked down. Gravity had taken its toll, the snail-slither stretch marks shining in stripes under the overhead light. Mercifully the steam began to obscure her reflection. She turned off the tap. She could hear the rain lashing against the windowpane.

She stepped into the bath and slowly let the water consume her, grateful for such simple pleasures, the fact that she was able to wash away the day, unlike . . . well, unlike many of the people she saw. She hated that place. She always left with a headache. It was too warm; they didn't open any of the windows. She closed her eyes and slowly dropped deeper into the water, leaving just her face exposed, blocking out the rest of the world, letting her body float up to the surface, cross-legged. She took some deep breaths. She *must* start those classes again on Saturday morning; she could really feel her back tensing up. She opened her eyes. She stared at the crack across the ceiling. It was no good; she couldn't escape it. She could still feel those unblinking, bloodshot eyes watching her every move; the way they followed her across the room, taking everything in, assessing her, continually silently commenting. This was ridiculous. *Emma* was the assessor, the commentator, the evaluator. But if Connie wanted to play these games, so be it: Emma would be forced to play them too.

Later, downstairs, soft-skinned and perfumed, Emma ate her Charlie Bigham lasagne slowly and methodically while she knocked back the rest of the Sancerre. She spent the evening looking over various court reports and papers for an upcoming mental health tribunal. Every now and then she'd change the Spotify playlist, alternating between Babybird and Joy Division. When she'd finished, she couldn't help herself. *Just one more time*, she said to herself, and clicked on Connie's document.

'Hi, darling, you're still up?'

Emma jumped. She hadn't even heard the latch. She looked at the clock on her computer. It was nearly midnight. Si was soaking wet and dishevelled.

'Good evening?' she asked, closing her computer, turning her chair. There was something loose and attractive about him like this. He kissed her on the forehead, like one might a child. He reeked of beer.

'Yeah, I'm starving,' he said, putting his bag down and opening the fridge. 'You smell good,' he added, but she could tell he meant nothing by it.

'Who was there? You can have the rest of the lasagne. Put it in the microwave.'

'Usual crowd. Oh, and Adrian brought his new girl-friend along.'

'I thought it was just the boys,' she said. 'What was she like?'

'Really nice girl . . . too nice for him. What have you been up to?'

'Oh, just work. What was her name?'

'Samantha? Something like that. Susanna, maybe.' Emma watched him rooting around in the fridge looking for the lasagne. He ran a hand through his thinning hair. *I am attracted to him*, she thought with some detachment. He used to have a good body but in the last few years his belly had bulged (good Lord, who was *she* to complain?). He was tall though, and still wore his clothes well. Like everyone, she took the positives for granted.

She got up, poured herself a little more wine and settled herself on the kitchen island, slowly swinging her legs. As he moved from the fridge to the microwave, she stuck out her foot and rubbed it up and down his thigh. In their relationship, a gesture like this could not just be what it was; it had to be loaded with meaning. She knew that; she was feeling reckless. He turned to catch her eye.

'Hey!' he said. 'What's all this?'

It was so easy. He moved a step in towards her. She put her hand on his crotch and rubbed his cock a little. He stiffened almost immediately. 'Is it my birthday?' he said.

That annoyed her. She let it slide; she was surprising herself with her own forwardness. He had lost all interest in his supper. She opened her legs a little. This unusual location for proceedings made her feel risqué and adventurous, like someone else. She pushed her breasts against his chest. She had good breasts; everyone had always told her that, even her mother. She was enjoying her own daring and yet, as she took off his jacket and damp shirt for him, she was aware that she was *playing* this role of seductress rather than *being* it. It was all a show, it wasn't *her*. It was almost as if she had an audience and several critics in.

Fortunately, Si needed little encouragement and he took over. He undid his trousers, pulled off her knickers and was trying to get inside her, his hands up under her T-shirt. It hurt a little – she wasn't wet enough – but they both knew what the protocol was: he spat on his fingers to ease things along, then he bent down to take her nipple in his mouth and sucked hard. She let her head fall back and sighed, as was the appropriate response. She was determined to stop judging herself, to stop being part of the audience, and told herself to just *feel* his mouth on her breast. As she did so, somewhere, deep down beneath the veneer of pleasure, a peculiar sorrow had been triggered. She was glad that the position was uncomfortable for him, that his mouth had to move up her body. She should kiss him now, she really *should*, but he was not expecting it and to her relief it was not on his agenda, so they made love intensely in the way they knew how, only this time she was trying to be someone else.

This is good, she thought, hearing her own gasps – she was making all the right noises. *This is spontaneous.* She didn't mind the smell of beer because it created a distance, almost like a third person was present, something 'other' than just the two of them. It was less exposing. *But I ought to kiss him.* Bravely, her lips sought out his. The thinness of his lips was something she had never got used to; their tongues met and explored but it felt cold and wrong – reptilian. Instead, she tried to concentrate on him inside her and managed to discreetly pull her lips away from his, burying her face in the safety of his neck as they moved together to the rhythm. She looked past his shoulder out into the garden beyond while the rain gusted against the windowpane. She cried out, partly because he was deep inside her now, and partly because it felt like the right thing to do. She was almost convinced by her own performance, but not entirely. And the audience wasn't either. She could feel them shifting in their seats, a few low titters and then, quite distinctly, someone began to laugh. She recognized that laugh. Yes, Connie Mortensen was laughing her head off.

Emma wanted the sex over with now, she'd had enough. She wanted it all finished and to be in bed reading *Hotel du Lac*. But she and Si were always courteous with each other in that way; she knew he was going to wait for her to come. She'd better get on with it. She leant back, pushing him away a little so that she could slip her hand down between them and attempt to speed things along a bit on her own behalf. But it wasn't working; her orgasm was proving elusive. Faster and faster she went, for God's sake, *come on*, but now she knew for a fact that she was not going to come. And she certainly didn't want to go through soothing explanations and new efforts so she had to do what was most expedient: her gasps crescendoed, she cried out, she froze, twitched and shuddered appropriately. She had *as good as* come; no observer would know the difference. That was her bit over with. Then, as she knew he would, Si climaxed almost immediately, crying out, pulling that strange expression with his mouth.

It was all done now. The end. She was quite keen to get off the kitchen island but that would be rude; she let his judders draw to a close while holding him close in a suitable fashion until it was permissible to show discomfort. Finito. They needn't do that again for a while. Yes, that was great. They had a good sex life, one that anyone would be jealous of: after fifteen years they were still indulging in impulsive lovemaking on the kitchen island. Si and she were *good*.

However, in the sticky aftermath of intercourse, in that post-coital black hole, Emma didn't get off the island. She sat there, bottom cheeks glued to the flint worktop, while Si went through to the hall to charge his phone. Everything was quiet; it was barely even raining any more, just a few taps on the roof, like feeble applause after a particularly poor production. And there she was, standing on an empty stage, alone, while the last members of the audience filed out with mumbles of disappointment. They could spot a fraud. *Turns out we're all avoiding something, aren't we, Dr Robinson?*

Chapter 3

The Weasel has come to see me. The Weasel is my husband, my *ex*-husband. His given name is Karl. This is his second visit and, so far, it has been just like his first. He has been standing very still by the window, silently weeping. He's always been a cry-baby so it's not as bad as it sounds. Today he looks old and sad. He smells nice though. He's always smelt nice. He lets me hold him and smell him for a bit, although I know that he is uncomfortable and is exchanging looks with the Squeak behind my back. The Squeak is such a phoney. She behaves very differently in front of civvies. She's all shark teeth and consideration. She brings him a cup of tea and his reaction is so over-the-top grateful you'd have thought she'd wrapped those gnashers around his overused member.

'Tell Mental Sita I'll see her at six!' I say, dismissing her like a waitress. I can be a knob but she deserves it.

'Don't call her that, Connie,' she says. It's for the Weasel's benefit. She doesn't give a toss about Mental Sita.

She gives me a look and leaves the room and I turn my chair to face the Weasel. He says nothing, takes a sip of the tea. He's looking out at the tree, but not at my leaf, even though it's having an epileptic fit to get his attention.

'How's my mum?' I ask. His lips are at the edge of his cup; I notice a tiny pause before he takes another sip.

He ignores me. He barely said a single word last visit. I observe him. He is incredibly tall and has a fine lean body like a long-distance runner. He is fit, black-haired and easy on the eye. But his skin is deathly pale and mottled, like some oddity a trawler might drag up from the deep.

'What about Josh?' I ask. 'Is he going to come and see me? I miss the kids.'

He holds the cup in its saucer and squares up to the window like he's going to have a fight with it and *tea* it to death or something. Then he turns around and looks at me. It's me he wants to kill.

'Josh doesn't want to see you.'

I am taken aback every time I hear this. But I try not to let it show. 'And Annie?' I ask, a little desperation in my voice.

The Weasel is staring at me. His eyes are very blue and winter cold. 'Annie?' he says. He is about to say something else but stops himself. He is looking at my neck, at my throat. He shakes his head at me, or at himself, I can't tell.

'Right,' I say, not wanting to upset him. He can be very volatile. I am the adult where the children are concerned, obviously. And I must behave like the adult and take their anger on the chin. I know I've been an embarrassment to them. It's the most horrible thing in the world hearing how your own kids hate you; it's like trying to digest razor blades.

'I don't know if I'm going to come again either,' he

says. I am very surprised to hear him say this. Despite everything, he is fiercely loyal. I worry that something is seriously wrong, something that he isn't telling me. I get up and cross the room to join him. His eyes flick from my hair to my throat to my eyes. He looks *at* my eyes, not *in* them.

I stop just in front of him. He's welled up. 'Why?' he says. His voice is so weak, his energy so drained, I feel for him, although I am deeply bored by the crying. He has never understood how his own self-pity shrivels mine. I don't really know what to do, how to help him, but I make an effort. I put my arms around him. He flinches a little, and then slumps a touch. He lets me hold him. He really does smell good.

'I wish I'd never met you,' he says. 'I wish I'd never laid eyes on you.'

I'm aware that this doesn't sound romantic but in its own way, it is. He is telling me how *entirely* we know each other. You only ever get to really know your partner when you're splitting up from them. Rage is good; it's necessary for the wrenching apart and there can be no separation without blood spilt, without pain – we both know this. Only then do you see the person in their entirety. Desperation, fear: they make us strange and ugly. We have seen each other's ugliness but look! He is still here with me! You know, if you're even remotely kind, you can end up right back where you started: liking this person a lot.

Karl is a kind man. Despite everything, he is a good man. I hold his hand and squeeze his fingers.

'I brought you some things,' he says eventually,

unlinking his fingers from mine, getting busy, rifling through a paper bag. He pulls out a Twix and a pile of books and some crap magazines. He always buys me crap magazines. I have never been a reader of them but he has always bought them for me. It used to be a joke and then it became a habit. There are no jokes now.

I can tell he wants to go and I feel strangely low. That's the other thing that happens after you and your partner split up – it's hard to remember quite where you are in your relationship, which rules you are living by. Then I remember that I have no rules any more. Only it doesn't feel quite as liberating as it did earlier.

'When am I coming home?' I ask him weakly. I really do flit. He stops arranging the pile and pointedly scrunches up the paper bag with unnecessary force. (Although technically, *I'm* the one who should be scrunching up paper with unspoken anger, not *him*, but there you go.)

'Home?' he says. 'There *is* no home.'

He's prone to melodrama. He can't just have a headache or wind; he has to have a brain tumour or stomach cancer. I take a step towards him and he moves away from me, his hands held out as if I am going to attack. I am not a violent person. I see how much of a stranger I am to him; he can't even look at me. The sadness tugs at me; I wonder where all our love went. It must be somewhere – in the bits-and-bobs drawer to the right of the sink, perhaps. One day someone is going to open that drawer and say, *Oh! Look what I've found! A whole load of love!*

As he gets to the door he turns around. He looks about a hundred and two, a weary old coelacanth. 'Get a fucking *grip*, Connie,' he says.

I stand there after he's gone and feel his anger whirling around me, but it doesn't get through me. I try to let it permeate me, touch me, but no. Nothing gets through me. I am quite numb.

I wander over to the pile of books and magazines he's brought. I flick through them and sit down. I separate the books from the magazines. I recognize the cover of one of the exercise books. It is Annie's diary. On the cover it says *Annie Mortensen, aged 9 and a halve. Private. Keep Out.* She'd be furious if she knew he'd brought me her diary.

I remember her first diary; I gave it to her for her seventh birthday present. She was sitting at the table, still in Josh's camouflage dressing gown when she opened it. She wanted to start immediately. She wrote down: *Got up washed my face brushed my teeth* and then she looked at me and said, 'Aren't diaries a bit boring?' So we talked about how to make it interesting, so that one day she could look back and actually enjoy reading it. She suggested she could write down some things that were going on in the world. I said that was a great idea. I said she could just write down moments, maybe 'the best moment of the day' if she liked, rather than what she did every minute. From that day she has kept a diary religiously. 'I'm always going to tell the truth,' she said, and I agreed that the truth was vital in a diary. Polly started one as well, of course – Ness bought her it – although they were never ever allowed to look at each other's. Instead they would spend hours reading out agreed random dates – which was crazy really, seeing as they lived in each other's pockets and every moment was spent together anyway; just like their mothers. Annie now keeps her diary in a locked box, so how the Weasel got it I don't know.

I used to be a stickler for privacy. Not any more.

I pick it up and randomly start flicking through it. Various pages are stuck together, sticky sweet-smudged fingers. She has actually stuck in sweet wrappers in case she should ever forget her favourite sweets: Toxic Waste, Millions, Chocolate Oreo, Maoam, Fangtastic. Some of the days have both headings and dates. I smile. Annie has always had a grand sense of occasion. *April 7 How the Ipad really broke. March 1 Alarm Bells.* I glance down the page – she and Polly seem to have gone to a shop on the high street and set all the alarm clocks to go off at once. *March 21 The real reason Josh broke his nose.* She's a good little writer; I feel a familiar swell of pride in my gut.

I take the diary over to the window and sit down, settling myself in for a proper read. I open it randomly on *Feb 1 The lost swimming costume.*

Mum is v v v cross. She says I have no respect for property.

The true story is we were coming back from swimming doing the short cut when Polly says DID you know that EVERYTHING in the universe bounces? I said no it doesnt and she said yes it does (she is such a knowall). I said not elephants. Elephants DONT BOUNCE. She says yes they do. I say not HOUSES. Houses dont bounce. She says yes they do. There is no POINT in argewing with Polly.

We were going past a posh house with railings and some scaffolding up and a pile of bricks in a yellow skip and she leans right over the skip. Anyone can see her knickers. I did not TOUCH the brick. It was only POLLY. Polly climbs TEN FEET high up the scaffolding with a brick and she says to me Watch Annie. Then she throws the brick on the pavement HARD. It smashed into ten billion peaces and one of the bits broke the window.

A man starts shouting and we RUN AWAY as fast as we can and hide in the bushes by the bus stop. Polly is tired. I am not I can run for ages. She says DID YOU SEE THE BRICK? It BOUNCED didnt it JUST BEFORE IT BROKE?? And I think she was right but I didnt say so.

PS the point of the title. When I was running I dropped my swimming costume with blue dots on it and we didnt dare go back for it. I told Mum it was at the pool and she made me phone the pool and listened while I pretended someone had stolen it.

I laugh out loud. Not a sarcastic laugh, a real laugh. I sound like a dog barking. I am grateful to the Weasel for bringing me this. How I miss my naughty little Annie. I'm not allowed a phone in here. If I had one I would call her. Even if she doesn't want to talk to me right now, I would ring her up just to hear her voice. It is husky and always ready with a joke.

Despite the warmth in this place, I feel a little chilly. I pull the blanket off my bed and take it back to the chair and make myself comfortable; I start at the beginning.

Jan 5 Unfortunate events in the swimming pool

Today Polly and me went to the inside pool with diving boards where Josh did a poo when he was a baby (he says he never did but Mum always pulls a face behind his back). The lifegard with the pop belly and the black glasses was there. We played the DEAD game. You can play the dead game anywhere. In Scotland we do it on the sand dunes. Its best with makeup and ketchup. NOT IN THE POOL OBVS. We did scisser paper rock EVEN THOUGH it was my idea and I am a better swimmer but she says she is a better actress. She wins scisser paper rock so she gets to be the one. She swims out into the middle of the pool and I hide by the edge. When she is sure that the lifegard is watching she starts flapping her arms and doing a few spasms like she is having a fit like Phoebe B in netball. She goes on for ages then just did floating with her face down. It was a v good death I must say. The lifegard JUMPS off his chair and DIVES into the water with all his clothes on. His glasses fell off. Polly very dramatic rolls on to her back (she is not as good as me at holding her breath). She has her tongue sticking out and has made her eyes go all boggly overdoing it if you ask me. The lifegard looks really scared which makes me a bit scared. He picks her up and swims to the edge and plops her on the tiles. I must say she looked really dead, all floppy with her mouth hanging open. I did some crying which was sort of real. Then the lifegard turned her face up and HE TRIED TO KISS her on the mouth!!!! She screamed and jumped up like a FLASH. She looked at me and I couldnt help laughing and she started laughing. He started shouting at us. He said we were BANNED for life from the swimming pool which means never aloud back. We bought 2x millions on the way home and Polly dropped hers.

Jan 12 BEST DAY EVER

Me and Polly tried to get into the pool. We gave false names and had sunglasses on but the woman said you two arent allowed here. I pretended I was french and didnt understand her but Polly started laughing. I can fit twelve hubbabubbas into my mouth. Then the BEST THING EVER happened. We walked past this hotel called Holiday Inn and Polly said maybe it had a pool. So we pretended we are staying at the hotel. It turned out they DID have a pool. It was OK. But the BEST thing was we went up in the lift and found one of those trolleys that was full of free shampoos and little bottles of wisky which is DISGUSTING. Outside the rooms people left food on trays so we collected all the tomato ketchups and on the way home we did begging. We sat on the pavement near Rymans and put ketchup on our legs and pretended we were dying drinking wisky. To be honest Polly is not such a good actress as me. We begged 3 pounds 55p and had to stop because we saw Miss Major coming down the road arm and arm with her lesbian. We brought some more sweets (we got 3 cadbury dairy milk for 3 pounds and on Monday we will sell them at school for 20p per peace).

TOP SECRET Polly and I saw Josh and Evie kissing we were using Evies deodorant in the top loo and they came up so we had to hide. They sat on the bed and stuck their faces together. REVOLTING. We tried to work out what that means if they get married and we think it makes us sisters. Sort of.

Josh asked me to be his model for his art project. I dont know whether I am pretty or not yet. Dad says I am pretty. Mum says I have an interesting face, Josh says that means ugly. I have done my first SITTING. Its v boring actually and Joshes room is smelly. Portrait sitting is just doing nothing with Josh being bossy. Dont move. Chin up. Stop blinking. He wont let me see the picture until it is finished on Friday. He thinks hes

Piscasso or someone the way he holds his pencil out and shuts one eye.

Jan 26 Worst day EVER

I HATE my family. Most in the world I HATE JOSH. I wish he was dead. I would be happy if he was dead. I have done sittings ALL week for Josh and his stupid project. I have done 4 hours for him. Tonight he had a private view of his portrait. He stuck it on the wall and hung 2 tea towels like curtans on either side and Mum and Dad, Ness and Leah and Evie and Polly came to see it with red wine and ribena in wine glasses. When the curtans went back instead of ME he has spent the week drawing a hairy gorilla sitting in a chair in my school uniform. Everyone laughed. I HATE Mum the most because she laughed so much that tears were running down her face. She said the funniest thing is, Josh, you have caught something about Annie and they ALL started laughing all over again. Even Leah who is never laughing was laughing. I shut them all up when I said Josh and Evie were sticking their tongues in each others mouths and making mmm mmm mmm noises.

I look up at my leaf. It has stopped fluttering. Suddenly I miss Annie so much. I have an ache in my stomach. When she was born, when I first held her in my arms, it was like I already knew her. I can't explain it. I didn't feel that with Josh – he was brand new to me – but Annie, it was as if I'd known her for ever. We are like peas in a pod; everyone says so. My mother calls her *Connie* all the time.

I need to see my daughter; I feel the lack of her. She

needs her mother. Who is looking after her? The Weasel? My mother? When can I go home? I love Annie, I love Josh with every fibre of my being. My eyes sting and my throat hurts.

I cannot read any more.

Chapter 4

Dr Robinson sighs and leans forward on the little table. We have a session this morning and then she's coming back for another session in the afternoon when DS Allen gets here. Dr Robinson has told me that it will be a *difficult* day for me. But she is on perky form. Perhaps she lives for difficult days – she can go back home to Si Hubby and the kids and feel that she's really doing something with her life. She is more colourful today. She's in a different kind of uniform, very straight but trying not to be; she's wearing a dress with a jaunty design on it. She looks as if she's stepped out of a Boden catalogue. She might be a French teacher or a shop assistant. I like to watch her contained and measured movements. And there's something else about her that's different today. I'm still trying to puzzle out what it is when she smiles at me.

'Thank you, Connie, for the document. I found it very interesting. And you write very well.'

'Why, thank you, Dr Robinson. And may I take this opportunity to say how well you do your job too.' I have always had a problem where I sound sarcastic even when I don't mean to be. This time I do though. It all seems suddenly ridiculous.

I am smoothing out my magazines. I've read them all

and the sum conclusion I have reached is that big bottoms are *in*. What a relief, I can let mine out. I've hidden
Annie's diary; it is my secret. When Annie *does* decide to
come and visit me, I don't want her to think I've been
reading it. And I certainly don't want Little Miss Boden
forensically examining Annie's business.

Dr Robinson screws up her face. 'I was intrigued,' she
says, all Miss Marple now, closing in on the cracked vase.
'I wanted to know what happened next.'

'Ah, well, kind of a prerequisite for a writer's work, I
suppose.'

'How are you today?'

'Fine, thank you.'

'You're looking better,' she says. I'll take her word for
it; I don't look in the mirror.

'And so are you,' I reply. It's not exactly true. Her eyes
are puffy – she had a few last night – but she has a renewed
energy about her, a skip to her step. Then I get it!

'Ahhh!' I say, Hercule to her Marple. I chuckle knowingly, cross my arms and lean back in the chair so that
the front two legs come off the ground. I give her a
cheeky-chappy wink.

She makes the mistake of looking quizzical.

'So, Si Hubby got lucky last night . . . ?' I say.

Dr Robinson actually blushes. And her hair slips. Oh,
yes. I know I am right. 'That *is* good news,' I continue.
'It's great to think that our little chat had such a positive
effect.'

She has gone scarlet. She has that sort of colouring.
'I'm sorry, I didn't mean to embarrass you,' I say. 'It's
extraordinary, isn't it, how our bodies give us away.'

I leave a therapist pause in case she wants to join in with the topic, because it *is* a fascinating subject and she will be trained in spotting body language. But no, she is frozen in a parody of control, head cocked, pencil held out for effect, and rather sweetly she is still trying to maintain the eye contact that she prides herself on. She's unsure how to get back on track, so I plough on. 'Well done you, for putting in the effort! A little bit of Dutch courage and off you went? I like that about you: you're a real trier, aren't you, Dr Robinson?' I'm hoping she notices my parroting of her questioning technique but now she's busy pretending to rifle in her bag for something.

'You know nothing about me, Constance,' she says with a tight-rectum smile.

Gosh, she called me Constance; she must be annoyed. Yesterday she was trying to be so pally. 'It's just it's surprising to me,' I say, looking out of the window at my leaf, which is flopping around like a drunk this morning, 'given your line of work, that there you are expecting the truth from me, almost *demanding* it, and yet you yourself are content to be . . . well, there's no other way of putting it . . . a bit of a *fraud.*'

I want to get a proper grip of this woman who has been sent to assess me. I want to *admire* her; if her opinions are to have such sway, I do at least need to respect her. And I'm not quite convinced yet.

'I'll tell you what *is* interesting,' she says, cool as a cucumber. 'How you feel the necessity to transfer your own feelings on to mine.'

'Oh, it *is* interesting,' I agree. 'It's fascinating . . . but

not unusual in female relationships. We're always looking for links, connections . . . And I do believe you and I
have some.'

'We are not here to discuss my private life,' she says,
shifting in her seat. Her hair has slipped out of place
again and she hasn't corrected it. She's not looking quite
so perky now.

'Not essentially, no. Yet it might prove fruitful. I think
we need to get to the bottom of why we – you, I, so many
of us – feel the need to be fraudulent. I doubt your reasons are very exceptional. It'll be the usual trappings:
safety, financial security, better the devil you know,
mortgage, kids . . .'

She gives me a sharp look. She has no idea how easy
she is to read, how many *tells* she has. When she tried to
open the window yesterday, her shirt rode up and I saw
her belly. It was loose and as creased as a relief map,
stretch-marked, just like mine: the scars of child-bearing
that no amount of downward dog or sun salutations
or whatever the hell she does will rectify. I always like
that about Ness; she doesn't care about her mum tum.
I suppose the rest of her is so perfect it would seem
ungracious.

For a moment I lose focus. When I look back at Dr
Robinson, I see a shaft of steel in those blue eyes.

'DS Allen will be here this afternoon. Are you ready
for that? I warn you, he's not as nice as me. He's not going
to beat about the bush, Connie.'

'Is that what you do? Beat about the bush? I don't think
that's fair.'

She has a light glow on her skin; she is perspiring. It is

too warm in here. Her lips are puckered with intent and too many cigarette inhalations.

'Why do you think you're *here*, Connie?' she says.

I like her like this: hard, flinty. My respectometer goes up.

'You mustn't be so harsh with yourself,' I say. 'You mustn't feel bad. Everyone fakes it. Maybe the lucky few feel it. I hope so. God, I hope so. I hope someone out there is leading a genuine life. But for the rest of us, faking is so important. I understand that now. I'd go so far as to say faking is *vital*. It is the foundation we build our worlds on.'

I glance at my leaf. There's a silence. She's thinking. Then she makes a conscious decision to go with me. 'Are you saying that you believe there is no place for truth in relationships?'

It's a good question and it takes me back a year. I'm in bed, our bed – I love this bed: it's new, it's huge, it's so comfortable, it's like a home in itself – on a Sunday morning. Karl has brought me a coffee and it's a beautiful day outside. I'm utterly content. I can hear cartoons on the telly downstairs and the thud of Josh's football hitting the wall outside.

'One morning,' I say, turning to look at her, 'out of the blue, so it seemed to me, the Weasel woke up, sipped his coffee, and told me that he'd been unhappy for years.'

I pause; I can't speak. I still find it shocking. How can one be oblivious to one's partner's unhappiness?

'Go on,' she says. She's really listening to me. *Forensically*, you might say.

'I mean, I didn't expect him to be skipping about with jollity after fifteen years. But he had never struck me as *un*happy.'

She waits. 'And how did you respond?'

I pause. I think hard, remembering how we had sat side by side in bed, driver and passenger in the marital vehicle. 'I had to admire him for his honesty. But once those words are spoken, once those doubts are voiced, there *is* no going back. That is the beginning of the end of something . . .'

'But it could also be the beginning of something . . .'

I wait for her to expand on this.

She adjusts her hair. 'You think honesty stands no chance?'

'Honesty brings chaos.'

'But relationships change, they are evolving things.'

'Did you *settle* for Si Hubby?'

'Did you settle for Karl?' Oh, she's rising to my bait.

'I think a relationship stands more of a chance if you at least *once* had passionate feelings for each other. But our generation, who met our partners round about thirty . . . a lot of us *have* settled. Unlike our parents, we'd already known passion, and therefore we also knew when it wasn't there. And if you've *never* felt it with this person, I think you're pretty doomed. Did you and Si Hubby *ever* have passion?'

'So you are an advocate of faking it? Carrying on when you know you're not happy?'

I laugh. I look about the room as if surely my circumstances speak for themselves. She stares at me. In that moment, her eyes are rather beautiful, so alive and blue and full of empathy. But I'm wary; I've seen the steel in her, I know she can hurl daggers out of them.

'I'm just warning you,' I say quietly. 'Be prepared. Dib dob.'

'We're talking about you and Karl,' she says. 'Why do you think he was unhappy?'

I sigh. 'Why's anyone unhappy after all those years? Familiarity had bred contempt. He didn't feel loved any more, emotionally, physically. He needed to be desired. He irritated me. I nagged. Apparently I had *emasculated* him . . . funny there's no word for de-feminization . . . Our very language is misogynistic.'

'Sounds like you took all the blame?'

I smile. 'I didn't have all the facts.'

'Do you think we ever have all the facts?'

I laugh. That's the first really good question she has asked me. I wouldn't mind sharing my leaf with her. I look out. We sit in silence for a good minute – marvellous for her if she's paid by the hour.

'I think he's selling the house,' I tell her. I'm feeling low again. 'Will you talk to him? Ask him just to wait a while.'

'To wait for what?'

'To-wit to-woo.' I do an owl impression, just because I can – nothing to lose and all that. But it's not quite as satisfying with Dr Robinson as it is with the Squeak. Anyway, she ignores it.

'I don't know about that . . .'

She's such a jobsworth.

'Do you know why you're here, Connie?' she says again. She sounds genuinely curious. Not tricksy.

'I do,' I say.

'Tell me.'

'They found me naked by the river . . .' This is not the answer she is waiting for, I can tell by the way she purses her lips. I continue, 'There was an explanation for that, by the way.'

She shakes her head. She's not interested in my explanations. 'Do you know *why* you are here, Connie?'

We have a little eyeball-off. I shrug.

'A week ago you drove your car into the river.'

I stare at her. 'I think I would remember that.'

She has that wrong. She's got it all wrong. She gives a measured sigh that is difficult to read. Then she crosses those thick, strong legs of hers. 'OK,' she says. 'Let's get back to Ness.'

'Sure,' I say. She needs to get this right. Besides, I don't want her to leave. She's the only person I get to really talk to. 'What do you want to know?'

'What do you want to tell me?'

'I want to tell you the truth,' I say, like a very good girl. She likes me a bit more then; I see it in her eyes.

'That's what I want too,' she says quietly. I've given her control again; everything is how it is meant to be. 'So you met her in the playground, you got chatting, the kids are playing, you find out a few things about each other, she compliments you . . .'

'That's right. This is important . . . so the next time I saw her, it was a few weeks later. I was posting a letter at the corner of our street or something, I can't remember exactly – this is all years ago. Anyway, Ness was trying to get Polly out of her car seat. I didn't recognize her at first. I was just thinking what a funky car it was – retro and a nice blue. Then when she stood up straight, I recognized her and the funny thing was she'd had her hair cut – just like mine! With the fringe and everything!'

Dr Robinson leans in and slowly recrosses one leg over the other, smoothing out her dress.

'I commented on it. I expected her to refer to the fact that she'd copied my hairstyle, after our previous conversation, or . . . some reference to it at least. But she didn't.'

'And what did you think about that?'

'I just thought it was a bit odd. I thought that perhaps she wasn't very self-aware. Or that she'd forgotten that it was me that she'd copied.'

'Fringes are very common. People are always getting fringes.'

'Yes. That's what I said to myself. And so I helped her unclip the strap of the car seat. And there was something else about her that bothered me, something that I couldn't quite put my finger on. Anyway, that same week there was a Christmas Fair at school. Ness and Leah were quite a hit, this new 'celebrity' family. It was because of Leah. Leah Worthington, the newsreader. You know the one: glasses, cool, serious, clever, always looks a bit miserable . . .'

'I know who she is.'

Fame is such a head-fuck. Leah's just a normal woman; it's everyone else who acts differently. Or maybe fame had changed her, I don't know. She did have that aura of success, a kind of affected nonchalance. Being with her was so odd. Once you'd forgotten who she was, you'd see how people changed when they recognized her: shop assistants, waiters, postmen, bank clerks, teachers, the headmaster – *everyone* would get a bit giggly around her, a bit flirty. People behaved bizarrely once sprinkled with the fairy dust of fame. Evie and Polly have got used to having special dispensations and privileges they take for granted: straight to the front of queues, friendly faces. Ness is warier of people, doesn't trust them easily; they're suddenly much nicer to her when Leah turns up.

'They were an "unconventional" family, the Joneses. I'd heard people talking about them; everybody was falling over themselves to befriend them. They were *glamorous*, you see. They were an attraction.'

Dr Robinson hasn't moved a muscle, but her eyes are all lit up; I can tell that even she wants to ask me what Leah's like and all that bullshit. I mean, she's pretending to be cool about it but underneath that B-is-for-Boden dress, she wants to flash those B for bazookas.

'At first, I was definitely the exception. I stayed away from them once I realized Leah was famous.'

'And Karl? Was he impressed?' she asks.

'That's not the point. The Weasel does *the impressing*. And after much perseverance he succeeded with Leah. She thought he was *hilarious*. He can make anyone like him; he kind of hijacks them until they relent to the charm onslaught. That's why he's so good at his job, after all: getting everyone on side. It's odd, he even wants strangers to like him – he used to lift the kids up on to his shoulders with loud whoop-di-doos in public spaces, just to be sure everyone noticed what a cracking father he was . . . It's extremely important to him that everybody thinks he's fantastic. I expect you already do.'

'I haven't met him.'

'Oh, you will. And you'll think he's fantastic, he'll make sure of that. The irony is he *is* fantastic; he just doesn't need to try so hard.'

She cocks her head, her eyes not leaving mine. 'And why do you think he does that?'

I shrug. 'You tell me, Shrink.'

Dr Robinson nods to signify that the subject is now finished with and she will retain this information for a later discussion.

'Back to the Christmas Fair. Did you and Ness speak?'

'Not at first. But she seemed very different to how she was in the park. At first, I'd got the impression that she was a bit square – her clothes were pretty sensible, she seemed stilted. But here at the fair, she looked completely different. She was glamorous, more confident – perhaps because she was with Leah, or maybe it was the alcohol, I don't know. She wasn't nervy and twitchy at all. Anyway, later on, Leah had taken the kids home and some of us were in the playground, a bit pissed, and Ness came back from the loo with a piece of toilet paper hanging off her skirt and neither she nor I could get it off. We were laughing and mucking about; I smeared some chocolate soldier on it, just being stupid. That was when we connected, I'd say. She *was* really beautiful. I could see it now, this beauty everyone was talking about. It was quite extraordinary. How on earth could I have missed it? Anyway, she was laughing so much, leaning on me to try and pull it off. She was very close. And then, wham! My God! I got it! That scent! She was wearing the same Jo Malone perfume!'

'*Your* perfume? The same perfume she had commented on in the park?' Dr Robinson asks, reassuringly affronted. (That's all you really want from a psychologist: agreement.)

'Yes.'

'Did you say anything?'

'I did! I said, *Oh! You bought the Jo Malone?* But she looked nonplussed, as if she had absolutely no idea what I was talking about.'

'How peculiar.'

'Very. I thought it most strange that she made no mention of our previous conversation in the playground. It struck me again that she wasn't very self-aware.'

'And how did it make you feel, the fact that she was wearing your perfume?'

'I suppose I felt flattered . . .'

'Nothing else?'

'Yes,' I say. 'I felt a bit robbed. Like she was stealing from me by not acknowledging that she'd copied me.'

She nods. She's taking it in, frowning. 'Which scent was it, out of curiosity?'

I smile. 'Don't worry, it's not the same one you're wearing.' We're not allowed scent in here, so you can smell the outsiders a mile off. She looks caught out.

'Mine's bath oil,' she says, leaving us both with the intriguing image of her standing naked by a bath pouring grapefruit oil underneath a hot running tap.

'Did you feel jealous?' she asks.

'Of whom?'

'Of Ness and Leah, of their life together?'

I'd never been a particularly jealous person; I had

always been innately confident in myself. But I'm trying to be honest with my feelings. I was intrigued by them. And I thought I *did* see passion there, between Ness and Leah, and I was envious of passion. 'Perhaps,' I say.

'And were you jealous of Ness's beauty?'

I smile and shake my head. 'No,' I say. 'I'm a great fan of beauty.'

She glances at my scars as we both let that comment hang in the air, its repercussions wafting around the room with the grapefruit.

Chapter 5

I don't know precisely when I realized that I was developing a crush on Ness. These things happen so slowly. Looking back, it was probably the time we went for that long hike outside Bath somewhere. Do you know the Bath countryside, Dr Robinson? You should go. I was struck by how fearless, how in control Ness was, with the Ordnance Survey map on her phone, her sensible boots and her blue cagoule. I found myself quite content to follow those slender striding legs into the unknown and was enjoying this strange new feeling of being second in command. A strange thought kept occurring to me: *If I was a man this is exactly the sort of woman I would fall in love with.*

The trip was unplanned. Now that the kids were a bit older Ness had got a job managing a gallery on the South Bank – she was doing really well and had been sent out to visit an artist in Bristol to discuss an upcoming exhibition. The night before the trip she'd sprained her wrist playing netball. Leah had work commitments, so she'd asked if I was free to drive her there and back. I was free (I was procrastinating doing research for my book). Besides, it was just for the day and I know she would have done the same for me.

Initially, as we left London in the old RAV4, it had felt a little peculiar; Ness and I had always passed our time together in the comfortable context of our families and here we were: individuals again, in the big wide world, just two women in a car going on a journey. Within the familial context, we'd all grown closer, thanks to the kids dashing in and out of our houses without the reserve of adults. They'd broken all the barriers for us, resulting in many impromptu evenings spent together. Karl was unusual like that – he was perfectly happy in the company of women (as long as he was the centre of attention); he had lots of women friends; he genuinely *liked* women. And Leah and Ness were unusual in that they had quite a few straight male friends. And you know what? I'd even seen Ness being quite flirty with them – I suppose being in a lesbian relationship allowed her that safety.

Leah's brother and Karl had met and got on like a house on fire; they supported the same football team, knew a few *characters* in common. (What is it with men and *characters*? Why are they so eager to lay claim to them? Is it that they think a little of this *character* will rub off on them?) We knew Ness and Leah's story by now: the kids' biological father was a gay friend of theirs who now lived in France and Ness was the biological mother. Their past interested me: Leah had always been gay but Ness had only been in heterosexual relationships until they met; she'd been with her ex-boyfriend for five years. I assumed she must have always had a sexual interest in women, but she waved away my comments: *I just fell in love and it happened to be with a woman.*

I became quite fascinated by how they functioned as a

couple, eager to pin them down and define them in some way, wanting them to take on traditional gender roles, which they did to a degree. In some respects Leah was the more *masculine* partner: she wasn't vain, she never wore make-up when she wasn't on television, she never wore skirts, she was sporty and practical, she got drunk like a man, loud and leery. And Ness looked after Leah, shielding her from the public interest, buoying her up, batting away the depression that never seemed far from Leah's surface. Ness was somehow more *sensible* than Leah, more responsible. Apart from being gay, she was surprisingly straight. And yet every now and then she would take me by surprise: she was partial to a spliff, she could stay up all night, she had no qualms about breaking wind (a gentle inoffensive gust, but nevertheless she was unabashed); there was a subversiveness in there somewhere.

The journey flew by as we gossiped. Ness had plugged in her phone and was playing a Rufus Wainwright track; she'd unwound the window and was leaning out to feel the wind in her face. 'Going to a Town' – do you know it, Dr R? If not, Spotify it right now and think of us in the car, windows down, London behind us, singing along lustily to Rufus. It was one of those moments of happiness that seem to belong to a different lifetime now. I am smiling to recall it. I may not have been blessed with a melodious voice, but I'd been top of the queue when they were handing out gusto. Ness, however, had a sweet voice (*I know, I know*, what doesn't she have?). It transpired that she'd actually met Mr Wainwright at some celebrity do with Leah. As I said, she was *cool* in her

straight way, Dr R, or are you impervious to such things?
I think not.

I don't want to bang on about Ness's beauty because I
despise this whole beauty obsession, but I have to say,
after initially having been oblivious to it, I was now continually left-fielded by it: we'd be chatting away about
human motivation or medieval doctors or the extraordinary Caravaggio (her favourite), and I would get
distracted by the gorgeous tone of her skin, or those
large dark eyes, or those unnaturally red lips – the sort
that Shakespeare would eulogize about (where *did* that
extra blood come from?), or her perfect teeth, or the
petiteness of her, those high cheekbones, those full
breasts. Nature had been a little unfair on the donating
front; I felt crudely crafted next to her. Don't get me
wrong: she wasn't *perfect* but it would be mean to point
out that perhaps her hair was a little too frizzy, or her
fingers on the stumpy side, or her skin a little moley – all
that was lost in the glory of the whole. There was something undeniably feminine about her and *yet* she had a
solidity, a capability, an appetite, an athleticism which
was quite masculine.

At this stage I wasn't consciously smitten with her;
I was still representing myself quite well. I had yet to
be skinned, deboned and filleted. And I don't want to
give you the wrong impression – I was smart and cool
and pretty impressive in my own way (there is no room
for false modesty in these records, wouldn't you agree?).
No, I'd never doubted my own attractiveness; it had
never been an issue for me, but she was in a different
league.

It's surprising how much dancing can be done in a car. The Temptations were bemoaning frustrated love. Lyrics don't come much better than theirs. It turned out, to our mutual delight, that we were both pedants on the lyric front, agreeing that a bad lyric could ruin a musician's whole oeuvre; personally, I had never forgiven Prince for slipping the word *restaurant* into an otherwise faultless song. It's kind of inexcusable; the word had no business in a lyric at all. I'm digressing. My point is – it's an intimate act, sharing music, not dissimilar to Polly and Annie sharing diary dates. There is an element of risk in exposing your tastes but Ness and I appeared to be of one mind. If we quibbled about a song it wasn't a problem: we'd persuade or dissuade, pause the track, debate a lyric, look for consistency, laugh or change our minds; we were in harmony.

Ness did what she had to do in Bristol and I wandered around, had a sandwich by the canal, read my book with a coffee. And then we left to go back home. We could probably have made it in time for supper. But on the way, we got completely pelted by rain on the M4 and one of my windscreen wipers broke. It was quite dangerous – I could see nothing and we were in the fast lane at the time – but she was cool-headed, flagging the cars around us until I got us safely on to the hard shoulder, my legs a-tremble. She put her hand on my thigh and soothed me. I can't describe it, Dr R, but I felt *looked after* with her, in a way that I didn't with Karl. *Yes, if I was a man, she was just the sort of woman I would fall in love with.*

We called the AA and our partners and waited in the rain.

Looking back, what happened next seems entirely random. The AA arrived quickly and towed us for miles to some garage in the Bath countryside. It turned out they would have to order a special windscreen wiper (who knew such a thing existed?) which wouldn't turn up until the next day – if we were lucky.

So, there we were, stuck in the middle of nowhere. We had an empty slate. So we made the relevant phone calls home, organized the necessary childcare, and then found a surprisingly pleasant inn on the edge of the village recommended by the mechanic – an establishment favoured by walkers: low beams, flagstone floor, roaring log fire. The only room they had available was a double, which neither of us was bothered about. So we found ourselves drinking pints of local ale sitting by the log fire, feeling rather elated at the surprising turn of events. We were on our second round when Karl's texts started beeping through: *Where are Josh's shin pads? Annie can't find her blue wig? You haven't bought any washing tablets. How do you switch the dishwasher on?*

Ness was utterly incredulous that he didn't know how to use the machines. I wasn't. I saw it as a deliberate ploy. Karl was a grand master of lethargy; he'd made uselessness a tool in his bid for idleness. Most insultingly of all, he must have thought I didn't see through it. How, after years, could he still not manage to load the dishwasher with the plates at the right angle so the branch didn't get stuck? (Can *Si Hubby* do that, Dr R?) Or take the washing out of the machine immediately, so that it doesn't smell of old drains, and hang it out on the line in such a way that it won't need ironing? How could he not master these tiny, simple things when I have mentioned them four thousand times? I'll tell you why: because his over-riding aim has been for me to have to redo everything, so that he can throw his hands in the air, flagellate with hurt and despair, and cry, *Whatever I do, Connie, it's never quite good enough for you, is it?* As if it were *my* fault for wanting our fucking clothes to be clean and for him not to stink like a damp dog. He and I had always brought equal amounts of money into the house. At what stage during our relationship did I sign up to be the domestic slave?

You asked me if I was ever jealous? I'll tell you what makes me jealous: the sharing of domestic tasks. Imagine this: walking past the chest of drawers where you've left a pile of clean laundry and to find that someone *else* has put it away! That is foreplay in my book. To return home to a *wiped* table! That is nigh on orgasmic. You know what? Leah doesn't leave pee on the toilet seat, she tidies up the sofa before she goes to bed, *and* she reads the fucking news on the BBC. Yes! I'm jealous!

I'm working myself up into a state but you *must* understand, Dr R – maybe you do: it is these little slacknesses that kill relationships; that are the steady crunch of the woodworm, eating away at what might have been a sound structure.

We carried on drinking beer, ate a hearty meal – interestingly, Ness and I (unlike you, with your horse-food calorie-controlled nut bars) are in that minority of women who have never weighed ourselves or been on diets, which automatically eliminates an awful lot of those deeply tedious conversations I hear other women have – and crashed out, bloated and bulging, in the pillow-plumped four-poster bed.

The next morning we sat at the bleached wooden breakfast table, the whiff of toast in the air, the clink of white crockery and the rustle of newspapers. *It was all Gucci*, as Josh would say. At ten-thirty we rang the garage to be told that the windscreen wiper wouldn't be arriving until the following morning. After a minute or so of disbelief that our journey should be hindered by a windscreen wiper – it was *technically illegal* to drive without one, according to our mechanic, and it was looking like rain – neither of us actually minded that much; we were on an unexpected and welcome break from the old routine. My deadline for an article was not for another few days and Ness's boss was very amenable. We made the necessary calls home, got talking to a couple on the next table, and decided to go on a walk – a proper walk. Ness, as ever sensibly clad, was already wearing her walking boots and I had some trainers in the back of the car. So we took photos of the couple's Ordnance Survey map and pored over the route as we ate our porridge and boiled eggs. We decided on an eight-mile circular route to the lake and back. This was fun. In a way, I felt like I'd been waiting for Ness all my life: an accomplice, an adventurer, a partner in *carpe diem*.

The proprietor of the inn lent us a backpack and offered us some wellies, which we refused. I watched the way Ness efficiently packed the bag: water bottle, some Kendal Mint Cake that she'd bought at the counter, the way she carefully rolled up her blue Norwegian cagoule (the type that people die in on Mount Everest) and neatly stuffed it down the side. She methodically figured out how all the compartments worked. She was thorough. 'If I'd known I'd have brought my compass. Have you got a waterproof?' she asked me. I saw a new side to her: she was the tiniest bit *bossy* but I really didn't mind; in fact I was enjoying being bossed. Besides, it was a rarity for me not to ask three hundred times whether everyone had been for a pee, brought a jumper, etc. I only had myself to ask today.

I didn't have a waterproof.

'Not in the back of the car?' she asked me, surprised. I bet at home she had a proper hiking bag with a first-aid kit and a pouch where she kept her compass, a flare and a couple of crampons; unlike me with my strappy handbag, lippy and a couple of tampons.

We stopped at the garage, where she exchanged pleasantries with the mechanic while I put on the trainers and my Topshop bomber jacket, looking like an idiotic townie. Pathetic really – but in the event of an air ambulance rescue service at least I would look good.

Luckily for me, the weather turned out to be glorious (which actually meant we could easily have driven home). And the Bath countryside was magnificent.

We'd met each other late in life and we had a lot of catching up to do, so we decided we would tell each other our stories, interview each other, cover every stage of life, not necessarily in order. Whatever the interviewer wanted to ask they could ask; no questions were out of bounds, nothing was sacred. *What was said in the Bath countryside stayed in the Bath countryside.* That was our motto. I was to be interviewed until we got to the lake and she was to be interviewed on the way back.

We followed the river along the flatter land. Ness was so sure of herself and her map reading and I continued to enjoy being led. She knew about the Jurassic rock and the evolution of the land itself (her father was a geography teacher). We marvelled at the trees, which were shrieking reds and golds at us. It felt more like June than September and soon it became so warm that we stuffed our jumpers into the backpack. She checked her phone with the pictures of the OS map every time we came to a stile or a fork in the path. Already I was dependent on her; why was *she* the one carrying the backpack, holding the phone? But I liked the way she was a bit nerdy, the way she referred to the map, knowing what all the symbols meant, her finger following the dotted red line. Initially I wanted to double-check every decision made – I was used to being prime navigator of my tribe, after all – but I soon surrendered entirely to her control. And it felt good being dominated; a new and perhaps *feminine* feeling that I wasn't quite used to. I was giving myself over in a way I hadn't for many years.

So, I was the first to tell my story. Once we'd crossed the river, we began in earnest. She wanted to start with the meeting of my parents, so a couple of hours later, by the time we'd got to the top of the peak, I'd gone through the birth of my brother David, my own entry to the world, my early schooling, the important characters from my childhood, friends – she asked me a lot of questions about my greatest friends, Grace and Ally – the teenage years, my brief first marriage. Her questions were poignant but sensitive, her curiosity sharp. She was a great interviewer, able to keep the flow going, pull it back on track, create links and point out patterns, all the while handing me little bits of Kendal Mint Cake and glugs of water.

We were walking along the top of the dyke when we glimpsed the lake. It was as blue as the sky and took our breath away. It was wonderful to walk with someone who really felt the force of nature. It was a real connection. Karl was strangely impervious to nature; whether we were watching bursts of lava spewing from Etna, or just the last of the sun going down, I'd have to point the spectacle out, draw his focus. He'd stop and look and try to be impressed, because he knew he was meant to be feeling something. And the gap between us would increase. Then he would bring us close again with a joke, almost apologizing for his lack of wonder. *I wish I'd brought my watercolours.* We'd found a way that worked: we substituted laughter for connection. And so laughter *became* our connection, which in its own way is wonderful. But with Ness it was different. She and I spoke the same language: we both stopped and looked at the lake at exactly the same time, just because we both *did*.

By the time we reached it, we were boiling; we took our socks and shoes off and sat at the edge with our feet dangling in the water, basking in the warm sunshine. There wasn't a soul about. I splashed the icy water on to my face and hair and we ate the last of the Kendal Mint Cake. Then Ness sat up abruptly, rummaged in the backpack and pulled out her cagoule, unzipped a pocket and produced the remnants of a fat spliff and a lighter.

'Yes!' she said. 'I knew I had it! Leah and I smoked half of this last week!'

Weed had gone out of fashion for some reason – parenthood had made cokeheads out of everyone. (Well, smoking's so *bad* for your health, isn't it, Dr R?) She passed it under my nose and then lit up. This was a moment of bliss, the sort you crave for when you're stuck on a crowded tube.

We lay in the grass in an easy silence, our toes flicking the water, feeling the warm sun on our skin; bees and buzzing things meandering by, dropping in to see whether we were worth pollinating. I watched an eagle hovering above high in the sky and felt Ness shift on to her elbow at my side. She was close; I could smell her. She smelt of me. Me without the body odour. She passed me the spliff.

'When you met Karl, did you know straight away he was the one?'

I took a drag and softly blew the thick smoke out before turning to look at her.

'I'm not sure I believe in *the one*.'

She looked momentarily crushed. I didn't like myself for it: it's so easy to make people feel small. Yet my response gave away more than she heard, don't you think?

'I was still busy thinking I'd found *the one* in someone else,' I said, to make amends. She looked at me in that particular way she had, out of the corners of her eyes. It was alluring. 'It's funny how things work out,' I continued. 'The decisions you never consciously make. When I met Karl, I certainly wasn't looking to get involved with anyone. But he was like a breath of fresh air. Then he kind of set me in his sights.' I smiled to remember how, in those early days, he would turn up uninvited wherever I went. I was unfriendly, my brother was blatantly rude to him – he'd come over from Australia for a family reunion – but Karl never took offence. His pursuit was relentless. (In your profession you might call it stalking, but it veered just to the right side of it.) 'And he was so *funny*! I couldn't not be charmed by him.'

'Yes, he is charming,' she said. She had a slight edge to her voice so that I couldn't tell what she meant by that, whether she was being critical of him. I hoped not. I wanted her to be charmed by him; I wanted her onside.

'He'd been brought in by this magazine I was writing for; they were hiring and firing at the top. I was asked to show him around. We ended up having lunch together and he asked me out. We went on a few dates and soon it became apparent that we had similar outlooks on life, we both wanted the same things . . . it was all so *easy*. There was no reason *not* to be with him.' I laughed, feeling a wave of incredible fondness for Karl. (Interesting how we shape our own narratives to fit our stories. You mustn't take my version for the truth – I'm sure you don't.) For some reason I failed to mention to Ness that Karl had been a serial Lothario and during those first few months together I discovered at least three other women who thought they were going out with him. (Is this perhaps what kept me keen? Win the competition then let the cup gather dust? I hope I'm not that petty, but I might be.) I know why I didn't tell her: I didn't want to see her incredulity or hear her disapproval. I was protective of him, of us.

Ness was leaning on her elbow, facing me, one breast leaning heavily on the other. I took another drag.

'Then I found out I was pregnant . . . No, hang on, I'm missing something out. It was still early days when something really shit happened to him and I was just *there*, you know . . . it sort of made us a couple in other people's eyes . . .'

She was chewing on another piece of grass, her legs tucked forward a little, droplets of water caught on her calves, her hip bones jutting out through her jeans, her slender arms resting against the curve of her body.

'What happened?' she asked, because she could. These were the rules. I shifted position, leaning on my elbow and mirroring hers.

'He doesn't talk about it, actually, so don't bring it up.'

'I won't.'

'He was driving in north London somewhere and he knocked someone over. This woman. She died later in hospital.' (You'd have a minefield with him, Dr R.)

'Oh, good heavens!' Ness said. She often used rather sweet, old-fashioned expressions. 'How awful.' She covered her mouth with her hand.

'Yes.'

'How awful for him.'

'As I said, don't mention it, will you?'

'I wouldn't.'

I passed her the spliff. 'It wasn't his fault. It was a young woman. She was having a row with someone and walked out without looking and bam . . .'

'My goodness! Poor Karl.' This was the first time I'd heard her have empathy for him and I liked it. Sometimes I felt that she didn't really *trust* him in some way.

'He went into a kind of shock and then he just refused to speak about it . . . he still won't get in a Citroën,' I said.

'He's such a happy sort of person,' she said, somewhat incongruously. She sat up and folded her arms around her knees. I looked at her lovely smooth back. Her hair was up and some of it had fallen down. *If I was a man I'm pretty sure I'd fall in love with you.*

She turned and passed the spliff back to me.

'Is it hard, living with someone like Leah?' I asked her.

'You mean the fame? Or Ms Misery Guts?' She smiled, looking round at me. I meant the latter; she knew that. 'I suppose I'm so used to it. I don't think I could bear someone endlessly cheery. They'd get on my tits.'

Again, I took this as a slight dig at Karl, who had a peculiar habit of being relentlessly chipper in groups. He wasn't really like that in private. It was as though he had two distinct personas. In public he was Mr Joke-A-Minute, filling silences with whistled snatches of lift music. She was absolutely right: it really could get on your tits. I didn't mind it getting on *my* tits but I didn't want it getting on other people's tits, if you see what I mean, Dr R (maybe because it would reflect badly on me?). I wanted Ness to like Karl. We always want our female friends to like our partners in just the right way.

'Have *you* ever been depressed?' I asked. I was curious.

'Umm . . .' she said, but she shrugged her shoulders and had to think about it. No one likes to confess to *not* having felt depressed because that makes them seem insensitive and superficial, but on the other hand no one likes to say that they've been Prozacked up to the eye-balls, waking up wailing every morning at the prospect of another twenty-four hours to live through, because that makes them sound unhinged. You have to have felt just the right amount of misery to be socially acceptable to the Establishment, don't you agree?

'I always think of all the people who have it much worse than I do.'

I blew the blue smoke up into the blue sky. Yes, I could believe she did that. There was a slightly Edwina Currie-ish side to her, a no-nonsense, put-on-an-extra-jumper kind of mentality. It was the opposite of indulgent and I liked that, but it showed a thickness of skin that I'd noticed elsewhere in her character. Leah could be openly rude to her and it was like it meant nothing; she never reacted. She'd brush it off, seemingly unaffected. I would have been incredibly hurt or angry had someone spoken to me that way. Other people's relationships are anathema – face it, Doc.

I was envious of her too: of her mental strength. How wonderful not to have been to those dark places. It probably just wasn't in her nature. I liked that about her – she was straightforward. You'd know best, but I've come to believe that it's in the DNA, that self-destruct button; you're either suicidal or you're not. It doesn't mean that you've gone any lower than anyone else; it's just the way your brain is programmed to deal with things. To some of us, death feels like an attractive, proactive solu-tion to a problem. And at the time it appears to be by far the more sensible alternative to carrying on. It seems quite obvious to me that risk-takers are more likely to chuck it all in. My first suicide attempt happened at fifteen. I got pregnant the first time I had sex and it truly felt like the end of the world. I went to the bathroom cabinet in my parents' house and swallowed every pill I could find in the cupboard. Sadly for me, they were old hippies and it turned out I'd OD'd on tree bark and ginseng.

'I was on antidepressants,' I told her, just because I felt like it. 'After Annie's birth, I took a dip.' She didn't really react or appear to judge me. Thank God there's not quite the same stigma attached that there used to be.

We were both lying back on the grass, looking up at the sky, pretty stoned now, talking about cause and effect, accidents and fate, serendipity and coincidence. We were watching the eagle and the eagle seemed to be watching us. It kept swooping and climbing – we reckoned it was getting the odd waft of sweet sinsemilla up there, had the old rabbit-munchies and was boring the arse off the other eagles. We chuckled away for a while before drifting off into our own worlds.

'What was this guy like you were in love with?' she said, her voice breaking my reverie. I paused.

'Which guy?'

'The guy before Karl. You said you thought you'd found *the one*.'

I sighed. *That* guy. My God, how do you describe it, Dr R? Have you had it? Did Si Hubby make you feel as if you'd been half asleep all your life? Did he *wake you up* and fill you to the brim? Have you suffered from that particular madness? Or wasn't it Si Hubby at all?

'I'd known him years ago. He'd been my professor at uni. But then I bumped into him a few years later at a party and . . . it was . . . it was complicated.'

She was inhaling and turned her head to me with a raised eyebrow. 'You mean he was married.'

I raised an eyebrow back at her. 'It turned out he was, yes.'

'How long were you together?'

'On and off for four years.'

She whistled a bit and lay there looking up at the sky. 'I bet you had cracking sex.'

I laughed. 'We did.' We *really* did. I watched Ness stretch herself out, her arms over her head. She had rolled up the sleeves of her T-shirt and I was momentarily distracted by the curve of her breast against the side of her body.

'Wouldn't it be great if we were allowed just one day of pure passion, to shag our brains out, with no repercussions or consequences?' she said with a sigh. For a moment I thought she was talking about *us*, her and me, and my heart surprised me when it did a little cha-cha-cha.

'Who would you do it with?' I asked. (Yes, in my book, that is flirting. What do you think?)

'I don't know. Whoever floated my boat.'

The sky seemed to prickle with stars despite the daylight.

'Would you call yourself bisexual?' I asked her.

'I don't like all these labels.'

'Don't you miss sex with men?'

She looked at me and shrugged. 'No.'

'You and Leah have a good sex life though, don't you?'

I asked. Seeing as she'd opened the portal to this conversation, I stepped right in. I'd always assumed that they had, but now I thought about it, I hadn't seen much affection between them recently.

'Yeah,' she said loyally, but I heard the doubt in her voice. Well, you can't say *no*, can you, Dr R? 'You and Karl?' she asked.

'Yeah,' I said, because I was a liar too. 'But let's just say I might have to brush a few cobwebs off the old French maid outfit at the back of the cupboard.'

She sat up on an elbow and stared at me. 'Do you dress up?' She looked really flabbergasted. I told you, there was a touch of Edwina about her. But I also *liked* this about her, that she thought dressing up ridiculous. It suddenly felt very feminist and empowering *not* to appeal to men's fantasies. And yet, on the other hand, it seemed to me that there was an element of imagination missing from her make-up. (What about you? Do you carry on playing doctors and nurses when you get home? Does Si Hubby like a bit of sexy Santa?)

Ness was staring at me, waiting for an answer. 'No! I'm serious! Do you?' she repeated.

'I used to,' I said. Karl was into all that dressing up when we started. 'He has particular tastes. For example, he likes *white* underwear. It has to be *white*.' I kid you not, Dr R – he gives me some every birthday. To be honest, I don't really consider that a proper present, do you? He might as well give me a QPR season ticket.

'My God, I can't believe you dress up!' Ness cried, shaking her head, laughing with disbelief. 'Not me, no way, I can't bear any of that stuff. I'd just feel utterly ridiculous dressed as a schoolgirl or . . . or . . . what *do* you wear?' she asked, an uncomprehending grin on her face, the whole concept unfathomable to her.

I started laughing. 'Well, I used to have a kind of bunny girl thing . . .'

She burst out laughing now. We both did – we were pretty wrecked. We got up and started hopping about pulling our best fuck-me bunny faces. Which reminds me, Dr R, some free sex advice you can pass on to your clients: if you're on all fours, taking it from behind, never *ever* turn around and try to look sexy. It's not going to work. Ness and I proved it: we tried every angle we could and it really is impossible to look good. But it *is* hilarious to try.

We laughed until the jokes slowly petered out, and the birdsong and the buzz of the insects took over. Then we thought perhaps it was time to carry on our walk and we started getting our things together, without much success: I found her intently studying the map upside down. She pointed out that I had two socks on one foot. Eventually we *did* get our acts together and headed off again.

'So,' she said, after a little while; we were walking alongside the lake, ready to veer off. 'What was his name, this professor?'

I wonder what percentage of happily married people still have a small place in their hearts reserved for someone other than their partner. Not in a real way – they would never do anything about it, their lives are good – but in a fantasy way. Are you any good on stats? I'll tell you a secret: this man was capable of reducing me to nothing, to just an essence of being. You lot probably have a name for it, a condition, don't you? Or is it just *falling* in love? I was glad I wasn't that person any more. I did not want that kind of love again. I had lost myself in him. And then, when he went, he left a hole in me. I filled it up with concrete. I hardened up. I have rock in me now. Everyone tells me that.

'Jonathan Hapgood.' Saying his name was like lifting a buried artefact out of the mud into the light. Not necessarily a good thing – think of the curse of Tutankhamen.

'Jonathan Hapgood,' she repeated. How exciting to hear his name on her lips. The spliff had made me indulgent, for you must understand I was *very* happy with my life, with Karl, with my kids, with the choices I had made. That soft melting love was no basis for rearing a family. Families needed solidity. I had a past – that was all.

'What happened with Mr Hapgood?' she asked, looking at me in that sideways way she had.

'Oh,' I said carelessly. 'He finished it in the end. I've heard since that his wife went off with someone else.'

'What goes around comes around. Do you still see him?' she asked.

'God, no. I've not seen him for nearly ten years.'

She turned to look at me. 'Are you still in touch?'

'No.'

'Not at all?'

'New Year's Eve text maybe. Birthday email.'

'But you still *think* about him.' She was so insistent and probing.

I sighed. 'Occasionally.'

She was drinking from the water bottle as we began to head onwards. 'Like when?'

I felt guilty, disloyal, but also strangely free. I had *never* spoken of these things. 'I don't know. Actually I thought of him earlier, looking at this,' I said, gesturing to the hills, the lake, the majesty of the place. 'Or sometimes if I hear particular music . . . the usual corny old tosh. Anyway, it's your turn now.' I wanted to stop talking about me. I felt unnecessarily exposed, like I was having one of those naked dreams. I had said too much, made a bigger deal out of something than it was. Perhaps I needed to explain myself. 'Sometimes, Ness, I think it's because I'm not very good at letting go; I'm a fiercely loyal person. If I love someone I never stop loving them. Men, girlfriends . . . I have never fallen out with anyone . . .' (I realize that I was self-aggrandizing, making myself sound a bit special, that my *loyalty* was to blame, not my fickleness.)

We were walking side by side now and she laughed and took my arm in her hands. 'Constance – that is your name, after all. Don't worry! You're *not* being disloyal. I think you could be the most honest person I've ever met.'

It gave me a thrill to hear her say that and to see her looking at me in that particular way, although I have always believed that honesty is vastly overrated. (Loyalty, on the other hand . . .) Her hand was soft against my skin and she let her fingers stroke my inner arm all the way down to my hand, which she squeezed. 'Besides,' she said, 'there are lots of different kinds of love.'

Men will never understand the beautiful intimacies of female friendship.

Chapter 6

DS Allen has stains down the front of his cheap suit. I'm sure Dr Robinson has noticed too. I imagine her to be a clean freak, judging by the state of her handbag; it's lying open at her feet, the clasp not doing its job. Everything has its own little compartment. I see some antibacterial wipes, a plastic make-up bag, a low-calorie oatmeal bar, her menthol cigarettes, the spine of a book. I lean forward to read the title: *Hotel du Lac*. We read that in my book club. Ness hated it. Dr Robinson sees me looking, pretends she doesn't, leans down and snaps the bag shut, and places it on the other side of her chair.

We are in a different room; I have been escorted out of my own room and through various corridors by the receptionist, or jailer, whoever she is. Actually she might even be a man; it is hard to tell. Whichever, she's built like a rhinoceros. At one stage we crossed a courtyard and the fresh air took me by surprise. I paused. I turned my face to the sun and felt its rays on my skin. My hair is red but my skin is sallow; it craves the sun. I thought of all those times I have taken sunlight for granted. The Rhino gave me a little tug and I moved on across the courtyard, following the heavy roll of her bulk.

We passed Mental Sita in the telly room. I gave her a

little wave and she stared at me as if she'd never seen me before. But then she is mental. It's a veritable rabbit warren, this place, grey lino and mint-green walls. We passed the canteen and I saw the Squeak laughing with the chef. I make a mental note – looks like they've got a thing going on. She says something to him and he turns to look at me, his smile dropping. I see it everywhere; heads look up and necks crane as I pass and, to my surprise, I realize that I'm something of a celebrity. Maybe this is how Leah feels – except the smiles don't drop when she passes.

This room we're in now has an unbreakable glass panel on the window with that black squiggly thread going through it. Beyond the glass a goon is patrolling the lino in his polyester uniform and the Rhino waits. There are no other windows. The room smells faintly of Josh's feet and Monster Munch. Essentially it is a police interrogation room complete with recording equipment at the side of the table. I am on one side, DS Allen and Dr Robinson are on the other, and between us there is a screen. DS Allen seems at home here; he has loosened his collar and taps the lid of a small cardboard box in front of him. I am not at home here; they have handcuffed me to my chair.

I watch him as he leans forward to turn the recording equipment on.

There is nothing remarkable about DS Allen. He is pushing sixty I'd say, grey hair, red face, slightly bloated, drinks too much. If there were a policeman production line, he would roll out.

No, I take that back, there is something remarkable about him: he has a strangely breathy voice that sounds like the hand dryer in the visitor's loo. Everything he says seems a bit painful for him. I know the feeling. We could have a rasp-off.

'Beginning of session with Mrs Constance Mortensen. Present in the room with her are Dr Robinson, her forensic psychiatrist, and myself, Detective Sergeant Allen. The time is 14.55 and I am about to show Mrs Mortensen footage from CCTV cameras on Lower Bridge Road from the night of Thursday November 16th.'

With that he turns on the screen. After a dull stretch of black-and-white footage of an empty road in the dead of night, a car whizzes by. I know nothing about cars but it does look familiar. DS Allen pauses the tape, rewinds and zooms in. 'Is that your car, Mrs Mortensen?'

It could be, I can see that now. I squint at the screen. Then he zooms in on the number plate.

'Yes,' I say. I'm good with numbers. He comes up to the driver, who is in white, blurry-faced, leaning forward clutching the wheel, looking like something from one of those zombie shows Josh watches. I can't see anyone else in the car, only darkness.

'And is that you?'

Fuck. It *is* me.

'It might be.'

He zooms in a little more. I look ghastly. I have a vague recollection of it now. I nod.

'Yes or no, please,' says the hand dryer.

'Yes.'

'Constance Mortensen has identified herself as the driver of the vehicle on the night in question.' He seems pleased about this. Confident now, firing on all his Dyson cylinders, he pulls out a small pile of photos wrapped together with an elastic band from the box. For a moment, I wonder whether he's going to show me his holiday snaps. *Here's the wife and me in Margate . . . Here's a Boeing 747, transit number 0985 . . .* However, his face suggests otherwise. I watch him as he undoes the band. I try to catch Dr Robinson's eye but she is avoiding mine.

The band makes a snapping noise and he neatly puts it to one side. He looks at the first photograph for some time. I can't see Dr Robinson's expression; she has her head bowed but at an angle – she is looking at it too. DS Allen slowly turns the photograph around, places it on the table and slides it smoothly across to me. At first I only notice his stumpy bitten fingernails.

I meet his eye and then I look down at the photo.

It is a picture of Annie lying on a white sheet: naked torso, hair loose, eyes shut and mouth gently open with a tube coming out of her nose – it looks like she's taken that water tube from her hiking pack. She has fantastic bruises over her chest; they look incredibly real – dark reds and purples. I smile fondly: she's excelled herself with the game this time. Another photo is pushed before me. It's another one of Annie, from a different angle this time. I can see her felt pen-stained hand lying open at her side. She's wearing my black nail varnish on her fingernails; it's mainly chipped off. And her thumb is sticking out – she's probably just taken it out of her mouth. I look for evidence of her snuggler in her other hand, the bit of manky old fur she likes to sniff as she sucks, but I can't see it.

Another photo is pushed into my sightline. Ah, yes. It's

Polly. She's lying on a white sheet too. She looks more restrained; Annie's gone for the ghoulish look, perhaps overdone the bruising a tad. She too has a water tube coming out of her nose – they must have used Josh's. He won't like that.

I can't help but laugh.

I look up at DS Allen and Dr Robinson. They are not smiling. They are both staring at me with quietly shocked expressions on their faces. No one says anything.

Then DS Allen suddenly gets up, his chair making a loud scraping sound. He leans forward, placing those podgy fingers on the table, a little grey quiff of hair falling down the middle of his forehead, his face quite flushed and his strange voice oddly calm, 'May you rot in hell, Mrs Mortensen.'

I'm not sure policemen are meant to say things like this.

He turns around and walks out of the room, letting the door slam behind him. Dr Robinson lets out a kind of gasp, like a sob.

'Hey!' I cry. 'It's the death game. They play it all the time . . . they do it at the swimming pool, in the street . . .'

She bends down hurriedly to pick up her bag; she won't look at me. She is putting her jacket back on. The Rhino has come in and is uncuffing me from the chair.

'There were three of you in the car, Connie,' Dr Robinson says, her voice harsh and cracking. She's lying. Anyone can see that there was no one in the car apart from me. I haven't seen Dr Robinson like this before. She's really angry; she keeps dropping things on the floor in her rush. She is desperately trying to get away from me, to get out of the room as fast as she can. How dare she be like this? How dare they lie? I get up and rush after her, making the most of being uncuffed, but the Rhino grabs me by the wrist, spinning me round, making me cry out in pain. I lash out, I hit her. I scream after Dr Robinson.

'No, you wait!' I shout at her. 'What are you doing? Trying to make me think my daughter is dying? Fuck him and fuck you! You don't play with people like that. You don't tell a mother that her daughter is dying! You've got no fucking idea what that's like!'

Dr Robinson is in the corridor just outside the door but she stops quite suddenly and turns around to look at me, her face flushed and blotchy, her perfect shiny hair partly hanging over her face.

'You're wrong there, Constance,' she says. 'I know exactly what that's like.'

For a moment I don't understand what she means. Then I see it, her gaping sadness, the black grief that fills her up. And all my anger leaves my body; the Rhino seems to feel it too as she lets me go.

And slowly I move towards Dr Robinson. No one stops me. And she doesn't try and get away; she is staring at me, her blue eyes boring through me. I stop right in front of her. I reach out my right hand, the cuffs hanging off my wrist. I touch her cheek and still she doesn't move. She is trembling. Then she nods briskly, turns and heads off.

Chapter 7

The woman on Emma's left was a television producer and the man on her right was a gynaecologist. Emma had arrived late and missed the introductions and the Martinis. She missed the beginning of things because, however hard she tried to be on time, she always seemed to be late. It drove Si mad; he had argued vehemently once that late people were deliberately inconsiderate. She had been shocked – she hated to be thought of that way – and yet she never seemed capable of rushing. Perhaps she was on a different clock to other people. *Everything* took time: deciding what to wear, booking a holiday, having an orgasm.

Tonight, though, she had completely forgotten about the dinner party. It had been organized way too far in advance to remember. Hattie was good at cornering people; in the flush of a new relationship, she'd pinned Emma back in July: 'What are you doing November 28th?' It was designed to lasso the recipient into commitment. And Emma had not been quick-thinking enough to slip the noose. It was the last thing she had felt like doing but Emma was a reliable person: if she said she would go to something she always did. She got an Uber but the traffic had been so bad around Highbury and

Islington that she had got out and walked the last ten minutes, getting severely rained on and thus arriving with make-up running down her face – which Hattie had felt obliged to point out in a room full of dry, perfectly groomed, marginally pissed strangers.

And now here she sat, at the table on 28th November, having knocked back a catch-up Martini, asking polite questions of her neighbours in the way that she had been brought up to do. So far she had discovered that the gynaecologist was a misogynist and that the produ-cer made salacious reality shows where the aim of the game seemed to be to lure beautiful young people to have sex live on TV. Her name was Alba and she was also a vegetarian who loved animals, but appeared not to be very fond of human beings. Alba and the misogynist bickered across Emma's pea and mint scal-lops. She presumed they were married. She was relieved that neither of them had asked her a single thing about herself.

She caught Si's eye down at the other end of the table. He was sandwiched between Adrian and Adrian's girl-friend, whose name she didn't quite catch. Everyone agreed how nice the pea and mint scallop dish was and Hattie, without any qualms, was going into the details of the cooking of it, although Emma knew for sure that she would have bought it pre-prepared at some expensive eatery, because Hattie's driving force in life was expedi-ency. She had found the short cut to everything: why exercise when you can have the fat sucked off your buttocks?

The point of this dinner party was for everyone to

meet Blair, Hattie's new beefcake of a boyfriend, who was a perfect Ken to her Barbie. A long time ago Si and his sister had looked alike but Hattie had changed beyond recognition over the last ten years. She now resembled a doll. Her skin was permanently tanned and waxy, her lips looked puffed and painful, her hair was bleached blonde and of adjustable length, her eyebrows crawled across her ironed forehead, and her lashes flapped like crows' wings, casting shadows across her double-G breasts. The result of all the nips and tucks was that she had achieved a look of 100 per cent fakery and utterly indeterminate age – she could be anything from forty to eighty.

As the wine flowed, Emma slipped further and further out of the conversation. She couldn't focus at all tonight. However, she did notice that a game of musical chairs seemed to be going on around the table: people were up and down and moving about. She became aware of Si mocking his sister and knew he was about to tell the story of when they were kids and how Hattie had dropped his cigarettes down a gorge in the south of France. Emma had heard this story too many times. It wasn't even that good because Si was not a great storyteller. He was sweet and good but he didn't have what might be called charisma. Emma's eyes glanced across the room at the other guests as he began it. She smiled encouragingly. *This is the way we have to behave in couples,* she thought, *we support them in their delusions*. She wished *she* had a girlfriend to go on walking holidays with, to compare notes on their partners, to laugh about sexual positions, to feel part of some sisterhood. But all of Emma's friends had moved into a different world of parenting, sharing things that she wasn't a part of any more. They didn't quite know what to do with her these days, quite what to say. She had felt herself a cause of unease, an eggshell not to be stepped on, her very presence awkward and embarrassing. And nice as they were, they had stopped inviting her.

Emma stared at her glass. She picked it up and knocked it back. She looked over at Si. Adrian's girlfriend thought his gorge story was very funny so he was happy. How dare he be happy? She couldn't think straight; she didn't mean that. She poured the last of the bottle on the table into her neighbour's glass, feeling too self-conscious to share the dribbles. Ken, or Blair, or whoever he was, noticed and passed another bottle down the table; she was grateful for that and waited for someone to pour it into her glass. No one did.

Somebody else had already moved on to a funnier story. Emma missed the punchline but everyone was laughing a lot more at this story than the gorge one. She smiled politely; the men seemed to be getting louder and trying to top each other with who could be more outrageous, who could say the most callous thing for effect. There was a sort of frenetic flirtatious vibe in the room that Hattie always liked to create; the safety of couple-dom giving everyone a licence to flirt. Only when Emma spotted the white dust that circled Blair's nostril like a sugared doughnut did the penny drop; she took comfort in her Chardonnay.

Someone was telling a story which involved nudity and a goat. Emma found herself pulling suitable expressions at suitable moments but she had missed the gist of it and was looking around to see who else had gone off to powder their nose. It upset her – it wasn't the drug taking itself, it was the underhand manner of it, the exclusivity, the sneaking off from the table. It all seemed so childish. Worse than that, it was just plain bad manners. If you're going to take it, put it out on the table where everyone can partake or not as they wish. And for that matter, why had nobody offered *her* any? She wouldn't have had it (she'd had some once and been violently ill for days) but why did everyone *assume* that she was so square? She never used to be square. She and Sally Pea used to be quite wild in their teens.

'Sounds like the awful moment I found myself riverdancing in an Irish pub,' Blair said, and Emma watched as everyone decided at that moment that they liked him despite the fact he ran a battery-chicken farm and had voted for Brexit.

Emma helped the gynaecologist to some more wine, for courtesy's sake, then Alba the TV producer, then lastly herself. She was relaxing now. The stresses of the day had receded into the background, she was on to her second helping of bread and butter pudding – the cocaine-takers had all lost their appetites, so it was just her and Si who were having seconds – wondering whether she would draw attention to herself if she put her glasses on to pick out the raisins, when the conversation in the room hiccupped to a halt. Someone clearly said, 'You are kidding?'

Emma looked up, raisin on fork. All eyes at the table were turned on her. Her first thought was that they were all marvelling at her greed, or her manners. But something about their intensity said otherwise. Two things struck her: one, she was tremendously drunk, and two, someone was tightly clutching her arm.

The grip lessened. 'My God! What's she like?' Alba's eyes were all lit up, her palms clapping. Then silence.

'Who?' Emma asked.

'The Yummy Monster?'

'No, wait, the kids *survived*, didn't they?' someone else said.

'I think it's touch and go, that's what I read.'

'One of them's certainly in a coma. What's she like, Emma?' Emma stared at Alba, aware of a hot flush speeding up from her belly to her face. 'I mean she was just like a normal middle-class mum who lost it, wasn't she?'

'Yup!' piped up some scrawny-looking woman in the far corner whom Emma had only just noticed. 'You know Leah Worthington has left the BBC, don't you?'

'I thought she'd gone back?' someone else said, and for a moment they were all distracted by the scrawny woman. 'I know someone who used to do the park run with the Yummy Monster's husband. She said she was just a normal mum.'

'She was in a book club with Amanda Lewis's cousin.'

'Jesus!' someone said.

'Mind you, I'd kill my fucking children given half a chance,' said Alba, wiping at her plate with her finger. Several people laughed heartily. Emma caught Si's eye momentarily, then Si looked away, like he always did.

'Oh, Alba!' Hattie said. Her expression was almost

impossible to decipher since the surgery but her hairline moved up and down and her eyes flicked nervously from her brother to his wife.

'I'd love to make a programme on her.' The TV woman had refocused on Emma.

'Constance Morrison, that's her name,' said the scrawny woman.

'No, Mortensen,' several people corrected, but they were all still looking at Emma.

'Christ Almighty! What's going to happen to her?' someone else said.

Everyone was waiting for her to say something. She took a sip of her full glass of water. 'I'm . . . I'm just her . . . psychiatrist . . .'

'She should fucking fry, man,' said Ken, or Blair, the battery-chicken killer, whoever he was. 'Wait, frying's too good for that psycho. She should be stoned.'

Emma stared at him. The flush burned on her cheeks.

'Shut the fuck up,' Hattie said to her boyfriend, gently slapping him on his arm. 'Seriously though, Em, is she a monster?'

The room began to spin with their hatred.

'*Why* did she do it?'

'She's obviously insane . . . ? What will she get?'

'It's no use, Emma can't talk about work,' Si said, coming to her rescue. 'It's strictly confidential. I'm not allowed to ask her anything. Every time I walk past her computer, she slams down the screen as if she's having an affair!'

Adrian, the joker, the charmer, then took up the comedy baton and ran. 'I mean, attempting to murder your own child is bad enough. But someone else's! Can you imagine making that phone call to the parent?' He mimed being on the telephone. 'They had a lovely sleepover, super-fun, lots of crisps and pop, but just one *tiny* little thing . . .'

Everybody laughed and turned to see whether Emma was laughing. She hated Adrian then. Adrian, the caring barrister who defends trafficked women but visits prostitutes. She knew this because Si once let it slip by mistake.

Slowly, she got up from her chair; her voice was low and calm. 'Yes,' she said, looking at Adrian. 'Just imagine that.' She wiped her mouth with her napkin and put it down, tucking her chair in to the table. 'Excuse me,' she said, 'I'm just going to the bathroom.'

She hadn't meant to make a statement with it, but, nevertheless, she was aware of a momentary silence in her wake. She could hear the conversation pick up again by the time she got to the stairs. She went up slowly, hand on the banister. *Hold yourself together*, she said to herself. She got to the landing and opened the bathroom door. She went inside and locked the door behind her and leant against it, her heart punching fists against her chest. She went to the sink and clutched hold of the rim. She looked up at herself. She had drunk too much. Her hands were trembling.

A knock on the door startled her. She cleared her throat and turned on the tap.

'Just a moment!' she cried.

She flushed the loo for effect. She sat down. *Pull yourself together, woman*. She took a deep shaky breath. She could hear mocking laughter from directly beneath her and she hated them all. There was another knock on the bathroom door.

'Em?' Si tried the handle. 'You all right? Let me in!'

She thought about it and then got up and unlocked the door. She let him in and locked the door behind him.

He stood there looking at her. She felt foolish. She hated making a scene.

'Come on, Em . . .'

'Come on what?' She was torn: she didn't want to ruin the party but she was spoiling for a fight. 'They sit there, that bunch of bloody hypocrites, Hattie in all her fakery, with the meal she hasn't cooked, the hair she didn't grow, that moron of a boyfriend, making these judgements.'

'Woah!' he said. She knew he would defend his sister.

'They think *everything* is there to be joked about, to be mocked. Well, it's not, Simon. Everything is *not* funny. Some things are *not* funny.'

'That's just Adrian. You know how he is.'

'They're a bunch of frauds.'

'Right . . . Well, who's being judgemental now?'

She hated him, him and his stupid sister. 'She's worth ten of that lot.'

'Who is?'

'Connie.' She corrected herself. 'Constance Mortensen.'

He was looking at her in the same way she tried not to look at her patients. 'What did you say?'

Emma couldn't repeat it. She shouldn't have said that. She didn't even know what she meant. She had to do something decisive rather than continue in this vein so she went over to get some loo roll, snatched it off and blew her nose.

'You should be careful what you say,' he said.

'I'm always careful what I say! That's my fucking job!' she shout-whispered; even in this state she still worried about being overheard. 'I want some of that cocaine downstairs.'

'What? No you don't.'

Si sat down on the edge of the bath and stared at her.

She too sat down on the edge of the bath, knocking over a row of Hattie's expensive products as she did so.

'You've drunk too much,' he said.

'No, I haven't.' Obviously, she had.

'You've got work tomorrow.'

'No, I haven't. Not till Friday.'

They sat there for about a minute, side by side, both staring at the floor tiles. Her hair had slipped forward and he couldn't see her face, but she sniffed loudly.

'It's awful,' she said, her voice deep and angry. 'It's just awful.'

'What's awful, love?'

'Those little girls . . .'

Slowly, he stretched out his legs and crossed his ankles. 'You know you don't have to do this case? You could have it reassigned.'

Emma ignored him and stood up swiftly. She went to the little window above the toilet and opened it. She got out her cigarettes and lit up. She stood there, her back to him, and took a long soothing drag as she pulled herself together. 'I saw the forensic photographs today,' she said, turning around, glancing at him. 'We showed them to her. You know what she did when she saw the photograph of her daughter lying there in a coma?'

They held each other's gaze for a moment. 'She laughed, Simon.'

Emma looked back out of the window where a gust of wind was hurling the rain against the neighbouring brick wall.

'She's not of sound mind, love,' he said. He was ever the lawyer. Everything was so black and white for him.

'But she *seems* it. She seems far sounder than any of us.'

'Facts are facts,' he said.

'Those idiots downstairs,' she said quietly, so that the idiots wouldn't hear her. '*Are they dead? Are they in a coma?* They don't *care*, do they, as long as they get some gossip out of it . . .'

Emma blew the smoke in a steady stream out into the wet night and listened to the rain without moving, her eyes looking through the brick wall into a bleak beyond.

'No,' she said quietly, more to herself. 'A dead child is just a dead child.'

It was a cruel thing to say. She didn't turn but she heard him make a strange sound, an audible exhalation, like a punctured ball slowly releasing its air. As usual, she felt the distance between them.

Chapter 8

Feb 10

Leah was going out to play tennis and told me and Polly to be good for a few hours. Polly asked her for some money but she told Polly to stop being so bloody cheeky which was good because there is a swear box that Leah has to put money into. She put 10p in then we both did begging noises and got on our knees and tried to make her swear again. I like it when Leah laughs. She said Polly had no understanding of the valew of money (because she had given her 20 quid last week and she dropped it out of her pocket. It must of been when we were doing chalk circles round the dog poos in the park). Leah said if we wanted money we would have to work for it and told us to tidy the house while she was out. She looked silly going off down the street in white nappy nickers tennis costume. We collected all the money we could find in the house. Down the sofa. In the pencil pot. In the desk. By the bed. We found LOTS of interesting stuff in the draw by the bed. They have an ENORMOUS plastic toy willy on a short lead thing that buzzes and dances on the floor!! Polly strapped it on her back and we put an egg cosy on its head and we pretended it was a baby.

Then we got bored and decided to make a shop. Polly said Ness has loads of things she never uses so we had a look in her cubbard and found lots of stuff. Some gold boots that she only wears at Christmas. And a whole see threw zip bag full of clothes. Then we found Leahs golf sticks, Polly said she will never notice if a couple of them went missing and some nice big books from the top shelf. Polly says no one EVER looks up there. And we took the dancing willy. ANYWAY we found so much that we ended up borrowing a trolley from Sainsburys and we put everything in it and pushed it to the park and we made a stall by the market. Some boys from year 7 bought the willy for 2 pounds!! And Sashas mum came by and bought Nesses leather jacket. She was modelling it all like a model and we were going yeah it looks really good on you, although to be honest it didnt because she is not the slimmest of people ahem ahem if you know what I mean, but you have to lie in shops if you want to be a seller.

We made LOADS of money. 46 pounds 35p (minus 10 pounds because Josh and his smelly friends came by and said theyd snitch on us).

Anyway when we got back to Pollys Ness and Leah were having a row. We could hear Leah shouting from outside the house. At first we thought it was because of us and our shop but it wasnt. They didn't even hear us when we came in. So we tiptoed up the stairs and they carried on argewing.

Polly says she thinks they are going to devorce and then she would get two summer holidays instead of one. And more Christmas presents and two Christmas dinners. And maybe go and live in Jamaica. I said why Jamaica. She said thats just what people do when they get devorced. I dont think shes right. Mum says Polly has a very active imagination which means she lies. For example Polly once told me that when her aunt was in hospital, she suddenly pulled out all her tubes and

*got out of bed, peeled an orange ate it and died on the floor.
I hope she is not going to live in Jamaica. I hope they dont
devorce.*

*I hope my mum and dad are not going to devorce. I feel sorry
for all those people in our class whose parents are devorced. I try
and pretend its OK to them but I would hate it. Alice says you
have no idea at all that its coming but Phoebe P says you can tell
its coming because first of all you notice that your mum and dad
are never in the same room (mine are). Then you notice that
they are never holding hands (mine still do sometimes) and then
they are always banging things (mine do that) and the big clue
is that they dont sleep in the same bed (mine do!!!). Polly says
she doesnt think mine will devorce because everyone is always
laughing in our house. It is full of jokes so we are OK, pleeeease.
Polly says Ness and Leah are never laughing only when they are
with other people. She says Ness is nicer when Leah is away
otherwise Leah just sits on the sofa watching golf and tennis.
Polly likes to climb up to the biscuit cubbard to make her shout
at her.*

These are things we hear Leah say to Ness in the row.

*1) That she cant bare her stupid family and that she should
try climbing out of her own arse some time. ???*

*2) That they have NOTHING in common. (Wrong. Polly
and Evie and two hamsters.)*

*3) Why doesnt Ness ever show any emotion?? She called her
a fuking robot. (Polly and me like robots.)*

*Ness didnt shout back at Leah at all. I would of done. I
would of said get off the sofa you lazy poo. Actually I would of
said the BBC news is rubbish. She cares about that shes always
on twitter swearing at her phone.*

4) Ness says to Leah, I think you better calm down before you say things you might regret.

5) Leah says to Ness, Stop being so fuking patronizing.

6) Ness says to Leah, You can be quite a kleeshay yourself, Leah. (Polly and I dont know what a kleeshay is and it is not in the dictionary so it is probably rude.)

7) Leah says to Ness, Your so passive aggressive. (Which Polly said means sometimes you want sex and sometimes you dont.)

Then I dropped my tube of gobstoppers down the wooden stairs and Ness came out and said hello girls perhaps its time you went home, Annie. I said no I didn't have to but Leah said I did. When I went home, Granny and Grampa were in the kitchen and Granny said hadnt I grown and was I still good at maths. I said I havent grown since yesterday and I am as good at maths since yesterday. I sat on Grampas lap and gave him some starbursts. He likes the orange ones best. Mum said to Grampa have you seen Doctor Timmins? And Grampa said I did what up the chimney? And Granny said oh yes we must get it cleaned. Mum and Dad were laughing so much I knew they werent getting devorced. Phewyyy!!

I feel sad reading this. I shut the diary and look out of the window for a while. It's a grey lifeless day, with a smothering dark blanket of a sky. Oh, Annie. There is nothing worse than your child's unhappiness. I don't mean when they've lost a football game or hurt their knee, I mean real unhappiness with a damn good reason: a death, or discovering that their parents might be splitting up – which is just another kind of death. He was so angry; I hadn't anticipated that. I hadn't anticipated any of it; each blow seemed to take us all by surprise. A family in peril, hanging by a thread until it snaps and we're all tossed into freefall, landing randomly with different breakages. Josh's pain turned to fury at us. And rightly so: we were destroying the safety of his world. *We*, his parents, his protectors, were consciously choosing to hurt them: *we* were the cause of their unhappiness. How unnatural and perverse it is to do this to one's own kids. But how far are we meant to go for our children, how much can we take? I told him I felt so guilty. *Guilt?* he said. *What's the point of guilt? It's just you telling me that you're a nice person.*

I don't hear the Squeak coming down the corridor. I turn as she unlocks the door, my eyes glancing at the clock. It's not medicine time. Then I remember that a social worker is meant to be coming today and am surprised to see that it's not a social worker; the Squeak has brought Dr Robinson. She's not looking me in the eye.

'Need any more water, Connie?' the Squeak asks me. As if she cares.

'Yes please, ice and a slice,' I say, sounding cheerier than I am feeling. But I am pleased to see Dr R. The Squeak rolls her eyes at me and brings in a lukewarm jug and swaps it for the empty one on my side table. Why bother. Dr Robinson is smiling politely at the Squeak; she's being helpful, holding the door open for her so she can get back to her trolley. I notice that there is a stain on Dr Robinson's trousers and her hair isn't looking quite so glossy. It's matted a little at the back.

'Those fumes are pretty strong . . . could we open a

window?' Dr Robinson says to the Squeak. They're painting the whole place a happy yellow colour that isn't
fooling anyone. I can't smell a thing – I've got used to it.
It's pretty toxic; Mental Sita's gone berserk. She somehow got hold of a pot of Sunshine and tried to bury her
head in it. She's good at grabbing life by the balls.

The Squeak isn't used to anyone important bothering
with her but she shuffles into the room and makes a feeble attempt to open the window, knowing full well there
is no chance. She says something banal like she'll ask
someone at reception, but she won't. She's a lazy cow.

When she leaves the room, Dr Robinson gives me a
curt, brusque smile and comes over to our little table. I
feel a bit hurt that we have become such strangers again.
She regrets revealing so much to me. She takes her jacket
off and I'm intrigued by the fact that her jumper is on
both inside out and back to front. (She shops at Agnes B.)

'I only gathered this morning that I would be needed
today,' she says, seemingly by way of explanation. 'Oh,
those fumes!' She languidly waves her hand in front of
her face. 'They're unbearable.' I watch her go over to the
windows and attempt to open them herself. She *knows*
they're locked. I see the impatience in her body language.
Something's not right with her today. She sighs, smooths
back her hair and cautiously crosses the room to sit down
in her usual place. As she bends down to put her bag on
the floor, I get a whiff of her. And it all makes sense. She
is a drowner of sorrows. It is a much stronger smell than
the paint. When she looks up, something about my
expression makes her nervous and she leans over to get

something out of her bag. She pops an Xtra-strong mint into her mouth. It won't do the job; she reeks of wine. It's seeping out of every pore. I rather like the sweet sickly smell; it's reminiscent of those 1970s sweets – cherry drops. Karl used to smell of it regularly, every time he'd come back from a bender. He's a harmless drunk; stupid and boring, but harmless. I wonder what Dr Robinson is like when she's drunk. I bet she's a bit feisty.

She's trying to smile that professional smile but it's not really working any more. And her skin is going a strange colour.

'Constance,' she says, clinging to a semblance of control. 'I want to talk about your hair. When did you notice it starting to fall out?' She really is very pale; it occurs to me that she might be about to throw up.

'Dr R,' I say. I have never called her this to her face, but I am nothing if not opportunistic; she's weak and vulnerable right now.

'I think I've eaten something that has disagreed with me,' she says, a light sweat breaking out on her upper lip.

'Either that,' I say, 'or possibly the vat of vino.'

The mere mention of wine and all is undone. Suddenly she clutches her hand to her mouth. She, the Forensic Psychiatrist, is going to puke in the Loony's room. It is quite marvellous. I gesture magnanimously towards the snazzy, shiny, silver, suicide-proof toilet like an airy hostess and she gets up. Even in her hour of need she does not appear to rush and therefore does not quite make it across the room. A little vomit slips through her fingers on to the lino floor. Poor Dr R, she is on her knees, clutching the rim of the lunatic's toilet, heaving like the wino she evidently is. I think I like her more right now than I have ever done before.

I follow her to the loo and place my hand on her back. It feels so good to have human contact. Her back is broad and strong. With my other hand I hold back the strands of her hair that have slipped forward. Her hair really is very soft. I feel good. I am a natural carer. I am a mother again. She pauses before heaving again and when she next pauses I flush the toilet, rid her of her spewing mess.

When she has finished, she slowly sits back on her thighs, shaking her head, wiping her mouth. 'I am so sorry, Constance. I am so sorry, this is inexcusable.' She is mortified with embarrassment, unaware that there is no need – bad behaviour is my comfort zone. 'I thought we didn't have a session today. The phone call woke me up . . .'

'Ssshh,' I say. 'It doesn't matter. Are you going to be sick again?' She shakes her head. She is unsure.

I leave her there and pour her some plastic-jug water. She rinses out her mouth and spits into the loo. She tries to get up.

'You need to wash your hands.' I stand her up; she is as meek as a little lamb. I take her to the shitty little sink and she washes her hands and splashes her face. Then I escort her over to my bed and tell her to lie down for a minute.

'No . . .' she murmurs. 'I'm so sorry, this is inexcusable. I do apologize.'

'I just hope the evening was worth it.' She lets me lay her down on top of my bed.

'I better . . .' she says, the impropriety of the situation

getting too much for her. She struggles to sit up. I lay her down again and she lets me.

'Just for a minute,' I say, 'while I clear things up.'

She relaxes a little and I turn off the side light and take off her shoes (Russell & Bromley). I put them on the floor and then I tug out some paper towels from the dispenser and clear up the vomit on the floor and around the toilet. I wash my hands and run my flannel under cold water. I return to the bed and press it on to her forehead. She opens her eyes briefly and touches the flannel and makes a few mumbles of polite protest.

After a minute or two, when I think she has actually fallen asleep, she says, 'It wasn't worth it, no.' Then, rather sweetly, she tries to carry on a normal session. 'I got your next missive. Thank you.'

I spot a bit of vomit on her chin and wipe it off for her. She tries to open her eyes but decides against it.

'Was it beautiful?' she says sleepily. 'The walk? What's the countryside like around Bath?'

'It's stunning,' I say. 'If you haven't been, you should go.'

She smiles, still with shut eyes, and nods her head a little. 'How nice to have a friend . . . was the dinner good, in the inn?'

'Yes, it was hearty.'

'And the room? Was it nice?'

'Oh yes, we slept in a big four-poster bed.'

She is nearly asleep but she raises an eyebrow there in a questioning fashion. I like her like this, I really do. I'm smiling but she can't see me.

'You dirty shrink,' I say to her, quietly moving the chair from the table to the bedside. She smiles. I sit down and very gently begin to stroke her hair. We are very close. A muscle twitches on her face and I remember Ness lying there next to me in that big four-poster, inches apart, like this. And I remember something she said as we lay there in the great leveller of darkness. She told me that she had something to confess – how excited I'd felt to hear those words. She wasn't sure exactly *why* but she couldn't help feeling jealous of my best and oldest female friends, Ally and Grace, of the place they held in my affections. She'd met them at one of my birthday drinks at the house and I'd noticed she was odd with them. I understood, or I pretended I did, for I felt flattered and tried to cover up my coyness with a pretence of understanding; we talked about female friendship for a while but it was ages before I could fall asleep. This . . . whatever it was that was going on between us . . . this *tenderness*, was not easy to categorize. It felt precarious, unsettling. Ness on the other hand had no trouble sleeping; at one stage, breathing heavily, she turned in her sleep and wrapped her arm around me, her hand cupping my breast. I suddenly became wide awake, aware of every single nerve-ending, every rise and fall of my chest. I could hear an owl in the woods beyond. She must have thought I was Leah. After a minute or two, I gently crawled out from beneath her hand, got out of bed, tucked her in, and took a blanket and went to sleep on the sofa.

'Just because we might *feel* these things, it doesn't mean we have to act on them,' I whisper, but Dr R too is sound asleep now. That mantra I have oft repeated sounds hollow now in this sterile room, my voice just a rasp.

'I never wanted mess in my life, you see,' I say to no one. 'I've always been very clear about that. I *hate* mess. I hate deception. Karl deserved so much better than that . . .' I sit back. I look around and think about the mess my life is in right now. 'I hate mess,' I repeat quietly, confused by everything.

The greyness outside is oppressive. I'm looking at my leaf for comfort. It is immobile. I feel so incredibly sad for everything that's gone, everything that's lost. I look down at Dr R, lying there, breathing deeply through her parted lips, finding respite from her own losses. How much younger she looks when asleep, now that the frowning and fretting has left her face. I stroke her silky hair, noticing that she dyes it – expensively. Right at the roots I can see the thinnest line of grey. She begins to snore gently.

I shouldn't waste this time. I get up and go over to the chair and look at her things. I pick up her jacket and try it on. She's broader than me. I put on her shoes; they are a size too big. I walk around the room feeling professional and dapper, organized and successful. She is in a deep sleep. I do a little tap dance; my grandmother taught me to tap dance in nothing but her tights. The shoes seem to come to life. I sling her Mulberry bag across my shoulder and give it some jazz hands. It's amazing what clothes can do. I could walk out of here. I could slip past the moron outside the room and make my way down the corridor. They'd stop me at the door though; it's like Fort Knox down there. But I don't leave. I don't *want* to leave. I need this little hiatus in my life.

So I move the chair back to the table and I sit down

and begin to go through her bag. No keys or sharp objects – she would have had to hand them in at reception. There are a few gluten-free oat-bar wrappers folded neatly at the bottom, her Xtra-strong mints, a couple of Tampax in a case, the usual things. I find a couple of receipts: Wagamama (chicken ramen £9.95, smoothie £4.75 – eating alone), Boots (ah . . . to get that silky look she uses a John Frieda intense treatment for brunettes £9.95; Braun toothbrush £74.95 – wtf? They're paying her too much.) Her bag is neat and tidy, not like mine. Where is mine? I am not a handbag person any more. Handbags are not for asylum dwellers.

I open a zip pocket and find her phone. It takes me a while to work out what the cover photo is of – I'm too immersed in the detail. Only when I move back can I see it. It's a child's handprint in white clay, the kind that new parents have done – so dizzily in love with our new-borns and for the first time understanding the fragility of time, already lost in a future nostalgia for *now* because the horrific reality is unignorable: one day this perfect tiny miracle will become an ugly great mess of humanity. So, desperate to preserve this momentary perfection we press their little hands into white clay as 'concrete' proof of it.

I look at my leaf and the stupid leaf is looking at me, waving merrily. But I am not merry, I am far from it. I feel a panic and a sadness swirling inside. Where does all the love *go*? Where has everything gone? Where is my mother? I swipe away the handprint. I want to speak to Karl. I want to hear his voice. I need him. Right now I can't quite remember why we have split up; the reasons don't seem important. Perhaps he and I are salvageable. I must speak to him.

I stare at the keypad. I have no idea of Dr Robinson's code. So I continue looking in her bag. In another zip pocket I find her wallet. Inside is a photograph of a balding man playing some sort of wind instrument, presumably Si, looking like a chipmunk. I find her driving licence; it takes a while for me to realize that it is a picture of her. Time has not been kind to her, or me – it has slapped us both about a bit. She looks so young and happy in the photo, plump and glowing, full of life's potential before disappointment management becomes the name of the game. Maybe she and her musical husband have been backpacking in the Himalayas, or helping starving orphans, or rebuilding earthquake-ridden towns. Yes, I bet he's a doctor, working for the Red Cross or something heroic.

Her full name is Emma Elizabeth Davis. As I thought, she is English through and through. She's forty-seven. I find her date of birth and try various combinations of it in the phone. Nothing. I take out her iPad mini and try a few combinations of her birth date and bingo, I'm in. There's no wifi so there's little I can do. I check out her Safari history – which is interesting, and I look at what she's been watching on BBC iPlayer – which is not. I sit like that for a while, in her clothes with the contents of her bag strewn across my lap, and I imagine that I am her, with her successful life and her inner sorrow. I imagine I am someone else, a normal person capable of managing my misery. But who is a normal person? And what exactly is the difference between them and a mentalist?

One of us is drowning, that's all. One of us has slipped beneath the surface, unable to bear the load any more. I feel afraid. I want to do something but there is nothing I can do. My mother would know what to do. I miss her so much. I will ask Karl to bring her here; she will be worried about me. Maybe she's visiting David in Australia. Yes, that must be it.

I should wake Dr Robinson up now, but I like watching her and it seems almost cruel to snatch her from this sweet slumber. I have put her things back in the bag and moved my chair beside the bed again to watch her for a while longer. It's been an unusual session, to say the least. But the hour is up.

'Dr Robinson?' I say gently, my face very close to hers.

She opens her eyes and looks at me. For a second she has absolutely no idea where she is, or who I am. Then she remembers. I see the panic set in. It must be confusing; I am wearing her jacket.

'You're wearing my jacket,' she says guardedly, climbing off the bed, the intimacy we shared an hour ago all gone. I take off the jacket and put it at the end of the bed. To be honest, I'd totally forgotten. I hope I haven't made it smell.

She takes the jacket and goes to her bag. She pauses there; I know what she's thinking. I see her check her phone, the time, the code, her driving licence; she gathers her things, crosses to the bathroom and tries to smooth her face in the metal smear of the mirror. She doesn't look me in the eye. Then she goes straight to the door, clutching her bag tightly. She wants to get the hell out of here. She stops and turns around.

'Connie,' she says. She looks awkward, which given the nature of the session is fair enough. 'I've let you down and I'm so sorry. I'm going to talk to my supervisor.'

'No,' I say quite firmly, alarmed at the prospect. 'Don't talk to anyone. I'm not going to.'

She looks surprised. I think I see something like gratitude in her eyes. And a little fear. I frighten people now. I frighten myself. I feel so alone.

'All I ask is that you bring my mother to see me . . . please.' As I've said before, I'm an opportunist.

'I really don't think I can do that,' she says.

'You can. Just drop by – there's no point in making plans. If she's not at her house she'll be at mine. Just go and get her. Say you're there to pick up a nightie or something for me.'

She doesn't want to do this. Her eyes flit across the floor; she's remembering the vomit. 'I can't promise anything.' But she's thinking about it.

'I tried on your shoes, too,' I say.

She is quiet for a moment. She is looking at her shoes, perhaps wondering whether they feel different since being inhabited by a madwoman. I like her, I really do. She is vulnerable like me. I don't want her to go, I don't want her to leave me on my own.

'Can I ask you something?' I say, because it occurs to me that she really might know the answer. She looks up at me and gives a small nod.

'How does everyone else . . . function?' I say.

She frowns and cocks her head, listening for that familiar wolf.

'Why aren't the streets *full* of wrecked people?' I ask.

And I see something like recognition in her eyes. We stand there in a silence that only loonies, lovers and psychotherapists are comfortable with.

She shakes her head a little; she doesn't know. She is *so* sad; I think she's as sad as I am. Then, and I have no idea why *then*, because it seems indulgent and inappropriate, I start to cry. I cannot remember the last time I cried, but whenever it was I don't think it sounded like this: a ship's foghorn. And it feels so strange to be feeling something (and preventing a crisis at sea) that I feel almost triumphant in my unhappiness.

'It's all right,' I hear her say. And I don't know if I'm imagining it because she's not meant to touch me (or vomit in my toilet) but I feel her hand on my shoulder and it makes me foghorn again. I miss human contact so much. I miss my kids. I miss my mum.

'Please don't hate me.' I'm pathetic now, bleating like a lamb. I'm really letting myself down with this ghastly neediness, I know, but it suddenly seems vitally important to me that she doesn't hate me. If she leaves this room hating me, I feel I might go mad. Madder, I mean.

She shakes her head. 'I don't hate you,' she says, and these are the most beautiful words I think I have ever heard.

'Everyone else does,' I say. I notice her hand slowly falling from my shoulder.

'Perhaps they don't understand you,' she says. I can hear the Squeak coming down the corridor. Dr Robinson can hear her too and suddenly flashes me that professional tight-rectum smile.

'Do *you* understand me?'

She looks anxiously through the glass in the door.

'Mrs Ibrahim's on her way,' she says, and gives me that curt nod goodbye.

'Emma!' I cry, reaching for her hand. (I've never called her this before. It kind of stops her in her tracks.) 'Do *you* understand me?'

I get the connection I'm after; she holds my gaze.

'Keep telling your story and we'll get there . . .'

And then she's gone, leaving me standing in the middle of the room like an abandoned toy. But I'm worried now. I'm not sure I want to get to where we're going.

Chapter 9

The local surgery was a hit-and-miss affair, but you would know that already, Dr R. There were six or so regular GPs and unless you specified a particular doctor, you got whoever was next in line. My mother, however, had a specific appointment, an *important* appointment. The waiting room was packed and we had squeezed ourselves into a pew by the desk; unfortunately the receptionist, a woman with the voice and pores of a seasoned smoker, was hard of hearing and I learnt far more than I wanted to about the personal ailments of my fellow waiting-roommates. I was hormonal and stressed but had promised my mother I would take her. I'd picked her up from her house where she was eagerly awaiting me at the window. To my surprise, she was wearing her best earrings and her pink floral dress. She looked as if she were off to a wedding. I complimented her and saw her anxiety lessen a little. I asked how she was feeling, whether she was still having dizzy spells, but she wasn't listening; she was rather haphazardly putting on some red lipstick in the hall mirror. In the car, I noticed through her tights that her shins were covered in scratches; she'd been gardening, but what with the poppy smudge around her mouth, it made her

seem rather vulnerable in her battle against the professional medical opinion.

Patient after patient was called in, their names whiz-
zing by on the screen in jazzy dotted writing, my mother
reading everyone's name out loud (and commenting in
her not untheatrical timbre on possible parentages). By
the time her own name sped across the screen, we were
pretty much the last people there. With all the excitement of the lettering and the global mix of patients, we
had both rather forgotten the nature of the appointment.
You'll be fine, Mum.

We went in to see Dr Rhys Evans. Anita Rhys Evans. I
knew her: she was a mum at the school and the private–
public line had merged too much for my liking (I always
specified another doctor for my own appointments). It
had been embarrassing for both of us on the first day of
nursery to lock eyes as we rummaged about in the sand-
pit searching for plastic toys with Josh and Hannah when
the last time we had met she had been rummaging about
in my traumatized vagina post placental abruption. Awkward memories of concrete mammaries and septic
stitches came back as I blew sand from a plastic tractor.
We had further been thrown together in Year One when
Josh developed an obsessional crush on her minx of a
daughter. *I am the saddest man in England, Mummy*, he told
me coming out of school in tears one day, snot pouring
from his nose (not a girlfriend-keeping look, darling).
Hannah, the slapper, had been flashing her knickers at
Aidan O'Connor. *I'm afraid, Josh, Hannah can show her
knickers to anyone she likes*, I'd said responsibly. (I also had
a soft spot for Aidan; he was a fiery kid from the estate

who allegedly once told the headmaster to fuck off – hats off, that boy.)

Dr Rhys Evans (I needed to keep this professional) didn't seem to notice the immense effort my mother had gone to, which I couldn't help but hold against her. A fleeting comment on how well she looked, how pretty her dress was, would have gone far to soothe the nerves. However, her interest went straight to me as we walked in. 'Hi Connie, how are you?' She was grinning. She grinned a lot and spoke through clenched teeth like a ventriloquist. It was most disconcerting. I suspect she even gave grisly prognoses with that lockjawed grin, her hand flapping in a rubber glove. Anita Rhys Evans was one of those women who was desperate to be a hit on the social scene but unfortunately managed to get on everyone's nerves. 'I read that interview you did with er . . . what's his name . . . the disgraced MP?' she said. 'I *loved* it.' I murmured thanks. 'But Tom felt it was a bit far-fetched . . .' She always did this. She loved to deflate; I'm not even sure it was deliberate – it was probably part of her make-up. I was quite susceptible to deflation that day and I had an instinctive, almost visceral response to flee from Anita.

Anita Rhys Evans was a space-invader, always standing those few inches too close, and she had the most peculiar habit of looking you up and down as she spoke to you, her eyes settling on vulnerable parts of your anatomy for whole sentences. I'm used to men having conversations with my breasts but I'd never encountered it in a woman before. And she never actually listened to what was being said; to ensure that she didn't have to, she had developed an elongated blink that prevented interruption. She was a brain drain; I always left her company feeling emptied of life. And she certainly wasn't the one I wanted to hear bad news from; there would be an edge of glee in the telling.

So we asked after each other's kids. Hannah – not the sharpest tool in the box – had been force-fed tutors from Year Four and was doing *absolutely amazingly* at St Poshy-Posh-Posh School for Girls, while Josh – averagely sharp but lazy tool – was learning how to illegally download anything he wanted at Statey-McState Academy round the corner. I'd bumped into Hannah on the bus and been bemused by the new accent and the inordinate number of times she said *like* (actually she said *lake*) in one sentence. So within the first minute of sitting on the chair and listening to how Hannah had joined the rowing team and was climbing mountains for Duke of Edinburgh (what *is* that?) and was almost fluent in Spanish after two years, I felt a new component in my increasing unhappiness: *guilt* at the shabby education I was giving my son.

My mother wasn't helping matters by repeatedly saying, 'How marvellous! How clever of her! What an amazing school! Wonderful Hannah!' I wanted to bang the table and establish one important fact: let's not forget that Hannah shows the boys her vagina!

So, puffed up by her own crowing, Dr Rhys Evans eventually turned to my mother, lips stretched into an unmoving letterbox slot, eyes fixed on my mother's cut shins, and said, 'All right, Mrs de Cadenet. Are you ready?'

I haven't told you about Mrs de Cadenet, have I, Dr R? Let me try and summarize. My mother is a warrior. She has always been fearless. She swam across lakes, she dived off rocks, she lit fires, I saw her break the neck of a dying rabbit with her bare hands, she galloped on horses, she climbed trees, she peed in bushes (or worse), she would think nothing of approaching strangers, of fixing plugs or changing tyres, of sunbathing topless, of disputing authority. She prized initiative above all else and nothing annoyed her more than when we didn't show it. We didn't have boundaries like other kids did. It wasn't a considered thing; it was just the way she was. She had been brought up in the wilds of Northumberland under a rule of benign neglect, which she considered normal parenting.

She adored my father and he was indeed adorable. He was a fusty old academic who didn't really notice what we, or she, were up to. In fact, he didn't really notice anything at all if it wasn't in Latin. (A favourite pastime for David and me was to blindfold him and get him to describe what he was wearing. He would never have the slightest idea at all – I mean, not *at all*. *I'm wearing my tennis clothes,* he'd say proudly, sitting there in a three-piece suit.) Which probably explained why we lived where we lived: in an armpit of north London. They could have moved if they wanted to, but it didn't seem to bother them that our house was the only one in the street that wasn't derelict, or run-down council accommodation, or a squat, or a drug den, or the Hare Krishna house (goodness, Ganesha, did they like a drum and chant) or – somewhat bizarrely – a convent.

My mother formed ranting action groups that held meetings in our kitchen – usually consisting of just her, my father (smuggling in a book on Renaissance philosophy) and old Sister Gwendolen. They mounted campaigns, picked up litter, lay on the road to divert Heavy Goods Vehicles (also good reading time for Dad) and fought to keep bus services going. She took the council to court, refusing point-blank to pay our rates, and won the case, becoming the first person in legal history with the right *not* to pay rates. The local police all knew her by her first name (Julia) as she called them a couple of times a week over some incident or other that she had attempted to sort out: the ten-year-old glue-sniffer she found lying in his own vomit, the skinhead brandishing a weapon – *Put the gun down, young man!*

Nothing intimidated her; not even the man who jumped out from behind a tree as she and I were walking the dog in a particularly secluded part of the litter-filled, bombed-out, brambled green space further down the road. He was masturbating furiously at us. *Look at me! Look at me!* he cried proudly, clenching his prized possession in his plump fingers. My mother pushed me behind her (I was stock still, utterly mesmerized by the sheer monstrosity of it) and stepped right up to him and said in the voice she reserved for truly bad behaviour, *Shame on you! Put your penis away, you disgusting little man!* To my amazement, the disgusting little man promptly burst into tears and stuffed that thing away. It turned out he was indeed ashamed of himself, and she spent the next twenty minutes comforting him on a tree stump while I kicked some used condoms about. Are you getting the picture, Dr R, of where I've come from, of who this woman that bore me is?

Well, I am sad to say that my warrior mother has finally been defeated. Her brave heart is riddled with fear now as the Alzheimer's begins to shake her in its jittery jaws. Fortunately ten years ago they moved to a house near me, seemingly amazed that some people lived in streets where windows weren't smashed and people used toilets. But now, daily, sometimes hourly, she bikes round to my house – I know, I know, but there's no prising her off it – in a state of pure alarm. (What will she do if we sell the house? I have to be near her, don't you see, Dr R? She'll carry on turning up on her bicycle, oblivious to the new inhabitants and their differences: she'll sit in their kitchen, make their beds, get in their baths.) For she is stuck in a cycle of breathless panic: confused, shrunken, stuttering, swallowing, fear and worry oozing from her every pore. I try to calm her, soothing sweet nothings as she tells me of the latest molehill now become a mountain: she can't find a stamp, or her soap, or her handbag; she doesn't know how many teabags to put in a cup. Life itself has become the enemy, ambushing and assaulting her with its every terrifying move.

And yet, despite it all, Dr R, my mum is still there. She has retained her empathy, her emotional intelligence, her loving, caring soul. She is still the port in all my storms, my anchor, my sanctuary. She is my true north.

I clasped her hand in mine, overwhelmed by a fierce protectiveness towards her as I explained to Dr Rhys Evans that before we did the test I just wanted to mention that she'd been feeling faint and weak. She flashed her teeth and raised a finger and rang through to the nurse, and asked whether there was time for a quick blood test. Then Dr Rhys Evans looked down at the dreaded notepad.

'All right, Mrs de Cadenet, shall we begin?'

My mother was very anxious now but she concentrated as hard as she could.

'I want you to remember three words for me . . . and I'm going to ask you to repeat them to me at the end of the test. OK?'

'OK,' my mother repeated, as if it was one of the words.

'Apple. Horse. Tuesday.'

My mother laughed, delighted that the test she had been dreading was going to be so absurdly easy. 'Apple. Horse and . . . Tuesday,' she said, her lips repeating the words several times.

'Right,' said Dr Rhys Evans. 'Can you tell me what day it is today?' (Slightly mean, don't you think?)

'Tuesday!' My mother said with great confidence. It was Friday.

'OK,' said Dr Rhys Evans. 'And can you tell me who our present monarch is?'

'Of course I can!' said my mother, rather enjoying herself now. 'Queen Elizabeth the Second.'

'And what might you put up in the rain?'

She was thrown by this and killed some time with repetition. 'What might I put up in the rain . . . A shelter?' she said, as if it were an initiative test. It was a vaguely sensible answer, wouldn't you say, Dr R? 'I might light a fire,' she continued, confident but in the wrong vein.

Dr Rhys Evans flashed those teeth. 'All right. And what is nine plus eight?'

'Um . . . nine plus eight . . . is, ooh. Eighteen . . . no . . .' She was beginning to panic. She wanted to pass this test so badly, to be told that everything was all right, that she wasn't losing her mind. 'I just can't think for the life of me.' She laughed.

'Never mind. Can you spell the word "difficult" for me?'

'Difficult. D-i-f-f-f . . . c-l . . . t.' I smiled at her encouragingly. She had always been an excellent speller. I felt humiliated for her.

'That's wonderful. And what were the words I asked you to remember at the beginning of the test?'

'Oh.' she said. She looked quizzical. She had no idea what the doctor was talking about.

'Remember, Mamma?' I said. 'You had three words at the beginning to remember?'

'Oh yes,' she said, glad for my intervention. 'Thank you, darling. Now what were they? . . . Now, hang on . . . Oh bugger! . . . Starlight?'

'Yes!' I said to her, and she looked so pleased with herself. Starlight had been the name of her pony as a child. Horse-Pony-Starlight. There was a logic to it; I'd have given her half a point. But Dr Rhys Evans did not look impressed.

'Don't worry,' she said. 'You did just fine.' But my mother seemed downhearted despite fond memories of galloping across fields on Starlight. Just then the nurse came in with her blood test paraphernalia and sat down next to my mother. 'Thank you, Sebo,' said Dr Rhys

Evans, and let her eyes settle on mine after noting the make and model of my shoes.

'So how's Ness doing? I haven't seen her about,' she asked, while Sebo rolled up my mother's sleeve. I could tell Dr Rhys Evans had been waiting to ask me this and was delighted to have me cornered in her surgery. She wasn't asking in a concerned way, she was asking in a gossipy way; there was that undeniable edge of excitement in her voice. I'd heard it in a few others when they asked about Ness and Leah (I seemed to have found myself being their director of communications).

'I saw Leah at parents' evening . . .' she continued in a leading manner. (She was still milking the state system for all she could get with her younger two children before swanning them off for futures of entitlement.) That was the other thing about Dr Rhys Evans: she was a complete star-fucker. Even as she rolled out the list of Hannah's achievements, she couldn't resist dropping a few names – celebrity parents of Hannah's contemporaries, chefs and footballers (does that count?) – until my face had run out of impressed expressions. Poor Leah – Dr Rhys Evans was all over her like an oozing dose of herpes.

'Ness is fine,' I said. I was not going to discuss the matter with her.

But my mother evidently still felt as if she were in an exam environment and had stumbled upon a question she knew the answer to (by nature she was never indiscreet).

'She is *now*,' she said, 'but it was awful for her!' Every now and then, my mother pounced on a memory as it passed through her head with the agility of a wildcat upon its prey.

I knew exactly what she was remembering. The day that Leah left her not-so-happy home, Ness had wandered round to my house, barefoot and bemused. I was out interviewing an oil magnate up in town and my mother happened to be in the house looking for something, but had long forgotten what. She was the perfect person in a crisis, with her heart full of compassion and her head full of muddle (perhaps an unriddled mind cannot offer the same simple solace). She received the distraught Ness, no doubt enveloping her in her bosom. Later – I came in through the downstairs door; they hadn't heard me – I stood in the portal of the sitting room to find them on the sofa, Ness half tucked, half sprawled, like a lazy old dog, across my mother's chest, with my mother running her capable, practical fingers gently through Ness's hair, softly singing the same lullaby she used to sing to me as a child, 'Golden Slumbers'. (My dad, unmoved by post-fifteenth-century music – except for a brief yodelling stint – was always adamant that the Beatles pinched the lyrics from an ancient anonymous poem.) At first, bizarrely, I thought Ness was singing too for she was making an only just audible whining sound, but I soon realized that it was the sound of misery, of sobs almost turned to sleep. Neither of them noticed me. I stood there taking it in, this tableau of tenderness between two of the people I loved most in the world, and I knew exactly what had happened. Then behind the door at my side I noticed Karl sitting in the chair, headphones on, playing *Football Manager* on his phone.

I look back now and can say that even in that moment I was aware of the day's significance, although, I might add, not where it was going to lead. This was the end of an era. Leah had moved into a flat on the high street. Ness was beside herself. However, the tragedy appeared to have ignited something in my mother: a purpose, perhaps. I hadn't seen her so clear-minded for a while. When I came into the room, she signalled for me to run Ness a bath, which I did. And make her a cup of tea, which I did. She placed the tea next to the sleeping Ness and slithered out from beneath her, and took me through to the kitchen with an almost military focus. I trotted along behind, always amazed at the youthful appearance of my mother from the back; she could pass for a woman of thirty. In the kitchen she told me to make some lunch for the children – Evie had gone out but Polly was upstairs with Annie.

For the briefest twenty minutes I had my mother back: the brave heart, the compassionate practicality. She asked what had happened and listened without judgement as I explained that none of this was out of the blue, that they'd been fighting for a long time; on our last summer holiday Leah had barely said a word to Ness for the whole two weeks. This all appeared to be news to my mother although I had told her several times that their relationship was getting worse. 'Poor Ness. Poor children. Poor Leah,' she said without sentiment. After a moment or two of staring out of the kitchen window, she said, 'Leah has guts' – which struck me as odd. Then she held me close and said, 'Oh darling, this will be strange for all of you.' Then she started clearing up but I noticed that she put the milk in the cleaning cupboard, and when Ness staggered into the kitchen she turned to her and said, 'Vanessa, you look awful, are you all right?' That's the worst thing about Alzheimer's – it makes you appear unfeeling. Which is just *not* fair.

'Was there someone else involved?' Dr Rhys Evans asked my mother, a gossipy glint in her eye. Everyone assumed there was someone else. And there usually is, isn't there, Dr R? It takes a third person to really motivate us, to kick us up the derrière. What *had* motivated Leah? I can only think of how unhappy she must have been to inflict this on the family. She *was* unhappy, we all knew that, but it was kind of accepted, almost a joke: one New Year's Eve her resolution had been to start walking with a spring in her step; she thought it might help to cheer herself up. I had never known her any different. I was sure there wasn't anyone else involved. That's what I liked about Leah: she wanted a clean life, no mess. She wanted to make a change in her life so she had done so.

On the way up to the bathroom later, where I'd left Ness to blub in bubbles, I'd popped in to Annie's room to find her and Polly sprawled on the bed as they watched something funny on YouTube. I gave Polly a hug. She smelt of chocolate. After a moment or two she said, 'I can't see the screen, Connie,' so I let go.

Ness lay motionless in the bath with her head turned to one side, one hand lying across her breast, like a wounded St Sebastian. It was an inappropriate time to take advantage of, I know, but Ness had always been strangely coy about showing her body; and despite the fact that we had been on many holidays together and lain on numerous beaches, this was the first time I had actually seen her form in all its naked glory. And it *was* glorious, complete with stretch marks and wayward hairs. Karl was bored of me always going on about her perfection and kept pointing out to me that she was like a boy, straight up and down and had no arse, nothing to grab hold of. (But I thought that was *good* – blimey, we women really get mixed messages. And when did he last *grab hold of* me anyway? He's all talk. In actual fact, we had never really had that *grabbing hold of* kind of sex; we indulged in pleasant perfunctory intercourse once a month, much like you do, Dr R. Or hey, let's go crazy, perhaps a two-night flurry. By the way, I'd recently asked my mother how often she and my father made love and she'd said, 'Oh, hardly ever these days, darling, about once a fortnight.' WTF?!)

'How's Poll?' Ness had asked, turning to face me, the bags under her eyes a pretty greeny-brown.

'Watching YouTube. Evie and Josh are still out.' (Evie and Josh were now officially boyfriend and girlfriend – weird, slightly incestuous, but nice.)

'It was awful, Con. Polly just ran off and hid underneath her bed crying. Evie marched out of the house slamming the door.'

'They'll be all right, kids are resilient,' I said. Sometimes we all need a platitude to keep us going. You could do with using a few more of them, Dr R. If you're not careful, you can come over a touch frosty.

'I'm going to be that single person that no one invites to dinner parties . . .' Ness said.

I squeezed her toes. 'No, you won't.'

'Promise you'll invite me.'

'Of course I will. You can come and eat round here every night, my love.'

'I don't want to be on my own.' She was so broken, so full of pain. It was alarming but, I must admit, fascinating to see such rawness.

'You won't be on your own, I promise.' I got on my knees at the edge of the bath and wanted to cry myself.

The whole thing was so profoundly sad. Karl and I lay in bed that night, pretending to read, both of us staring at the ceiling, silent, in our own worlds, the repercussions beginning to sink in; little waves kept hitting me. My own foundations had been shaken. It's selfish, I know, Dr R, but I was gutted for *our* family. The eight of us were such a safe unit. We had become inseparable, we lived in each other's houses, we'd holidayed together for the last five years – in fact we *preferred* to holiday together. Over time we had merged and the eight of us got on better than in our separate fours. Leah and Karl would go off for hours to play golf or tennis while Ness and I went for long coastal walks or lounged around reading. And so the big question was: what were we without them? I wasn't sure. We would be left alone to face the reality of our own relationships.

There was something else going on in my head too: I felt slightly *envious* of their freedom. Leah had broken the chains; she was free of all the cosy conventions of our comfortable little community. She wasn't in love with Ness, so she had left. She had taken a gamble. My mother was right: she had guts.

Karl and I should have lain there in the increasing

darkness holding each other tight saying *we'll never lose each other, we'll never break*, but we didn't; we bobbed about individually on our ocean of a bed. Perhaps I should have seen it all coming then.

'We have to look after her, Karl. I'm worried about her.'

'Well, she can come and hang out here, she can eat with us, the kids can stay here . . .' He was so kind, as always. He'd even told me that my parents could come and live with us; if my father couldn't cope with my mother she could come and live here. (His intentions were good but in reality I knew that meant *I* would be looking after her, as Karl was frequently away with work and, lovely though he is, Dr R, you and I both know he didn't know how to use the washing machine, so the burden would all be mine – and how was I going to cope with the pressures of work, the kids, the house *and* my mother?)

Lying there in that crepuscular light, I felt suddenly terrified by the precarious nature of the future. I reached for his hand and he squeezed my fingers, both of us ignoring the enormous elephant padding about beside us in the room: it was blindingly obvious that we should make love – that we needed a display of unity – but neither of us was able to muster the necessary enthusiasm.

Dr Rhys Evans was listening to my mother's every word as she showed off her remarkable powers of recall with detailed descriptions of *that* day, the tea mug, what Ness was wearing, what she sang to her – but she was soon repeating herself and abruptly stopped sharing information when she caught sight of the huge needle the nurse was brandishing. My mother cried out and grasped my hand. 'It's all right, Mamma,' I said. A fear of needles seems entirely sane to me: only a nutjob welcomes a stabbing. 'Just look at me.' I stroked her papery skin. Her eyes were suddenly pale and watery and full of alarm, her shiny blue eyeliner had slipped and smudged, and somehow she had managed to smear some of that lipstick across her nose, lending her an air of tragic comedy. She winced as the huge needle dug into her skin, so pallid next to the ebony darkness of the nurse's hand.

'What was I saying, darling?' she asked me.

Initially, Ness's misery had been intense. But she soon pulled herself together, sensible girl that she was. After we'd both finished work she and the kids spent most of their evenings round at our house doing homework, she would make work phone calls at our kitchen table as I cooked. We'd share a bottle of red. If Karl was around he would sometimes make us something fancy. He was mean with a wok. Sometimes we'd watch a film. Both families – minus Leah, of course – would huddle around the TV on a Saturday night to get our fill of modern-day bedlam. This set-up soon became normal. During this time my sweet father had to have a pacemaker fitted and I noticed he was having a few memory problems himself, so I flitted between houses and doctors, worrying now about the care that I would inevitably need to get in place for my parents.

My mother would turn up at the house whenever she felt like it and ask Ness how Leah and the children were. Every time Ness would patiently re-explain the break-up of her marriage until she couldn't be bothered any more and said they were all just fine. I missed Leah far more than I expected; her brooding negativity had become surprisingly comforting. Eventually she came back to the house to pick up all her furniture and possessions, leaving gaping holes on the walls and in the rooms in her wake. Ness and I sat and looked at the blankness for a while. Then we drove to Ikea and chose cheap and cheerful pieces to replace them with. On a whim she bought herself a cheery little cuckoo clock with a bird that flung itself out on the hour and screeched *Cheep Cheep*. It made her smile, she said. Smiling was good, I agreed.

I have to confess: occasionally I wished she would just give us a little space. I don't think a day went by without her and the kids appearing in our house. Just *sometimes* I wanted to spend the evening alone with Karl or be able to have other people around without Ness there as well. I'd begun to feel just a bit suffocated. And perhaps I was starting to get on her nerves too; I remember her getting quite short with me. On one occasion, the three of us were walking to the pub one evening and she said *I really hate my hair* – which was a strange thing for her to say, primarily because it was so girly, and secondly because I knew she liked her hair; she thought she had fabulous hair. She had a particular way of twiddling it that I had begun to find just a *teensy* bit annoying. It was self-consciously flirtatious – I'd seen her turn on the charm with various people at school, men and women, flick flick twist twist, and they were putty in her hands.

Was I jealous of her freedom? Perhaps I was. But I was also looking out for her; you must understand that. In my heartfelt opinion she deserved only good things. I did all I could to cheer her up; we spent one weekend painting her floors white and her walls blue, de-Leah-fying the place. I suggested we do a makeover on her as well; I'd always been dying to dress her, as she didn't have much sense of style. We shopped; she looked fantastic. I bought her some make-up: smoky shades that she said she liked on me. And it worked; she did cheer up. She began to have fun again. It was like watching a flower blossom. Within four months she was blooming. I hate to confess it, but I preferred her un-cheered up, when she was low and needy, enabling me to excel in the friendship stakes. She'd started going on dates. It was one thing her being with Leah but altogether something else when she spent the evening snogging a waitress. I wasn't adapting very well.

I just hate my hair, she'd said, tugging at her locks. *It's all . . .* She was searching for the word. We were walking along the towpath; I was behind her, Karl in front. She was wearing this beautiful dress I'd found for her in Urban Outfitters and I was marvelling at her petiteness. *Frizzy?* I proffered, because her hair *was* quite dry and flyaway and I did genuinely think that this was the word she was searching for. She *did* have faults, you see, I wasn't blinded. Well, she turned round sharply, her face full of indignation. She was insulted and shirty with me all evening. In the pub she pointedly ignored me, turning her chair away from me to face Karl.

'Apple!' my mother cried jubilantly, as the blood spilled from her arm down the plastic tube. 'Apple was one of the words!'

Dr Rhys Evans smiled and passed the nurse a swab of cotton wool. 'Very good! Apple!' I didn't like her patronizing tone. 'Thank you so much, Sebo,' she said, dismissing the nurse.

My mother was in good spirits now. 'Oh, yes. Thank you so much, See. Eee . . .' She was smiling at the nurse but then found herself struggling for the name she had just heard. 'Eee . . . Ebola,' she cried, pretty sure she'd nailed it. I could see the crossing of the wires in her brain: the vowel sounds, the endless threat of disease in the news, the colour of Sebo's skin. Again, there was logic to her thinking. I felt suddenly terribly moved by my poor little old mum, with her clownish make-up and her accidental racism, for the terrifying loss of herself that she was experiencing.

'I think I need to spend a penny,' she said, standing up on her thin scratched pins. And I got up to help her but Dr Rhys Evans stopped me with a hand on my forearm and asked Sebo whether she wouldn't mind doing the honours, which was a bit much given the insult she had just received.

They left the room. I wasn't comfortable it just being the two of us. Unwillingly I sat back down and rummaged for my phone in my bag to signify that I would wait patiently for the return of my mother, and then to make up for the implicit rudeness of my gesture I said, 'Yes, I know, she's getting worse.'

Dr Rhys Evans stared at me – not my breasts or my shoes, but my eyes. It was an uncomfortable silence so I broke it. 'But, hey ho, none of us are getting out of here alive . . .'

'And you?' she said, like a real doctor, which I kept forgetting that she was. 'How are you coping?'

I was surprised by the question. 'Me?' I said.

'Yes, how is everything with you?'

I was stunned. For a long time, no one had asked me this. They asked me how my parents were doing, how my children were doing, how Karl was doing, how Ness was doing. But nobody asked me how *I* was doing.

'Yes . . .' I said.

I felt exposed; my eyes began to sting. She saw it. Oh no. I would for ever be cornered in the deli section at Sainsbury's.

My woes felt small in comparison but ever since Ness and Leah had broken up, I hadn't felt *myself*. My resistance had dropped. I felt like I was crumbling, not dramatically, but in little pieces. No matter how hard Karl and I worked, we were always stretched financially. Every month we were sliding further and further into debt; there seemed to be no way out of it, as we lived way beyond our means. And work itself was challenging: I'd written a piece on the CEO of a pharmaceutical company for a broadsheet and had been bombarded in the comments section by the most vitriolic, personal attacks on a thread that just kept spinning. I know this is how it works now but if you've never been on the receiving end of it, Dr R, it's really hard to explain. As a journalist, I'm supposed to just take it on the chin – it's your own fault for putting your opinions out there. But I've never been great at taking anything on the chin and fatally, I got involved, defending my point of view. And then things escalated, culminating with rape threats and several poisonous comments about how I was too ugly to be gang-raped. Who the hell *are* these people?

Another thing was unduly bothering me – and this really is rather pathetic and adolescent. I'd seen photographs on Facebook of all my uni chums at a party to which I hadn't been invited and I was surprisingly hurt by this; in the dark hours of the night, it plagued me. On top of this, Karl was doing a lot of consulting abroad. He seemed to be away all the time so I was single parenting and trying to cope with my increasingly deteriorating parents. I was getting more and more concerned about their future and what was going to happen with them, and was spending every spare hour I could trying to sort through their house and its endless junk. Josh, now sixteen, seemed to have decided I was a fool – everything I said appeared ridiculous to him and was received with a snort of derision. The school was complaining about his behaviour, and Annie was also in trouble – she'd got into a fight in the playground and had sent one boy to A&E. I seemed to be failing on every front.

I was feeling more and more distant from Ness. Her life had changed now and she was making the most of the weeks without the children. She had a new-found freedom and was frequently off for weekends with her old mates at spas, always trying to get me to come along too, but of course I couldn't because I was the fort-holder. I felt a little ousted; I was no longer her priority, her life had moved on. I felt isolated and lonely on all fronts, actually. I was losing too many things at once and had woken up that week with the distinct whiff of *it* – that old tidal wave of misery on the horizon.

'You've got a lot on your plate,' Dr Rhys Evans said. 'It's not a crime to struggle.'

At that moment Sebo poked her head around the door. 'Did Mrs de Cadenet come back in here?' she asked. Dr Rhys Evans and I looked at each other and then got up quickly. My mother had gone AWOL; we rushed about the building and eventually found her talking to the greengrocer round the corner about aubergine recipes.

There we have it, Dr R. So that was the day my mother started knocking back the Floradix for her lack of iron and I started knocking back the Lofepramine for my lack of happiness.

Chapter 10

Emma was unfamiliar with this part of London and if it wasn't for Google Maps and the efficient female Australian voice giving her directions, she would have absolutely no idea of how to get there. She'd only decided an hour ago that she was coming. Despite leaving numerous messages, no one had returned her calls. She had planned to go to her yoga-meditation class and then spend the rest of the day with Si. Emma liked to have a clear agenda, but Si, without putting it in the diary, had gone off to a day's orchestra practice – their annual concert was coming up and this year the bassoon actually had a solo.

She decided against the yoga. The central heating was playing up and there was so much preparation involved for a class before the humiliation of piling herself into her yoga clothes. Shaving and hair washing were vital – mid-lizard pose it was possible to find yourself alarmingly close to random parts of strangers' anatomies. Somehow she always seemed to end up next to twenty-year-old contortionists in spray-on stretch suits who made her feel huge and ancient with the malleability of a crowbar. Then there were further embarrassments in the tiny changing rooms as naked, nubile, rippled, perky-breasted girls with no hang-ups and topiaried little mounds chatted loudly by the cubicles while Emma, clasping a towel to her roll-over tummy and untamed bush, tried to squeeze past to the showers.

A long time ago, when she and Si were first together, she used to get her bikini line waxed. She couldn't remember when she stopped; she cited feminist reasons but really it was laziness. But why was she lazy? When did she stop bothering? When did she stop thinking of herself as a sexual being? How had she lost her libido? She knew it was still there somewhere, lying latent; she still had occasional urges, but the urges had become secretive, not something to be shared with Si.

Did you and Si Hubby ever have passion?

'Turn right on to Fulham Palace Road,' said the Australian.

Emma didn't want to think about sex; it made her uncomfortable. Far too much importance was placed on it; we were cluster bombed by it wherever we looked. She had decided somewhere along the line, manipulated by the media and advertising, no doubt, that sex was the terrain of the young. Connie was right, *the body didn't lie*; now that her periods were deeply painful and erratic, it seemed that her own uterus was conspiring against her, and her vagina had joined in the rebellion by becoming paper-dry. And she didn't know whether the cause of it was physiological or psychological. Oh, the joys of the menopause knew no bounds: the hair that fell out when she washed it, the sudden claustrophobic sweats and the indisputable fact that her biological purpose on the planet had come to an end, all spoke of mortality. She, as a human being, in essence, had become obsolete.

Emma had been putting off going on HRT; she had been putting off labelling herself as going through the menopause full stop. But she was. These days she wanted to concentrate on other aspects of herself: the meditation, the effort to try and change her habitual thinking, to have more self-belief. But in actual fact, despite trying for a year now, she felt she hadn't progressed at all. She wasn't sure she had any graspable technique or aptitude for it. The moment she sat straight and closed her eyes in a search for stillness, it eluded her. Her thoughts played havoc, her mind a whir of daily problems, self-doubt and guilt. The book by her bed was reinforcing the fact that she must be kind to herself, not be full of blame towards either herself or anyone else.

But her behaviour in Connie's room the other day was shameful, whatever the book said; even thinking about it set off a profound embarrassment. It had been horribly unprofessional – Connie could have done anything. She could have escaped (she'd already escaped once from Milton House, for God's sake), she could have attacked someone, stolen a car . . . the consequences could have been unthinkable. Afterwards, Emma had driven straight to her supervisor to confess. But when, at the end of a long day, she'd arrived at Tom's office, one lone light on in the building, her tread silent with the shame of her deeds, she had found him playing *Call of Duty*, a duvet laid out on the sofa. She'd suspected he was having marital problems but hadn't realized that he was sleeping at the office. She had discreetly exited and re-thought her own bad behaviour, and Connie's future. The psychologist assessing Connie was getting nowhere – she was refusing to even speak to him, or the social worker. The CT scans showed that there was nothing neurologically wrong with Connie's brain. Emma knew, in fact, that she had come a long way with her, that things were progressing. There had been reported a noticeable change in Constance's behaviour at the clinic; no *incidents* recently, which meant no fitting, no public urination or defecation, no fights, no inappropriate sexual behaviour. She was taking her medication. If Emma was taken off the case, her assessment would have to begin all over again. It was one tiny lapse that no one need know about. She felt resolved. She hadn't had a drop to drink since then.

'In four hundred yards turn right . . .'

But Connie *hadn't* escaped or done any of those things Emma might have imagined; she had been kind and tender. And Emma had been quite thrown when Connie cried. This was progress; she was *feeling*. The sound she made was what had shocked Emma, that ghastly soul-wrenching sob, as if her body knew what she had done even if her mind couldn't remember it. Emma had wanted to take her in her arms, hold her, rock her and tell her everything was going to be OK. But it so evidently wasn't. In fact, everything was going to get a lot worse; so instead, she had scuttled out like a rat.

'In three hundred yards turn right on to . . .'

She found herself looking forward to their sessions. Connie's company, although unsettling, was strangely exhilarating. She wondered whether it was because Connie didn't lie. *The rest of us are all plausible liars.* When she was with Connie she felt like she was following a straight line in a world of angles. She couldn't veer from it now; she'd gone too far down it to turn back. Now she found herself conscious of the *lack* of her; she missed Connie's ruthless, rasping commentary.

'Carry straight on for eight hundred yards.'

She'd rowed with Si this morning. She'd picked a fight with him. And he'd accused her of getting obsessed with *this psychopath*. But was he right? Was she obsessed? She had always been somewhat obsessive: from Enid Blyton and Agatha Christie to Siouxsie and the Banshees and serial killers. But what he didn't seem to understand was that this was the way she *had* to work: she had to get inside this woman's head, slip her feet into Connie's shoes. (*Had Connie really put on her shoes while she lay there crashed out on her bed?*)

'At the roundabout take the third exit on to Putney Bridge Road.'

She drove over the bridge, the uneven tarmac echoing slaps against the car's underbelly. She turned to see the view over the river. It was beautiful. The tide was high, the sun was out, and clouds moved fast across the sky. They'd found Connie somewhere down here, stark naked. She turned right and pulled up where she could. She got out of the car, did up her jacket. The wind was strong but not cold; it felt pleasant against her skin. She breathed in the air as she wandered down to the water and away from the bridge. There was a faint whiff of chimney smoke mixed in with river dampness and autumn leaves. The ducks were swimming between the sunken branches of the trees, the water beyond them moving at an incredible speed. She stood there, hands in her pockets, mesmerized by it. Flotsam and jetsam drifted past her and she felt comfort in the transience, the assurance that sooner or later we would all be swept away and replaced. She thought of Connie. The report said she'd fought the police off and in the end they'd had to taser and sedate her before she was bundled off and sectioned.

Emma stepped back to let a procession of bikes go past in a blur of lycra. The scent of male sweat engulfed her and she felt irritated by the certainty with which they occupied space. Why did no one ring bicycle bells any more? Were they not aerodynamic enough or was she just old? Beyond them, she focused on a log in the middle of the river, almost the size of a tree.

'Emma?' She turned to her right. One of the cyclists had stopped and turned around to look at her.

'Emma Davis?' He was clad in skin-hugging black and yellow, like a thin wasp.

'Yes,' she said, curious. No one called her *Davis*. Something about his smile was incredibly familiar. He took off his helmet. Oh my God. It was Dougie.

'Dougie?'

'Yes!'

'Dougie Thompson? Oh my God!'

She couldn't help it, she felt herself flush profusely. At school, she had had a crush on Douglas Thompson so intense she had been flattened by it, rolled out like a piece of unleavened dough. She had not been the only one. Everyone was touched by him, with his quiet confidence and his sense of self.

'Wow . . .' she said, stupidly seventeen again.

Dougie hadn't just been the coolest boy in school; he

was also the *cleverest*. Not as clever as Emma, but only because he didn't work as hard.

'I thought it was you!' he said, lifting one long leg over the back wheel and picking up the bike as if it were no heavier than a bag of crisps. He brought it back to where she was standing. 'I thought, I *know* that girl . . .'

Girl. It hadn't been until the first year of A-levels that he'd even noticed Emma. He was going out with Deborah Jenkins at the time – he only went out with cool girls, not Goths like Emma and Sally Pea – and the rumour was that he'd got Deborah pregnant. Emma remembered the day when the maths teacher had given him a hard time for not handing in his work and she had passed him hers under the table. They'd hung out a bit after that and Deborah Jenkins had got her to be a kind of go-between. And she did get between. She and Dougie would get so carried away talking that they'd both completely forget to pass messages back to Deborah. And when Deborah began to freeze her out, Emma had understood for the first time the powers of her own attraction.

'You look really well,' he said. What he meant was: *you used to be so fat.* Puppy fat, her mother had called it; pointing it out the very day Emma had begun to appreciate her own contours.

'I mean, I liked the Goth look and everything . . .'

Any personal comment made her blush – she no longer had the white make-up to hide behind – and she felt the second wave of blood rush about her body and settle on her chest. There was nothing she could do about it; it betrayed her time and again, announcing her inner feelings to the outside world.

'How are you? Do you live round here?' he asked.

'Thanks. Fine. No . . . Do you?'

'Yeah, not far. Battersea. You're a doctor, aren't you, a psychiatrist . . . ?'

'That's right.' She was flung back to the contradictions of her youth: the self-assurance masking the vulnerability, the cliques, the passions, the stuttering, that heavy weight of the future brimful with possibility.

'Sally and I always thought you were going to be prime minister!' he said. She laughed. *Had they really?* 'But I'm not surprised you've gone into people's heads; you were always curious. And kind.'

The flush on her chest burned again. 'And you?' she asked. 'What do you do?'

She switched off after the letters 'IT'. *Always curious and kind. Dougie Thompson. Sally Pea. Deborah Jenkins.* How had she lost touch with everyone? Where had all the years gone?

'Did you hear about Sally?' he was saying, still smiling at her.

'No, I've lost touch with lots of people . . .'

'She just won a hundred and fifty grand on the lottery.'

'What? No way!' Emma shrieked. It was incredible. He was laughing, they both were. He had always had that effect on her, relaxing her in a highly unrelaxing way. He moved a little closer as another stream of bikes passed by.

'Honestly, that girl!' he said, shaking his head. 'She's throwing a huge birthday party – she'd kill me if I told her I saw you and didn't ask you. You've got to come.'

'That's right! Her birthday. December 14th!'

He was getting his phone out of a bicep pocket. His skin was smooth and brown. 'What's your number, Dr Davis?'

'Robinson,' she corrected, and immediately wished that she hadn't; she'd brought a kind of *otherness* into their conversation. This was no place for husbands. It wasn't fair that a man could keep his mystery but a woman had to be branded. She watched him tap the number into his phone as she told him the digits, noticing and remembering his ease of movement, the grace of his fingers and how, to her delight, someone had once mistaken them for a couple. She wondered whether he remembered that night at Jamie Storm's party, how they'd talked all evening on the sofa and their legs had been touching for hours. She never knew whether he was aware of it or not.

What a fool she was; of course he wouldn't remember. That was thirty years ago.

'Yes, you're married, I knew that. You've got kids, haven't you?' he asked.

She stared at him. Her head went blank. The blush drained away.

'Yes,' she heard herself say. 'And you?'

'Yeah, two boys. What about you?' he asked.

She paused. 'Just one. A girl. Abigail.'

Just for a moment she wanted to be like a normal person.

'Lovely name,' he said. She looked at him and nodded. Yes, it was a lovely name. 'How old is she?'

'Nine,' she said. It was as if Emma was watching the conversation from one of those speeding clouds up there.

Afterwards she sat in the car for a long time without moving, staring at the steering wheel. *Why aren't the streets full of wrecked people?*

*

It wasn't until the parking attendant tapped on her window that she came out of her reverie and started the engine. The cheery Australian voice, impervious to loss, took her by surprise.

'Rerouting.'

Yes, she thought, *rerouting.* She looked at her phone, noticing that her battery was about to die. It was eleven. Still no response to her messages. She would make it a brief visit.

Emma parked up in Allinson Road, as near to number five as she could. It was a gentrified Victorian terraced street. She had once hoped that she would live somewhere like this, where blonde women pushed prams, kids left unlocked bikes outside jolly coloured doors that were left open, window boxes bloomed, bins lived in painted kennels nestled beside olive trees wafting in lavender, and neighbours popped in to arrange dinner parties, postmen whistled and left packages next door. Bad things don't happen in places like this.

Oh Connie, how did you let it all go so wrong?

She watched the road in her wing mirror: muddy boys in football gear climbed out of a four-by-four. Two girls whizzed round the corner on skateboards in tutus, followed by a woman with neatly messy hair being tugged by one of those non-moulting poodles on a lead, a small boy bouncing a ball behind her. Emma watched them go. She had always wanted that: to be part of a busy, bustling family, like the one Si had come from. That had been a strong part of her attraction to him – his family: the noise, the jostling, the jibes and the effortless love.

Her own mother's love had always felt conditional – on Emma making her mother feel good, on Emma being clever (like her), on Emma being thin (like her). And it had just been the two of them for most of the time. It wasn't until she was older, when she was an undergraduate and had come across the personality of a narcissist in her studies, that she had begun to make sense of her mother. When Emma had failed to get pregnant, her mother would constantly remind her how easily she herself had got pregnant, keen to remove herself from Emma's failings as a woman. And so it had transpired that all those years of taking contraception and morning-after pills had been for nothing, because Emma's body ('such child-bearing hips', 'such a maternal bosom') wasn't up to it. And what joy, what extreme happiness for her and Si, when the second round of IVF had worked. And so the blow had felt even harsher when it came.

Why had she lied to Dougie?

She got out of the car. She locked the door, ran a hand through her hair, and slung her bag across her shoulder as she approached number five. The de Cadenets' house had an air of neglect: overgrown acer trees spilled on to the pavement, a mound of dead leaves made the front tiles slippery, the curtains were drawn, the front door was black and chipped, and the glass was thick with dust.

Emma rang the doorbell. It was dark and quiet within.

No response. She stepped back to look and see if there was any life upstairs. Dots of rain prickled her skin and speckled her pale grey jacket. If no one was in then she would leave a note for them. She'd take a sheet from their recycling box, which was bulging with loose-lined pages covered in neat ink-penned handwriting. *From the point of unity, the same self may retreat . . .* The rest was hidden under a *Wetlands* magazine. She rang again and peered through the panel. She was about to leave when she saw a figure slowly approaching. She stood back. With much unlocking, the door opened and an old man stood there. It was clear from his eyes, dark and fiery, and his skin, sallow and swarthy, that he was Connie's father. He blinked at her.

'Hello,' she said. 'I'm sorry to disturb you. I did try ringing several times . . .'

'Hello,' he said. There was a smell of mustiness and drains.

'I'm Dr Robinson.'

'Is this bad news?' he asked. He looked scared.

'No,' she said. 'I'm from the Tatchwell, I'm working with Connie.'

At the mention of his daughter's name, a weighted sorrow seemed to seep through his features; his shoulders dropped, his head hung, his mouth drooped.

'Come in,' he said, opening the door wider. She stepped inside. It was dim in the house. The walls of the hall were crowded with paintings and prints, and the floor was lined with piles of books in Sainsbury's bags. He moved awkwardly through the hall, leaving a faint waft of urine in his wake. She wondered whether there was a carer in place or whether he was trying to care for his wife alone; she would ring social services when she got back and find out exactly what was going on.

'Is your wife in?' she asked, but he had bent down to move a heavy metal doorstop and it fell over with a bang, drowning out her voice.

She glanced up into the darkness of the floor above. No curtains were open; the house was still, the green carpet worn on each step. A painting caught her eye: Connie and her brother as teenagers, lying on a sofa reading books.

'Your son David lives in Australia, is that right?' she asked.

'That's right,' Mr de Cadenet said, pausing mid-shuffle, sounding most surprised that she should know.

'No one else is in?' she asked, as they turned left into a sitting room where piles of clothes spilled out of black bin bags. They were having a sort-out. Every cranny of wall space was filled with paintings or prints and every inch of the floor appeared to be occupied, either with the bags or piles of books that grew in towers across the carpet and upon the sofa and chairs. *The Life of the Medici*, *The Letters of Marsilio Ficino: Volume V* and *Ramses* lay on the tops of the nearest piles.

'Gosh,' she said. 'You're certainly having a clear-out!'

'Yes, we've been trying to . . . sort things out,' he said, looking about the room confusedly while a telephone began to ring. He didn't seem to hear it, or he ignored it. Her own calls had obviously been similarly left to the ether.

'Are you here to take the books?' he asked.

'No,' she said. 'I'm here to talk about Connie . . . I'm the forensic psychiatrist?'

'Of course you are.'

Dust lay thick about the place. The paintings were skew-whiff, revealing darker stains on the walls behind. Her eyes followed a trail of crumbs across the carpet that led to a half-eaten lemon drizzle cake, which lay in its Sainsbury's box on a chair. A faux fire glowed dimly but the room was cold and his hands were purple, trembling slightly.

He set off across the room. She noticed how his cardigan had stains on the back as if someone had been hurling mess at him. She thought of Connie and her brother and the game they would play with him, making him guess what he was wearing. It was hard for him to walk, and looking down she noticed why: his shoes were on the wrong feet. She would ring social services as soon as she got back to her car.

'But I can definitely take some bags to the charity shop if you need me to,' she said. 'And here, let me take these plates and cups to the kitchen.'

He stopped mid-voyage and turned to her. 'How very kind of you,' he said, surprised by the offer.

She picked up the cups that were lying around, all of which had congealed mould at the bottom. She scooped up the lemon drizzle and found a couple more plates amongst the piles. 'You've got some lovely paintings,' she said as she did so. And he stopped and looked upwards around the room as if he had only just noticed them.

'Yes, we've always enjoyed art. Not me so much, but I enjoy other people enjoying art . . .' He smiled at her and his eyes almost disappeared.

She took the crockery through to the kitchen, which was in an equal state of disarray. Emma put the soiled things to soak in the sink and filled up the dishwasher, which was half full of dirt-ingrained plates. She turned it on for them and on her way back through to the sitting room she was distracted by a photograph stuck on a cupboard: the whole family, wrapped up in scarves and hats, stood on a windy British beach somewhere. It could have been an advert for life insurance or a bank, manipulating happiness into money: everyone was laughing, smiling, all eyes on Annie, who was kicking a leg high in the air, grinning a toothless grin, her red hair blown wildly up by the wind. Emma felt her heart beat fast in her chest. The abject finality of loss still struck her with the same force as it had all those years ago. The phone began to ring. She stood there listening to it for a moment before coming back through.

'Do you want me to get that?' she asked. He was sitting down on the small two-seater; he'd cleared a space for them both and had poured two whiskies, which sat on either arm of the sofa.

'Oh no, don't bother. I can't understand a word they say . . . Please sit down. Have a drink,' he said. She sat down next to him, shifting one of the bin bags at her feet.

'Has Connie remembered anything yet?' he asked, tapping his elegant but stiff fingers against his glass.

'Things are coming back,' Emma said, straightening her skirt, turning to face him better.

'The car?'

'We've shown her photographs of the girls . . .'

She saw it then, the incomprehension and bewilderment. He looked pummelled by shock. With a shaky hand he drank from his whisky glass.

'She's in denial,' Emma said.

'Karl said you called it something, her condition . . . ?'

'Dissociative amnesia. It's one way of dealing with trauma.'

'He thinks she's faking it. Do you?'

'Well, *faking* it is comparatively unusual. Dissociative amnesia is more to do with the brain protecting itself, locking traumatic events away, as it were, into a box, and pushing it to the back of the brain,' she said. It was something she herself had become quite adept at, in a conscious way, of course.

'And what's wrong with that?'

'I'm sorry?'

'*Must* she remember?' he asked. 'No good is in that box. Just pain. Wouldn't you agree that perhaps there is *enough* pain about already? Why bother?'

She wanted to take a sip from her glass. She could imagine how good it must taste; she could almost feel the burn in her throat.

'I have to assess her mental state at the time of the offence and whether she is fit to stand trial. At some stage, Mr de Cadenet, she has to be held accountable. If Connie doesn't acknowledge her actions, how can there ever be recovery?'

'Recovery?' he repeated, taking his glasses off and pinching the skin between his eyes. He was from another generation: war children raised by parents who kept whole worlds locked away in boxes.

'I think we all have to face pain, Mr de Cadenet,' she said, like the hypocrite she was.

'I'm sorry to be disrespectful but I don't trust you doctors,' Mr de Cadenet said. 'Connie wasn't herself, you see . . . Those drugs that silly grinning GP gave her . . . they did something, I'm sure . . .'

She knew exactly which drugs Connie had been taking at the time of the offence: aside from the Lofepramine for the depression, she'd been prescribed a benzodiazepine for her anxiety. Nothing unusual.

'That's very unlikely, Mr de Cadenet.'

'They all think I don't notice anything, but I *do*.' His voice faltered, his lip quivered. He was looking right at her now. 'She just wasn't *herself* at all.'

He pulled out a grubby grey handkerchief from his pocket and dabbed his eyes. Emma reached out and touched his cold shaking hand. *Where was David? Where was Karl? Where was Mrs de Cadenet? He shouldn't be here on his own.*

Her touch, her empathy, elicited a release and the old man hung his head and began to weep. She took his hand in both of hers and smoothed it and squeezed it. 'Connie was most likely suffering from a psychotic episode . . .'

'That doesn't mean anything! What did we do wrong?' He was crying like a child. 'I don't know if I can forgive her. I thought I was a Christian . . . but I just can't . . .'

Emma gripped his old mottled hand in hers. She said nothing.

'I don't know what to do. Julia always knows what to do when things go wrong . . .'

There was a ring of the doorbell. 'That might be

her . . . I'll get it,' Emma said, letting go of his hand, getting up, making her way into the hall. She opened the front door expecting Julia to be standing there, but instead a tall middle-aged man with messy, dark, greying hair and paint-splattered jeans hovered on the doorstep, clutching keys in his hand. Behind him in the road was parked a van with its engine running, its back doors open and its hazard lights flashing.

'Oh, hi,' he said, evidently wondering who she was. 'Just come to pick up Andrew's books for the market . . . ?' He had a faint Irish accent.

'Oh, right,' she said.

A car horn honked. A car had pulled up behind the van. He turned round, whistled and raised his hand to the driver.

'All the ones in the Sainsbury's bags, apparently,' he said.

Emma held the door open for him and he stooped to pick up the first few bags. Outside, the car behind his van hooted again.

'Here, let me help,' she said. She grabbed another couple of bags and followed him out to the van. He was grateful and dealt with the driver behind calmly, gesturing that he'd be a few minutes. Then he turned to Emma and said, 'What a plonker,' under his breath. She smiled and went back in for the last few bags.

As she was putting them into the van, she managed to get her cardigan caught on something. She couldn't reach the catch. He leant over to try and help her free herself, gently tugging at her cardigan. He smelt of something musky but pleasant.

'Oh, sorry,' he said, only making things worse. The thread had come loose.

'Don't worry!'

The car behind revved its engine provocatively. He gestured politely and smiled at the driver. 'Take your time . . . wind the idiot up,' he said, his blue eyes twinkling at her. Emma smiled, freed herself from her cardigan and tried to unhook the catch but she was too close; she needed her glasses. He stood there patiently as she unhooked herself at last, then he slammed the van doors shut and thanked her for helping him.

She went back into the house and closed the door. What a nice guy. Some people just had a way of making you feel better than you felt before you saw them. The hall looked much better empty. She returned to the sitting room, where Mr de Cadenet was sitting in exactly the same position that she had left him in, only his whisky glass was empty. He seemed lost in his own world and for a split second he didn't appear to recognize her as she sat down next to him.

'Has Karl gone already?' he asked.

'That was Karl?' She could hear the van pulling away. She drew the curtain back and looked out into the street. She wished she'd taken more in, introduced herself. She wanted to talk with him. *You'll think he's fantastic. He'll make sure of that.*

She should get on with the business she came here for. 'Mr de Cadenet, I was wondering whether it might help if you came to visit Connie?'

He sighed and clasped his hands together.

'At the Tatchwell,' she added.

'No . . . I couldn't do that . . . no.'

'She'd love to see you . . .'

He shook his head. 'No.'

'Would Mrs de Cadenet consider it? Connie misses her dreadfully. I could pick her up and bring her back if that was easiest?'

Slowly he turned to face Emma; he seemed confused. 'Mrs de Cadenet?'

'Yes. Connie is desperate to see her.'

'Julia is dead,' he said.

Emma stared at him, at those eyes that could be Connie's eyes. She opened her mouth a little, but nothing would come out. 'I'm so sorry,' she said eventually. *Why didn't she know this?*

'She died two months ago. I'm glad she's not around to see what's going on now. She adored Annie . . .'

'Julia died two months ago?'

'She took an accidental overdose.'

'I am *so* sorry.'

'It was my fault.'

Emma turned sharply. 'No, no. You mustn't say that.' It was a stupid thing to say; those words meant nothing. People used to say them to her. 'When Julia died, was Connie in Milton House?'

'She'd just visited Connie, yes. Karl took her. It was a dreadful place. She came home with a terrible migraine. She went to bed and took some painkillers . . . I didn't put the pills away. I didn't understand about the Alzheimer's. She didn't remember that she'd already taken her painkillers . . . so she just kept taking more . . . I should have noticed,' he said, bringing his cold mottled hand up to his face and pinching the skin between his eyes again as if he could press it all away. 'I should have taken better care . . .'

'Oh, Mr de Cadenet, I am so sorry. Was Connie told about Julia?'

'Yes,' he said. 'But she wasn't allowed to come to the funeral.'

Why, in God's name, had no one told her that Connie was grieving?

*

Much later, after she had tidied up, cleaned the sitting room and the kitchen, and taken all the bin bags to a local charity shop, Emma drove back across the bridge in the darkness, a cigarette in her fingers, tears blurring the city's lights. She drove through Kew and hit the North Circular, past those grim grubby houses all the way back to Wood Green, eventually letting herself in to the ordered safety of her own house. She leant against the door, blocking out the day behind her.

In the kitchen she could see Si seated at the table eating and she remembered that hours ago she'd said she would pick up some lamb and make them supper. She walked down the hall into the kitchen. 'Hi, love,' she said.

'Thanks for letting me know you weren't going to be back,' he said, pointedly getting up and putting his scraps in the recycling box before exiting the room.

Chapter 11

May 25

Polly and me have decided that we are Christians. Weve chosen Catholics because theres more blood and snacks and its by the newsagents. We went to St Mary is a Virgin church. You have to shake hands with the people near you and say may the force be with you. Then they pass around some free money on a plate. Polly said I will go to hell because I took some (only a quid) and your meant to give some (no one told me). She said I will get hot pokers put up my bum.

We came back to my house where HORRIBLE Mum who I HATE started shouting strait away for NOTHING. She is ALWAYS shouting and grumpy about EVERYTHING specially dropping coats on floors and tidying up. Yesterday I left my lolly wrapper on the chair and she screamed at me PULL YOUR WEIGHT YOU LAZY GIRL CANT YOU SEE IM TRYING TO KEEP TWO HOUSES CLEAN!!! I said get a cleaner and she said you are a spoiled BRAT. I said well whose fault is that and then I turned the other cheek. Daddy who is MUCH nicer said there was no need to be a marter but in a voice so she couldnt hear him. Polly says marter is the Virgin Marys sister.

I will pray for my mum to be nicer. If she is Ive promised God I will be a nun. Polly says nuns have sex with Jesus. I asked how can you have sex with a dead man. She says he comes in

*the night with a turkey baster. I said thats impossible, why is
he cooking turkey before hes even invented Christmas?? I will
lock the door anyhow. We went to Pollys house instead. Later
Dad helped Ness put up some shelfs from Ikea. He was being
all bangy and hammering and making jokes until he banged
his thumb and said FUK!! His thumb went red and squashy
but he didnt cry at all he carried on making jokes. Not until we
got back home then he started moaning like a baby and Mum
had to take him to A and E.*

The door opens. I look up and see the Squeak holding
it open for Dr R, who is in a brisk and efficient mood
today: tight lips, clickety shoes, file under arm. She has
attitude, as if last Thursday never happened, as if she had
never kissed the rim of my toilet. She attempts to
exchange perfunctory pleasantries with me but I don't
indulge. I'm sitting there with Annie's diary in my hands
but she doesn't ask me about it. She has an agenda. She is
focused (after she zips up her bag and puts it down *behind*
her chair, well out of my reach).

'Do you remember when your hair started falling out?'

Instinctively I pat my tufts. They are very soft and
comforting. I shake my head.

'You know hair can fall out with shock.'

'So they say . . .'

She leaves a meaningful pause. And so do I. I look out
of the window. I feel so unshockable now; you have to be
so certain of something to be shocked. I wonder what
was I so certain about.

'Take me back,' she says, crossing her legs, 'to that
morning when Karl first told you he was unhappy.'

I admire that businesslike streak in a woman: no apologies. She's a survivor. But I can't help feeling a little hurt again; I thought we had established an intimacy.

'Did you see my mother?' I ask.

She ignores me. 'And for clarification's sake, *when* did this happen?' she asks. I sigh. I try and remember.

'It was the end of April sometime,' I say. It must have been a Sunday morning because the papers were sprawled over our bed, which means Karl had already been out, but he'd had a bath, made some coffee and brought it up. He was naked, a towel wrapped around his waist, when he dropped the bombshell of his unhappiness as nonchalantly as he did the sugar lump into my mug.

You're unhappy? I'd said to him. I was truly surprised, because it's the sort of thing you hope you'd notice in a spouse. It seemed to me that if Karl was unhappy, he'd done a pretty good job of covering it up. *Yes*, he said. *I've been unhappy for years*. But he didn't sound unhappy, or angry or sad. In fact he was calm, almost perky. But on he went: *I feel like I've lost myself*, he said.

I look out of the window at the dark low blanket of cloud. It's suffocating.

You silly idiot, Karl: we've all lost ourselves is what I was thinking, but I didn't say it. After you become a parent, that's just what happens, isn't it? You have to shed the skin of your old self, your old ways. You have to abandon that self. It's just called growing up.

But again and again I've asked myself how on earth I did not see his unhappiness. Sometimes I think it's because it wasn't there. He made it up and it has now become part of the narrative I tell myself to make sense of things. What I cannot understand is how I got from that conversation on the bed with Karl to this conversation in this place with Dr R. I look back at her. She's waiting for me to continue.

'"You're not happy either," he said. Of course I wasn't happy. Who is, Dr R? But we keep the peace, don't we? We don't *say* it. We struggle on with the hope that one day we might wake up and be happy. I had got so used to my own unhappiness, I had accepted it. I was doing what I could to tolerate it: I was taking my pills, I was trying to organize help for my parents, I loved my children, I opened a nice bottle of wine in the evenings, Ness and I went on long walks in the park, I looked for respite where I could. And look at me! There I was, sitting in my giant comfortable bed in my beautiful house, with two healthy children downstairs – what *right* did I have to be unhappy?

'"You're wrong," I said to him, "I *am* happy." I was in denial. I watched him as he got up to shut the bedroom door, running a hand through his messy thick hair. His naked body in all its slackening middle-aged glory was as familiar to me as my own – more so; I could see the back of his, knew every angle. He put on his shabby blue dressing gown and sat down at the end of the bed facing me, his balls resting snugly on the duvet like one of those peculiar hairless cats.

'"We're just like everyone else, Karl," I said. "Well, I don't want to be like everyone else," he said, reaching out to take my hand in his, squeezing it. I felt my heart contract with alarm; I had no idea where this was going. He was looking pained, anxious, as if this wasn't easy for him to say, but he'd clearly been thinking about it for some time. This was prepared, this little speech. "You and I, I feel like we're not living any more, we're just existing . . ." He paused to let me take this in. "Don't you miss . . . *passion* in your life?"

'Well, I did miss passion, Dr Robinson. I did indeed. But I was willing to sacrifice it for security. Just like you do, just like most of us do. But I thought I understood these worrisome words, what he was trying to tell me was that we had once been free spirits. And somehow we had caged ourselves. "You're an artist, Con!" he said.'

I peter out – it was almost beautiful, what he was *trying* to say. I glance out of the window at the cold grey day, at my warrior leaf. All the others have gone now, all of them except for my stubborn friend and some hoodlums around the trunk. A few drops of rain tap against the windowpane. I look down at my hands; they look like my mother's, the veins protruding, a freckle on my knuckle that hadn't been there before. Why am I here? I cannot fathom quite what happened.

'I wonder what it is that makes us so restless as a species,' Dr Robinson says. Her voice sounds different, as if she is talking to a human being, a close friend even, rather than a patient. I respond to it, I lean into it – it's like she's proffering a warm hand, pulling me up from the abyss. 'What makes us crave transcendence?' she continues. She understands what Karl was trying to say.

She too is looking out at my tree and it's hard to tell if she's speaking to me, the tree, or to no one. But then she turns to me and we lock eyes. It is the connection I have been craving since she came into the room.

'I presume it's just part of being human,' I say, and I know then that I will tell her everything.

' "Why don't we make love any more?" he asked me.'

He'd had no resentment in his voice. I'd replied, too quickly. *We do.* It was a feeble response – we both knew it, but it just sounded too impossibly sad to agree with him, to admit it; one of us had to protect our relationship with falsehoods. But inside I was marvelling at him, his bravery at venturing into such dangerous territory. *I don't know*, I said, because I too wanted to open the cage door.

'Then I heard myself ask him one of those questions that can never be unasked: "Are you having an affair?" I was no fool, Dr Robinson. You see, Karl had been away a lot. He'd been on several trips abroad and had been working for a company up in Edinburgh on and off for a year, and I had had my suspicions that something was going on up there. I'd seen a woman's name – Janine – come up several times on his phone and each time he'd angled the screen away from me and didn't answer the call. Then a minute or so later I would see him secretively sending a text. But I said nothing; if it didn't affect us here at home, I preferred not to know these things.'

'How did he respond?' she asks.

'He looked affronted. "No, I'm not having an affair," he said, eyeball to eyeball. "But you *fancy* other people?" I asked.'

I'd thought he was going to deny it. He shifted on the bed.

'It would hardly have been surprising – we'd been

together for fifteen-odd years, of course he was going to fancy other people. I said as much to him.'

I remembered that Karl had let out this long breath that he appeared to have been holding for quite some time. Fifteen-odd years, perhaps. His shoulders slumped with the relief.

'What did he say?' she asks, she's leaning forward on the edge of her seat.

'He said, "Yes, I do". And I was grateful for his honesty. I smiled "That's OK," I said. And he leant forward and clutched both my hands in his. "My God! You're amazing, I really love you, you know that." And I did know that. It was what he said next that really took me by surprise. "Connie, I know you've always held a torch for Jonathan Hapgood."'

I'm still stunned when I think of the nerve he had; at the time it seemed so left-field. It was a subject we'd always tiptoed around, never broached. But now Karl was telling me that he had always known there was some small part of me that he would never possess. And I *suppose* he was right. In the garden of our marriage, was there a body buried? I mean, we'd sown a lawn over it, grown flowers, put up a slide and hung washing on the line, but was there a body down there? In the garden of most marriages, aren't there bodies? Isn't that what fertilizes the soil – the past? I remembered how Karl had once found an email exchange between Johnny and myself; it wasn't explicit, but there was a *tone* to it which had been intimate – old lovers who, yes, still held torches and swung them about every now and then in cyberspace. But that was all.

'Had you talked about Jonathan Hapgood?' she asks.

'Barely. Wait for it, because then he said, "I think you should get in touch with him. Why don't you meet up with him and see whether those feelings are still there?"'

Dr Robinson crosses those strong legs of hers and leans forward, frowning, her chin cupped in her hand.

'I was astonished. "Hang on, Karl," I said, "this is dangerous. What exactly are you saying? Are we talking about having an open relationship?" He shrugged. "I suppose we are," he said. We stared at each other. There we were, perched on the bed sipping coffee, talking about having sex with other people like it was the most ordinary thing in the world.'

It was absurd. My God, even as we were having the conversation I could hear Ness's reactions in my head when I told her, how she would cover her mouth and yelp. What a peculiar concept: permission from your spouse to have sex with someone else. I knew other people did it, you hear of it all the time, but no one *we* knew, not in our lovely little community. It would be a little bit 'out there'. But Karl understood me; I *was* an artist. Artists aren't doctors, teachers, accountants, lawyers, plumbers or therapists. We don't have routines. We don't sit on packed trains. We don't have regular salaries or know when bank holidays are. We confuse the paper-pushers; we slip through bureaucracy without ticking their boxes. We spoil their systems. Our signatures are never asked for on passport applications because we aren't credible. There's nothing respectable about us. We aren't important. We are part of the brigade swimming upstream, taking risks, getting humiliated or riding high so that others have culture in their lives, books to read, paintings to hang, evenings with box sets. And to create we have to live.

' "Don't you want to feel alive again?" he said. Oh, how I yearned for it, Dr R. "Yes, Karl, I do." '

'So there I was, free to contact Johnny if I so chose. In actual fact, I didn't even know if he was with anyone since our last contact, whether he was remarried with children by now. Yet knowing that I could make love to someone else, *anyone* else, that I could go out and explore the world again, was like opening all the windows in a stuffy house and letting in a summer breeze. I felt elated.

' "But home is sacred, right?" I said to him. "What happens away stays away. Nothing must affect the kids." He was standing up now and I was looking at the back of him as he pulled up the sash window and let the fresh air in.'

For a while afterwards we sat there on the bed staring at each other and then all of a sudden we burst out laughing, so much so that Annie came in to see what all the fuss was about and started bouncing up and down on the bed. I felt closer to Karl than I ever had done. It was tangible, our love. It was unconditional, beyond possession, beyond ego: it was *real* love. And the weight of unspoken resentment and the next forty years of pretending had vanished. It was extraordinary. We were giddy with it. We were pioneers stepping into a brave new world, hand in hand.

I feel giddy now, as I recall it. We did indeed touch a transcendence, albeit briefly. And it was beautiful.

'What happened next, Connie?' Dr Robinson says.

I turn to her and I see it in her face: a sneer. And I hate her with a passion. She's a pretender, another backstabber. (To think, I nearly trusted her!) *Look at the mess you're in now*, she's thinking. Just like everyone else, she is glad that we failed. It justifies the necessity of clinging on to conformity, to stay in your joyless job, relationship, whatever. Aim low, risk nothing, stay under the radar. Well, take heart, everyone: we certainly failed.

'No need to be so fucking superior,' I snap at her. 'You've sold your soul. You live your double life, creeping upstairs to your bedroom with your iPad for furtive fiddles – which MILF will you choose today to get off to on YouPorn?'

Surely she must have known I'd been on her iPad history? But apparently she's no Sherlock: she looks like I've smacked her in the face; her jaw is hanging open. I lean forward, occupying her space now. 'You're a fraud. We were trying not to be.'

She looks crushed. I feel bad. I am discovering that I have a horrible, mean streak. She tucks her hair behind her ear. 'I'm sorry if I seemed superior,' she says calmly, despite her face flashing like a Belisha beacon. 'That wasn't my intention.'

The sky is dark now. It feels as if a great black mouth is about to swallow the entire planet. I jump as the rain hits the window like machine-gun fire. I can't see my leaf any more. It feels like I'm falling. Everything is always spoilt in the end, nothing good can last. We are born alone, we die alone and no one can be trusted. I hang my head. I can hear it first, a kind of roar. I have to do something about it; I have to stop it. I sit up straight and clench my fist. I punch myself in the jaw as hard as I can. It feels good. I try to do it again but she reaches out and takes my wrists firmly in her hands. We struggle for a moment. I can hear her calling out and someone opening the door. She wraps me up in those strong arms of hers. I'm still struggling. She's holding me tight; she's got more resolve than I do. I am weak. I crumble.

'You're doing so well, Connie,' she says to me. 'You're doing *so* well.'

Chapter 12

I've been thinking back, wondering what that first big *shock* was, Dr R. I was sitting at home with Annie on the sofa when the phone call came. It was dusk, but I hadn't drawn the curtains. Outside I could see a bright, sharp fingernail moon clinging on to the electric blue sky above the footbridge. Commuters trudged past our house in clusters from the station, their faces like ghosts lit up by their phone screens. Occasionally one of them looked up and glanced through our window and I was aware of how snug we looked, how pretty the room was, how fantastic my life was. I was feeling better than I had felt for years in the post-agreement high, you see. Life was suddenly full of potential. Josh was out at footy training and Karl had a meeting in Soho, so Annie and I had decided to watch *Toy Story 3* for the five-hundredth time. Annie was dressed as a nun. She was in a religious phase, aided, I now understand, by me. She and Polly had been rummaging around in my box in the attic and found a kinky little nun outfit that I'd forgotten about. She'd appeared in it (accompanied by Polly in a slightly soiled nurse's uniform, eek) and had been wearing it ever since. It fitted her much better than me but it wasn't a look I encouraged and I certainly didn't want her going out in it.

She was sprawled out with her legs on top of me, a bowl of popcorn balancing on her nylon fire-risk habit.

'When God's met a girl he really likes and respects, does he do sex with her?' she asked.

'What makes you so sure God's a man?' I said, in my responsible feminist mother voice. She sat up, stopped chomping the popcorn and thought about it. The whole of Year Four had had a sex-education class at school that day.

'He might be both. He might have a peanut and a womb so he could make babies with himself.'

'Penis. Yes. Makes sense,' I said, trying to picture it. I was enjoying *Toy Story 3* more than she was. She went for another handful and nestled her cold foot into my cardigan sleeve.

'I think I'll probably be quite good at doing sex when I'm older.'

'Oh?' She didn't lack confidence, my Annie. 'Why's that?'

'I like looking at bottoms and things.' It's hard to know exactly what expression to pull sometimes with one's children. I focused on the film. We were at the bit where the stripy bear turns out to be a right bastard.

'Danny thinks he might be gay,' she said. I turned to her, leant forward and grabbed a handful of popcorn myself. Evidently the sex-education discussion had continued out of the classroom and into the playground. I should check with Ness what Polly had been reporting back.

'Wow,' I said. 'That was brave of him. And did everyone react well to that?'

'Yes, of course,' she said. 'He says he might even be pansexual.'

'Jesus!' I said.

'Don't swear.'

'What the hell is *pan*sexual? Someone who's into nature?'

'Yup,' she said breezily. 'You know: snowmen and stuff.'

Everything was different in the house; there had been a fundamental shift between Karl and me. It was now a place of tolerance and kindness. This new way that we were living seemed to be working for everyone. I'd relaxed. I was getting on well with the kids. I was writing away like mad – I had the beginning and the end of a great story and had pitched it to my agent, who thought she could sell it. I was feeling generally inspired. Karl had been up in Edinburgh for a few weeks (I didn't ask any questions at all) and when he came home he seemed happy and loving and kind. One night we had actually even spontaneously made love ourselves. And it was so much better without the duty attached to it. Even my father noticed that I seemed happier. *Has something happened?* he'd asked, with a peck on my cheek. *You're shining, my darling!*

Karl had been adamant that we should tell no one about our new arrangement. I felt the same. Except I did tell Ness, obviously – but I swore her to secrecy. It was a Saturday and we were in her kitchen about to have tea. She was trying to fix the Ikea cuckoo clock; it lay in parts on the table. Once the kids left the room I made her catch me up on her latest romance saga – she'd been on a few dates, with women and men. She was pouring the tea, one hand on the lid of the Cornishware blue-and-white striped teapot.

'Ness,' I said, 'Karl and I have come to a decision . . .'
(She, of all people, knew how strong but numb our
marriage was.) 'We're going to take lovers.' She paused
mid-pour, looked at me and frowned. It wasn't the
reaction I was expecting. Not shock or delight, but disapproval. I always forgot how essentially prudish she was.
Or did she think I was coming on to her? *Was* I coming
on to her? What did the agreement mean for her and me?

'That's a funny way to put it,' she said primly. I felt flat.
I regretted saying anything at all; I was wrong to expect
her understanding. I'd wanted her to be happy for me, to
share my excitement. She knew how hard I'd been finding it coping with everything. She knew that I'd gone on
the antidepressants. The truth was that I had expected
her to be there for me. And she wasn't. I didn't seem to
register with her the way I used to. There had been a
time when she found me captivating. She had revelled in
me – I used to see it in her eyes. Perhaps there is a stage
in an intense female friendship when a sisterly *irritation*
takes hold: once we have shared all our secrets, told all
our stories, predicted each other's responses, adopted
the ones we like and discarded the others; when we
become more interested in impressing strangers than
each other; when we side with other people in discus-
sions, even dropping an acerbic word or a scoffing laugh;
when the solidarity has gone and a pointed neglect takes
its place. In short, had she fallen out of love with me?

After we'd fed the kids and I was leaving, she gave me
a big hug and said, 'You're an incredible person, Connie.
You're brave. You're unconventional.' (Appalling really
how quickly my ego could be pumped up again, but

I loved her saying this. I have a deep and visceral need to be *special*. We all have a driving need: Karl's is to be *liked* (obviously). Ness's is to be *safe*. And yours, Dr R, oh, it's easy-peasy; you need to be *needed* – don't you?)

When Karl left for Edinburgh, where he would be staying in a grand, romantic hotel that the company was putting him up in (I'd seen it online), we kissed each other goodbye at the door with a knowing smile and a little wave. I asked no questions. That was the deal. Alone in the house, with high-wire nerves, I had emailed Johnny under the pretence of writing an article about journalism. To my surprise, within the hour he'd emailed me back and we'd arranged to meet up in a bar near the LSE off Drury Lane on the Friday. I must have read that email fifty times. It was all so easy. I hadn't expected everything to happen so quickly and I regretted it. *What on earth were Karl and I doing?* Wasn't it enough just to *be* honest; did we really have to act on it? I texted Ness and she came round after she'd finished working. We drank wine and danced to Fun Boy Three on YouTube. For the next forty-eight hours I could think of nothing else, my imagination galloping off in ghastly *Fifty Shades* directions. Over the last ten years I had fantasized about bumping into Johnny, especially if I went to Brighton where I knew he now lived. In my fantasy I was cool and wisecracking and irresistible. In reality I would be no such thing. Even the thought of it made me a jabber. I'd lost my appetite. I woke up with my heart fluttering. It was ridiculous.

I'd googled him, of course. I'd seen a recent picture. He hadn't aged badly: he had a few more wrinkles, a wider girth and a thinner head of hair, as might be expected, but he looked more or less the same. Presumably he'd googled me and seen similar slappings from the hands of time. I found myself staring into Karl's shaving mirror with fresh eyes. My face used to be a simple affair: two eyes, a nose and a mouth. But now there was too much going on: eye bags, lines on my forehead, lines round my eyes, thin red veins and an albinic moustache which I swore hadn't been there the previous day. My face had become too *busy*. It was depressing. But I did what I could: I lotioned and potioned my skin, I waxed and plucked that tash, I dyed and curled my lashes, I shaved my legs *just in case* and even managed to find time to have my bikini line done (by an overenthusiastic beautician, might I add; now my pubis resembled a pig's trotter, which was certainly not the look I was going for). Don't get me wrong – I wasn't going to be *showing* it but I needed to be prepared for this new voyage aboard the good ship *Freedom*.

Then on the Friday itself I got seriously chilly feet. I nearly emailed pretending I was ill. I *was* ill; I felt sick with nerves. Ness came round when she got back from work to babysit and pass the once-over on my look. She'd been intrigued by the whole Johnny thing since I'd told her about Karl's Janine up in the Highlands.

I'd been counting down the hours to the date. I'd even bought new clothes for the occasion. I spent ages trying on various combos, eventually resorting to the trusted staple of smart jeans and a plain black top, that casual look achieved with Herculean labour. Ness gave me the thumbs up, a squirt of Jo Malone and a neat tequila before pushing me out of the door. I put my hair up and then took it down, then put it up again and continued to do so the entire tube journey. By the time I got out at Leicester Square, I was almost shaking. I considered turning back. As I walked northwards and down Old Compton Street, I could feel my heart trying to do a runner back down to the tube. But I'd got what I asked for: I felt *alive*. I felt *present*.

I walked into the bar.

Johnny was there. He had reading glasses on and was looking at his phone. He glanced up and saw me and smiled. I felt a rush. I walked across the room. He got up slowly and we hugged awkwardly across the little table. He was drinking a dry Martini and I ordered the same. He felt familiar and foreign at the same time, like going back to an old house you once lived in: you know the shape of every cranny, but the decoration's changed. Yes, I knew the shape of him: his voice, his laugh, the way he tapped his fingers together, the way he spoke, slowly, self-deprecatingly, those wry observations. But he was also different: he seemed smaller, his shoulders were hunched, his back stooped; there were marks around his mouth that spoke of disappointment and unhappiness; his spirit seemed heavier.

We had another drink and caught up on each other's lives in a prescriptive way. He talked about his work and I talked about mine. We talked about his two girls, nineteen and twenty now, who lived with his ex-wife. I couldn't quite bring myself to ask whether he had a girlfriend these days and he didn't mention one. He asked about Karl. I implied that we were living separate lives but bringing up children together. We asked after each other's parents. His mother had died and his father was in a home – we spent a long time talking about that; it's a preoccupation at this time of our lives. Frankly the hours flew by; our intimacy seemed entirely normal. At one stage he took my hand in his and looked at it carefully. 'I'd forgotten your hands,' he said, 'such pretty hands.' We talked about how we had ended and, strangely, we both seemed to think the other person had ended it. What is the real narrative of events, Dr R? Do you ever believe anyone at all? He asked me what it was that I needed to ask him about journalism. I bluffed about media training and said I'd follow up with sending him some questions.

We went on to another bar. It felt like we had to start all over again out in the street; our bodies had to readjust to each other. He was smaller than Karl. I felt tall at his side. We found a table near the back and talked and he ate and time went too fast. When the waiters started stacking plates at the bar, we were both of us reluctant to part and so he walked me slowly to Waterloo station. It was a beautiful warm summer evening, London looked stunning, and as we crossed Hungerford Bridge I stopped to take a picture of the view. It felt magical: the night, the skyline, the river, him.

'Hey,' he said, turning to me. And my happy heart sang a little song.

'Hey,' I said, leaning against the balustrade.

'I should go . . .' he said, but he didn't move. 'What a lovely evening.' He was smiling. He was looking at me. I mean *really* looking at me, Dr R, in that way only lovers are allowed. I remembered losing him all those years ago and a brief shadow of that pain passed through me. A group of twenty-somethings strolled past and I supposed we must have struck them as very old, but we didn't care; we let their voices peter out. He moved closer in towards me and touched my face. I kissed him. How soft and full and familiar his lips were, how I remembered and had forgotten them. The way he held me, the smell of him, the taste of him, can you believe we forget these things? And what a kiss that was, to feel my whole being centred in my mouth. I'd sacrifice years for a kiss like that.

But then he pulled away. 'I can't,' he said, but his arms were still around me.

My lips stung. 'OK . . .' I replied. 'Why not?'

'Well . . . I'm . . .' He looked awkward; he shuffled his feet. 'I'm with someone . . .'

'Oh,' I said. 'Right . . . of course.'

'Um . . . It's fairly new . . .'

'Right,' I said. I looked over at St Paul's, at the bend of the river, the night sky, the lights, the water, the boats – they'd all lost a little of their majesty. I smiled at him. 'Lucky girl,' I said. I meant it.

'I should have said. I just thought . . . Sorry. I wasn't expecting this . . .'

'Oh God, no,' I said. 'I wasn't either . . .' I wanted to leave now. 'Look, thanks for walking me this far . . . I should go too.'

'OK. Let's be in touch,' he said.

'Yup,' I replied, walking off backwards, thinking *no, let's not*.

'So good to see you!' he said. He waved.

I stared out of the window on the train trying to make sense of it all. I'd got what I'd asked for, or had I asked for it? I felt alive all right: buzzing and excited but also sad and frightened. Thank God I had home and my lovely family to go back to. I checked my phone. A message from Ness: the kids were asleep at hers. Another earlier message: they were all going round to sleep at hers as our telly seemed to have lost its connection.

So I let myself in to a dark empty house. I went down to the kitchen and cleared things up. I turned off the lights and went upstairs, picking up various discarded garments of clothing en route. In the bathroom I washed my face and brushed my teeth, cleaning the sink with the other hand as I did so. I went back to the bedroom, drew the curtains, undressed and climbed into our huge cold bed, and lay there in the darkness listening to the noises of the house bereft of inhabitants; it felt strange, alien, lacking.

Yes, everything had changed now.

Annie had finished all the popcorn and we had slunk further down the sofa. We were sucking on Fab ice lollies and watching the climactic moments for poor Buzz and Woody trying to escape from the recycling machine, when I felt my phone buzz in my back pocket. I took it out. Karl's name was on the screen. He was taking clients for dinner in Soho; presumably he'd finished early and fancied a pint. I swiped and answered. 'Hello, love?' I said.

I couldn't hear properly because of the film. I covered my ear. 'Hi!' I said. He didn't answer.

'Hello? Karl?' I said. I could hear him faintly, as if he were a long way off; I thought he was laughing. I unhooked Annie's legs from me and got up from the sofa, phone pressed to my ear. I went into the playroom. 'Karl?' I called. And then I shouted, 'Karl!' But still he didn't hear me. I listened carefully.

'Oh, baby,' he said. I thought he was messing with me.

'Yes, baby?' I said.

'That's it, baby,' he said. He wasn't messing; he sounded really intense. 'Mmmm . . .' he went, as though he was eating something delicious; pistachio ice cream, perhaps – that was his favourite. Yes, that's what I honestly thought. And as a greasy feeling of dread slid through me from the pit of my stomach, my head kept whispering that this was the deal we had made.

'Uhh . . . yess . . . that's good . . .' He wasn't eating ice cream; it sounded more like kissing. 'So good . . .' he moaned.

Wrong again, not kissing.

'Oh!' he said. 'Oh . . .'

No prizes here: those were the undeniable sounds of fellatio.

I know I should have just put the phone down, but there was something mesmerizing about it. I couldn't. I stood there in the playroom, my foot on a Twister map, one hand holding a Fab lolly, the phone pressed to my ear, listening to my husband getting a blow job, unaware that I was in his back pocket, my ear and her mouth only inches apart, my heart punching against my breast, as it is even now as I write this. And still I listened.

'Oh, you angel,' he said.

He used to say that to me.

'Oh, you sweetheart,' he said.

He used to say that to me too. Why didn't I just put the phone down?

'You're the best,' he said.

He hadn't said that to me for a very long time.

'Stop! Stop!' he cried, and for a moment I thought perhaps his conscience had got the better of him – he was thinking of me, he couldn't go through with it. 'I have to fuck you!'

I know, put the phone down, right? But I couldn't, Dr R. Instead I listened to the muffled sounds of clothes being shed, zips being opened, snatched frenzied breaths. I'd been thrown on the floor now.

'Oh my God, you do it for me. Oh those knickers, those white knickers, you just do it for me . . . everything about you does it for me . . .'

I stood there rigid, phone at my ear, listening to the frantic gasps, the little shrieks to the peaks, the painful pleasure at the summit, the shudders and sighs of satiation during the long trip back down.

And then I heard it: *cheep cheep, cheep cheep* went the cuckoo clock.

Yes, that was the *shock*, Dr R. That was why my hair fell out: my husband and my best friend were fucking.

Chapter 13

That night, Emma lay in bed, *Hotel du Lac* in her hand. She was so tired. She'd worked a fourteen-hour day: after she'd left Connie she'd had meetings – they were expecting a statement from her soon on the Mortensen case – and a brief appearance in court on a case that had been dragging on for months, plus a mountain of paper-work. Her eyes had slipped across the same sentence for the umpteenth time before finally closing. Her current page rate was pathetic – not even a page a night before she conked out – but it helped distract her mind from the indelibility of the real plot: what pushes a loving mother to breaking point. In this slumber her mind began to free-flow: the night sky on Hungerford Bridge, that kiss, *real* kissing, white knickers . . .

She let the book rest on her chest for a moment, vaguely aware of the sounds of Si pottering about next door. She didn't have the energy to think about it but something wasn't right between them; they were distant with each other and what was worse, neither of them appeared to mind the fact. This had become the normality; when he wasn't working he was playing squash or was at rehearsal, and she barely seemed to be at home; her work was more demanding than ever. She would put some effort into *them* tomorrow. They really should do something together. She would make sure they did – the cinema perhaps, or a play. What was it Connie had said about art? She couldn't remember.

She heard the flush of the loo from next door and with only a faint hum of irritation, her brain proceeded to clock Si's movements in the bathroom and their inevitable consequences: tomorrow before work she would have to pick up the wet bath mat left skew-whiff on the floor, the towel stuffed across the bar, the tiny splashes on the mirror from his electric toothbrush, detritus left unrinsed in the sink, the small drops of pee around the toilet – the minute but continual daily male trail. After all these years, these things had only just begun to consciously bother her. She had always felt it was *her* problem, her fastidious tidiness, how difficult *she* must be to live with. Was it Connie who had awakened her to protest? With closed eyes she reached out and turned off her light.

She was nudged out of sleep by a hand resting on her hip. She was aware of the darkness of the room, the clicking of a radiator, the coolness of his fingers on her skin, making soft almost imperceptible movements that could only mean one thing. Wearily she knew that she had two choices: she could feign sleep, which would hardly even be feigning because technically she *was* asleep; or she could respond in an infinitesimal way and thereby give him permission to make love to her – she might not even have to open her eyes. She *should* choose the latter; she should try harder. Then in that murky shapeless twilight, neither awake nor asleep, another choice stepped out of the shadows: she thought of those smooth artistic fingers on the handlebars of his bike, the way he stood there on the towpath in his lycra, and she remembered how he had once looked at her many years ago; she recalled the night of that party when his knee had been pressed against hers on the sofa – she could even remember the sofa's fabric, a thick brown corduroy – *of course* he had been aware of the fact that they were touching. When she left the party he had followed her and hovered around to say goodbye and if she had had more confidence, she could have let it be known that she wanted to be kissed by him, but instead she had scurried off.

But supposing she had *not* scurried off – supposing he had kissed her, those full lips gently brushing her own. What if she had changed her mind and stayed on at the party; if they had returned to that sofa, carried on drinking, thighs touching until they crashed out on that soft corduroy with all the other teenage bodies scattered about the room. She might have woken in the night to feel Dougie's hand on her hip, just like this; *his* fingers stroking her skin, awakening every nerve in her body, setting off this sharp throbbing between her legs.

She shifted minutely to say *yes* to this touch on her skin and his fingers slipped over her hip, up the contours of her body to the fullness of her breast. He firmly squeezed her flesh in his hands, pinching at her nipple, quietly, so as not to wake the other inhabitants of the room. She opened her mouth to let out a silent moan in the safe confusing blindness where she felt free to express and suppress. She bit her lip so as not to wake the others, feeling him hard against her back in the confines of this small sofa. She placed her own hand over his, guiding it from her breast downwards, opening her legs, instructing his fingers on how to relieve this jabbing teenage ache. She moaned, barely audibly.

'Turn over,' Si said, and for a moment his voice broke the illusion and briefly her pleasure dimmed. But no, she did as he bade; she turned over. To her surprise, she was wet enough and soon he was inside her. Dougie was back, touching her as Si made love to her. And she was going to come. For sure. The whole thing had taken less than one minute and she was going to come. And he was going to come. They both cried out with pleasure.

Yes, all was well in their marriage.

★

When Emma got to the unit the next day, she was told that Connie was lying comatose on her bed; she'd had a seizure at 4 a.m. This was not good news – firstly for Connie herself, but secondly, the clock was ticking for Emma's statement on the case. And she still wasn't in possession of all the facts. Before Emma went in to see Connie, she asked for the CT scan and was told she could watch the fit on the camera footage from the room.

She sat down to watch it in the security room with the guard. From the way he looked at her she wondered whether he had seen the fateful footage of her vomiting in the toilet. She was sure not; this CCTV was perfunctory most of the time. She sipped at the sweet tea brought to her by the tea caddy guy on his rounds. It tasted institutional but good. She rewound the footage. The last person in the room was Mrs Ibrahim, handing out pills for the night. At this point Connie was sitting up in bed. Their interaction seemed brief and functional with Mrs Ibrahim pausing at the door as she left the room, and saying something over her shoulder to which Connie flicked her two fingers before lying flat on her back and looking up at the ceiling – nothing unusual.

Then for five minutes Connie lay there unmoving until the fluorescent glow that was in all the rooms was dimmed to signify that it was time to sleep. Obediently, Connie slept. Emma fast-forwarded to 2.20 a.m. when Connie woke up, got off the bed and wandered over to the window, where she stood staring out into the night for an hour and five minutes. She then turned around, went back towards the bed and pulled out a book from underneath the mattress. Emma leant forward to see if she recognized the book but the quality of the recording was poor. Connie moved the chair from the table towards the dim glow of the light, sat down and began to read. She was side-on to the camera. She barely moved. Every now and then she seemed to smile, or she turned a page. No one entered the room all this while.

Then at 3.50 a.m. Connie looked up from her book and stared straight ahead for some time before leaning backwards rigidly. She then went limp and slipped off the chair smoothly, like melting wax, the back of her head banging the chair on the way to the floor, the book hanging in her hand, a page torn. Then she began to fit, her limbs flailing, her head hitting the ground again and again. Four minutes later two nurses rushed into the room, one of whom straddled the fitting Connie in order to hold down her arms and legs, while the other twisted Connie's body, pulled down her pyjamas and injected her in the bottom. They stayed like that, riding the bucking bronco, until Connie stopped moving and slumped. Another nurse entered the room and Connie was then lifted and taken out on a trolley.

The CT scan in front of Emma showed no aberrations. It wasn't epilepsy. Emma got up, thanked the security guard, tucked her hair back behind her ear, popped the scan paper under her arm, and was taken down to Connie's room by a different guard. Her room smelt different today, more clinical. Connie lay on the bed unmoving, facing the window, eyes open; she appeared not to notice Emma's entrance. She'd been sedated. She looked dreadful, pallid and frail with fresh bruises on her face. The red tufts of hair lent her an air of neglected absurdity. Emma stared at her. She had not seen Connie this vulnerable.

She cautiously approached the bed, reached out and let her hand rest on Connie's arm.

'Hello, Con,' Emma said gently, pulling up the chair, surprised at her own familiar tone. 'I hear you had a bad night.'

There was no response.

'Oh, Connie,' she whispered. 'I'm so sorry.'

Still no response.

'What happened?' she said, more to herself than to Connie. 'You were doing so well.'

The sadness of the whole situation suddenly hit her full force. Emma let her hand drop from Connie's skinny little arm and stood up. She went over to the window and looked out at the naked winter tree. There was still that one lone leaf which hadn't let go. It was a beautiful day out there. She leant her head against the pane. It felt cool against her skin.

'Next time I come, I'm going to take you out of this godforsaken room,' she said to the pane, to the Connie inside her head who was listening. 'You need some air . . . how is anyone meant to get better in here?' Her words formed a patch of breath on the glass. She wiped them away with her finger.

When she glanced back at Connie, she noticed a faded red exercise book lying skew-whiff under the bed. Emma went over, squatted down beside Connie and reached for it, her face inches from Connie's. She pulled the book towards her with her fingertips and held it in her hands: *Annie Mortensen, aged 9 and a halve. Private. Keep Out.* She looked back at Connie: no acknowledgement. She smoothed the cover with her fingers. Little Annie Mortensen – the real victim in all this. She opened the diary and scanned the neat nine-year-old handwriting. She flicked through the pages. Annie had been prolific. Emma sat back down in the chair and began to turn the pages. What she was looking for she didn't really know. She flicked through to May, when Connie had discovered the affair.

May 10
  Mummy wore her pijamas all day long and to be honest, she is smelly. She is not using beodorant and she doesnt brush her hair or put on lipstick. Her voice has gone all wierd, it is so quiet that I cant hear her. It feels like she isnt my mummy any

more. I dont like being left with her. When I ask her whats wrong she shakes her head. I dont like her like this. She is HORRID to Daddy whatever he does and wont let him sleep in his own bed. He has to sleep on the sofa which isnt fair as half the bed belongs to him. Last night she called him rude words. She said she had NO respect for him NONE NONE NONE. I got out of bed to watch through the crack in the door. She was crying and she started hitting Daddy and he let her and then suddenly she stopped and dropped to the floor and he picked her up and carried her like a doll into the bed. I am scared of her. And he is so NICE to her he brings her tea and makes the dinner. The worst thing is she doesnt even know what I know. Daddy is planning a SURPRISE BIRTHDAY PARTY for her!!!!!!!!!! I forgot to say!!! He swore Polly and me to secresy because we bumped into him and Ness when we were at the Holiday Inn. They were at the bar then he tried to hide from us behind a palm tree. Which was funny because we tried to hide from them because we didnt want the hotel staff knowing who our parents were. But then Daddy pretended he wasnt hiding and so he HAD to tell us about the secret surprise. He didn't even ask us what we were doing there (we have started a business by selling the little wisky bottles to the tramps by the station for 50p each). I am very excited about the party. I said it should be a swimming party. I love surprises but I promised I wouldnt tell Mummy. She doesnt deserve it if you ask me.

May 12

When Mummy was picking me up from circus club after school we were walking home. Polly and Ness ran to catch up with us and Ness took Mummys arm but Mummy jumped

Natalie Daniels

away from Ness and said something to her in a nasty whisper voice and she dragged me hard by the hand and started walking really fast. Ness tried to follow us and she looked like she was going to cry. OF ALL PEOPLE I THOUGHT YOU WOULD UNDERSTAND Ness shouted at Mummy. And Mummy stopped dead still without turning round and started laughing in this way that wasnt laughing at all. I said understand what? But Mummy said grown up stuff. She doesnt seem very grown up to me. Frankly if I was Ness I would cancel the surprise party (but I hope she doesnt. Polly and I are bringing our swimming things to it even if its not a swimming party). Then later she wouldnt let me go round to play with Polly. She is a smelly poo and I hate her.

Emma looked at Connie, her glassy stare; she was miles away, oblivious. She flicked through to the last entry in the diary: 16 November. Gently she touched the blank paper, her fingertip running across the lines, the abrupt ending, the words unwritten, the life on hold. She noticed one of the pages was not aligned. She let the book fall open at it. It was half ripped; presumably the page Connie was reading on the CCTV last night. Emma slid the two sections together.

Oct 10

Josh and me saw Grannys dead body today. She was lying in bed in her nighty all white with her mouth open and no makeup on her face and wrinkles by her ears. She still had joolry on. Granny died in the night yesterday without waking up. In the morning Grampa thought she was sleeping and brought her some coffee in bed but she had cold skin. He wont

190

*let the undertakers take her away. Uncle David arrived this
evening. He has a prickly face.*

Oh God, Connie, she wanted to say. You *knew* this; you
knew your mother had died; they told you, at Milton
House, I've checked the notes. What a peculiar way to
rediscover her mother's death – from her daughter's pen.
But everything about Connie's life was peculiar now. She
read on.

*Polly came with me. She was scared by Granny and her mouth
open. Grampa isnt crying he just sits beside Granny and says
sorry my darling sorry my darling. Because it is his fault.
Daddy said no it wasnt and Uncle David said it was because
Grampa didnt notice all the pills Granny was eating. The doctor said she ate at least thirty. Daddy told him not to say that
and David started shouting at him and I started crying because
I miss my mummy. I want my mummy back home with me. I
want everything how it was before with Mummy home and
Granny not dead. Josh is letting me sleep in his room tonight.*

*P.S. Daddy just told Josh and me we must treasure our last
memories of Granny. Mine were on Monday when I rang to
say happy birthday to her and she forgot I was on the phone
with her and started having a conversation with Grampa.
And when she carried me around with her while she made a
cup of tea and ate a biscuit and then went to the toilet and
peed like the pony in Dartmoor outside our tent. I shall treasure my memories.*

Emma looked up from the book and out of the window. Then she looked down at the broken bird of a

woman lying on the bed, her twig-thin battled arm resting on the covers, the lifeless pink palm on the sheet unfurled to the world. Emma reached out for that hand and took the cool fingers in her own and squeezed them tightly. Connie blinked slowly, heavily. Emma saw it as a glint of hope. Hope for what? How was Connie going to put the pieces of her life back together again? She had no one. That was the truth of it. Mental illness was the greatest isolator of all; it terrified people, it had made a *monster* of her. And how was anyone meant to survive such isolation?

Emma wanted to go. 'I'm going to leave you to rest now,' she said, giving her hand another squeeze. 'I'll be back tomorrow.'

She thought she felt a pull from Connie's hand and it was enough to make her pause. 'I'll stay a little longer, if you want.'

And so she sat there, hand still clasping Connie's, and closed her eyes and listened to the faint institutional sounds beyond the room: doors closing, shoes squeaking, a phone ringing. She drew her focus back into the room. The light was making a very faint buzzing sound that Emma hadn't noticed before. It was impossible to hear anything beyond the bulletproof windows so instead she focused on her own breath. Then suddenly she felt it, the connection, the absence of fear, the freedom beyond the confines of herself. It was as if it had always been right there, just waiting for her. But in her momentary joy she became conscious of the experience and immediately disconnected from it.

Emma put the diary down. She got up again and went

to the window again and looked out at the beautiful day. 'Actually, sod it,' she said decisively, turning back to Connie. 'Let's get out of here!'

Emma buzzed herself straight out of the room and when she came back in she had a wheelchair with her, some blankets and a male nurse. Together they lifted Connie and got her into the chair. Although she was quite tall, she weighed nothing; it was like lifting a child. Emma tried to be gentle – her damaged body made her a liability, but she didn't make a sound. It was as if she were beyond caring. The nurse put socks on Connie's feet. Connie let them move her about. Emma wrapped the blankets around her and pushed her out of the room.

Despite having worked here for eight months now, Emma had never actually been out in the grounds before. The gardens were well kept, the grass mown, the bushes clipped. There was nothing fancy or ornate, no actual flowers, but it was pleasant enough. A path ran down the middle towards the old wall at the end where the brook ran by and where the huge trees stood. Connie looked different outside, more pathetic, like a gawky bird fallen from the nest. The cold air was turning her nose and her cheeks red, the sunlight making the tufts of her hair glow a coppery brown. Emma pulled out her woollen hat from her bag and put it on Connie's head. There was a bench halfway down the path and Emma stopped there, putting the brake on the chair and sitting down on the seat. Emma glanced back at Connie's wing of the building, its ugly uniformity, its electronic doors, its peculiar turrets. She turned Connie's chair away from it so for one moment Connie might forget she was in an institution. And maybe it worked because shortly after Connie twisted to the side to feel the sun on her face. She shut her eyes. There was a beauty about that face, a nobility.

Emma got out her cigarettes and her lighter. The Connie of yesterday would have commented on this. She missed the Connie of yesterday; she missed her barbed comments and her piercing search for authenticity in the everyday.

'There's something nice and paradoxical about a cigarette in the fresh air,' Emma said, expecting no response and getting none. She lit up and put her cigarettes back in her pocket, glancing at her phone as she did so. There was a message from Si on it: *See you at orchestra X.*

She stared at the text. What did he mean? Was it the concert tonight? She checked her phone diary. No, it wasn't for another couple of weeks. There was only one conclusion: he hadn't meant that text for her. She read it again and stared at the kiss in particular. He never sent kisses after messages. If it wasn't meant for her then who had he meant it for? Who was in that orchestra who received his kisses? Emma looked up into the cold blue sky. And down again at the screen.

I doubt it, she wrote, and then deleted it. Then she texted again: *Was that for me?* And then deleted that as well and put her phone away. She was paranoid. She was counter-transferring. Just because she fantasized about other men during their sexual intercourse, it did not mean her husband was being unfaithful. She took a long deep drag, crossed and uncrossed her legs, and shifted herself so that she was facing Connie.

'I know it's not going to be today, Con. But you'll have to start communicating with me again, love,' she said. 'It's the only way I'm going to be able to help you.'

Small birds were fixing a nest in the bush to her right. There was much twittering and excitement and Emma watched them for a while. A bold bee in an out-of-season venture flew out from the thicket and began inspecting Connie's blanket. Emma brushed it off.

'OK, well *I'm* going to carry on talking; you can just listen. Firstly, I want you to know that it is not surprising you couldn't cope when your mother died. You'd lost your people, your props. You were grieving, Connie. You're still in grief. A triple grief . . .'

Still no response. Emma turned her attention back to the busy little birds in the bush. 'I know what grief is, Con . . .' she said in a small voice. 'I know what self-hatred is.' One of the birds hopped out on the grass and was looking at Emma, cocking its head at her. She smiled. 'But we are made of resilient stuff . . .'

She took a long slow drag, exhaled slowly and sat there for a while, the two of them statue-still. But time was running out.

'You know you're going to have to tell me at some stage what happened at the Harvest Festival, Connie. What you did to Ness . . . There are several statements; there were many witnesses. So I know what *they* say. But I need to hear it from you; I need to know what was going on *inside* your head . . .'

No response. She reached out to tuck Connie's cold hand back underneath the blanket. She wasn't going to get anything out of her today.

'I told you, she pressed no charges,' Emma coaxed.

She took another deep drag and studied Connie's face. What pushed her to it? What was the trigger? She tried to imagine what the daily reality of life must have been like in that comfortable area where people said *good morning* and *how's so and so* and picked up each other's kids from school. She wondered how she herself would have coped. Ness was part of the infrastructure of Connie's life: their children, their houses virtually next door, the school gates, posting letters, at the shops, getting into her car. What had it been like when word got out, blinds opened and closed, the scandal, the tittle-tattle, the pity, the judgement, how people would *know better*, say they *saw it coming*. How humiliating it must have been.

High up she watched a bird soar across the blue. She needed to be patient with Connie. She thought of her as a ball of tangled string that could only be unpicked slowly, methodically, keeping hold of the loose end, nails in the knots, teeth if need be.

Emma checked her watch. It was almost time to go back in; as she turned to get up, she was surprised to see that Connie's lips were parted. She was trying to say something.

Emma moved closer. 'What, Connie? Tell me.'

She put her ear close to Connie's lips. 'Or . . .' Connie whispered huskily. 'Orchestra!' Emma looked at her sharply, eye to eye. Connie was smiling. She gave a puny, rasping laugh.

Chapter 14

Since the fit I have been given more freedom. Now I have made myself pathetic it appears that they are prepared to trust me a little more. Ideally for them, I would be a static blob on the bed, mouth agape, popping pills in one end and popping pellets out the other. As it is, the Squeak reluctantly takes me out into the garden into the recommended fresh air – presumably recommended by Dr Robinson. I'm glad of it. It's a sunny day and surprisingly warm with the blankets wrapped round me. The Squeak is not a nature lover; sunshine makes her sneeze, she says. Fresh air does not *agree* with her, she says proudly, like she has a diagnosed condition: Arselazyitis. So we head straight for the bench so that she can get on with her word-search puzzle. I'm out of the wheelchair now but we walk slowly, as if I am an old person. Even the laptop feels heavy in my arms. My body is feeble. I looked down at it in the shower this morning – tepid, as I'm still sensitive to hot water – and it was unfamiliar: I'm translucent, scrawny and sexless. Like an alien, without the benefits.

But I do have an admirer. Mental Sita is in the garden too. She has a visitor, her mother, I think – an oval-shaped woman in a sparkling sari who appears to be neither cold nor self-conscious about the copious rolling folds around her midriff. This must be where Mental Sita gets her sense of abandon from. She herself is frolicking about the lawn collecting blades of grass, leaping from one patch to the other, confused and marvelling all at once for it seems that she cannot work out how the grass is greener on her left than her right. Look up at the light, lunatic!

The Squeak directs me towards another bench as Mental Sita's mother got there before us. She's gorging on a bar of Cadbury Dairy Milk, unconcerned with the prancing goat before her.

How nice for Mental Sita to have a visitor. I haven't had anyone since the Weasel and that seems a very long time ago now. I cannot stop thinking about my old dad and how he is coping without my mum. Not well, I know that. He can't even get himself together to come and see me; it would have been nice for the Weasel to have brought him along.

My mother is dead. My mother died over two months ago, they tell me. I will never see her again. Never. That is not a concept I can grasp. Dr Robinson says I have locked the information away. She's right. It feels like somebody told me in a dream; as if another Connie knew it, another Connie in another dimension. I feel divided up: *this* Connie, *me*, is occupying only a small part of myself. If I were a house I would be in the hallway surrounded by doors that are all shut. I have curled up in a ball on the floor.

I want a visitor. I'm so lonely I'm forced to have a conversation with the Squeak. She's head down in her word search now and has chosen 'Modes of Transport', for crying out loud.

'Do you know if my father's going to come and see me?' I ask her.

She runs her short triangular finger up and down the letter columns and shrugs. 'I'm not psychic.'

I miss my mum.

'Have you ever seen someone overdose?'

'Yup,' she says, carefully circling the word *dumptruck*.

'Is it a painful death?' I ask her. I'm really hoping not, I'm hoping she just went to sleep.

'It's agony,' she says. She's on a roll: *caravan*. 'You puke up your guts.'

I try not to think about it. I shut that door and open my old Dell.

*

I puked up my guts, Dr R; I did it there on the Twister mat after listening to them fucking. It was a visceral thing, a great purging from my centre. It's a blur now, what happened straight afterwards, but somehow I must have mopped it up and I remember watching the rest of *Toy Story 3* with Annie in my arms, resting my chin on her wimple, feeling like I'd been punched hard in the face, my eyes stinging. At some stage Josh came back from footy and he seemed different to me, like he had grown since he left the house: his voice was deeper, his hair darker; he had become a man in those few hours. 'You all right, Mum?' he asked. 'Fine,' I said, smiling, and that seemed to suffice. I watched a version of myself making him some beans on toast. He thanked me, ate it, got out his phone and went up to his room. I took Annie upstairs too. She chatted away, making the most of my vagueness, asking me if she could borrow £100 to set up an ice-pop business. With difficulty – for she was practising being chewed to death in a garbage-crushing machine and was acrobatically rolling about on the top bunk – I got her into bed and tucked her in to her unchanged world, and then I sat on my bed, where nothing was familiar at all.

Even my hands seemed to belong to a stranger. They were the hands of the old me, of a few hours ago, an innocent. *She* was there, on my hands, on the fourth finger of my right hand, to be precise – my beautiful petal ring. She had given me that. I spun it around on my finger and removed it, put it on the bedside table and stared at it. I loved that ring. She was there too on the bedside table: three of those books were hers; I slowly reached out my hand and struck them hard and they fell to the floor. She was there on the floor too where the book-mark fell out, a David Hockney postcard she had given me. I picked it up. *Darling C*, it said on the back, *I am eternally grateful for your love and friendship. Love, as ever, Ness.* I looked away. She was there on the dressing table: my make-up bag a birthday present. And there she was hanging on the door: my kimono – a gift from Karl. She was the only person, including me, to have worn it. My eyes stung again, I was still reeling from the punch. Even the ceiling wasn't safe from her – the lampshade was made by her sister-in-law; I'd bought it at a private view that we'd been to. Ness had permeated everywhere, everything, even my husband.

Here's the thing I can see clearly now when I look back at my idiot self sitting in that bed: of all the conflicting emotions rampaging around me, the root of it was simple. I felt *left out*. The two people dearest to me had excluded me from their club. I was surplus to requirements. I simply wasn't wanted. Or needed. I had valued my own worth as being far greater than they had. What a fool! On how many occasions had they wished I hadn't been around so they could relish each other's company, sharing grimaces behind my back? The sheer ridiculousness of my presence embarrasses me even now.

I sat there on my bed waiting for hours, head hurting, thoughts that cut like shards of glass while the kids slept peacefully in their rooms. Nothing was as it seemed any more. I kept tripping up at every remembered happiness; how could I not have seen what was right before my eyes? All those people I'd sneered at when they'd said to me, *I'd never let my partner go to the cinema/theatre with another woman*. How superior I'd felt at such small-mindedness, such possessiveness, such lack of trust. Turned out they were right, and how the disappointment stung.

I couldn't compute. It was all so *messy*. I hated *mess*. I had thought that my arrangement with Karl was specifically so as *not* to have mess in our lives. He could have chosen anyone at all, so why her when it was so clearly a destructive move? Or had this been part of his plan all along? How had I been so easily manipulated?

I heard him letting himself in at last, closing the door, locking it behind him – the guardian, the protector of the house returned. I listened to his footsteps climbing the stairs and I thought I was going to panic, be unable to hold it together. I quickly grabbed one of the books and pretended to read, the bookmark now on my lap, her words of love scrawled across me. He was on the landing outside the bedroom. I wondered how on earth I was going to be able to look at him.

'Hi,' he said, hanging his jacket over the kimono. 'Good evening?' he asked with a yawn.

'Yup,' I said, my voice surprising me with its calmness. It turned out that I *could* bear to look at him; it was *he* who couldn't bear to look at me. In fact I became mesmerized by him. How often in life do we get to knowingly observe a con, to witness the enacting of pretence, the lie so blazingly authentic? Momentarily I felt lofty, from up here on my high horse trotting along the path of righteousness.

He yawned again. Yes, he always yawned when he lied, I'd noticed that when he was on the phone to his family. I just hadn't noticed it in relation to *me* before. He was putting on a great display of tiredness as he got undressed. He was nearly naked now, fresh from her touches and clutches; I searched his coelacanth skin for mating marks. He would not be getting in *this* bed, that was for sure.

'How was work?' I asked, again surprised by my own voice. I sounded casual. I put down my book for the showdown. If he hadn't been so pickled in his own deviancy he might have noticed that it was upside down and my hands were trembling.

'We met in a pub actually.'

'Oh, which one?'

'Coach and Horses.' He was quick.

I let him see me clocking my phone. 'That's late, was there a lock-in?'

'Yeah,' he said. He was taking off his socks now, sitting on the bed, his back to me.

'You didn't pop in anywhere on the way back home then?'

'No,' he said, pairing the socks, rolling them up, leaning over to put them in the drawer in a suspicious display of tidiness.

'Not even Ness's?'

He paused. *Squirm, you fuck-face.*

'Oh yeah,' he said, suddenly remembering; the rat didn't know he was cornered. 'She needed a hand getting the boiler working . . . the ignition had gone . . .' *Blah blah blah bullshit* (macho bullshit; it was *me* who worked boilers).

'And then you slipped and accidentally your cock fell in her mouth?'

He turned with a twitch. 'What?'

'Your phone rang me, you fucking prick.'

We were eye to eye now. He'd been caught out and he knew it. I shook my head slowly and watched it all fall away: my hauteur, his pretence, my respect, his dignity, my control, our deal, our striving for truth and honesty, our intimacy, our family. I felt it all tumbling away from me. I welled up, my voice cracked. 'How *could* you?'

For a second or two he fumbled about looking for words that weren't there and then, oh, how quickly he turned things around. 'I didn't think you'd mind,' he said breezily. 'This was the agreement, wasn't it? Why *should* you mind? I don't ask you what you get up to . . . you're fucking that Hapgood guy . . .'

Why should I mind?

'I thought we weren't going to talk about it,' he said. 'What happens outside the home stays outside the home.'

'But it's *not* outside the home, is it?' I shouted. 'She's my best fucking friend!'

'I knew it! I knew it!' he sounded strangely jubilant. 'Face it, Connie. You were never going to hack it, who-ever I chose.'

'I *was*. I *was*! Just not her!'

'Sssshhh . . . !' he whispered sharply, patronizingly, glancing at the door, as if I was being hysterical, as if my behaviour was unhinged. 'Keep your voice down!'

'Oh *now* you care about the fucking children . . .' I was crying now, I couldn't help myself. Tears of outrage streamed down my face.

'I don't understand why you're so upset,' he said, faux bafflement on his face, hands raised in innocence.

'She's my friend,' was all I could muster. My God, he was going to deny me my own feelings, my rightful pain. I couldn't keep it together at all; I was twisted and wretched, sobbing and snotting.

Then, cautiously, like he was approaching a rabid dog, he came towards me and sat down on the bed next to me, reaching out a hand to comfort me, or to smother me, for it felt as if he was pressing a pillow over my face.

*

I gasp for air. Mental Sita is standing beside me. She has a crush on me. Recently she's been leaving love tokens about the place, sanitary wear scrawled with messages pushed under my door. *You have nice bits of hair. You have nice nose. You have nice bra strap* – sophisticated literary erotica. Still, it's good to know I haven't lost the old magic.

'You lovely,' she says as she sits down beside me, handing me a bunch of grass. I can't breathe, my heart is beating too fast. I'm having a panic attack; I need my pills. I take some deep breaths and press my nose to the grass. There's nothing like a scent to bring you back to the present, or to waft you back to the past for that matter. Mental Sita's mother hovers and wobbles at her side and they both seem to be expecting a reaction from me, I don't know what: a proclamation of undying love? A bended knee?

I get my breath back and wonder about eating the grass, chewing it up and spitting it out, but I haven't got the energy for pranks like that any more. The Squeak wouldn't even notice – she's just found *long haul vehicle* and, full of the glory of her achievements, rises to her feet. 'It's time for your scan, Connie,' she says, shark smile intact for Mental Sita's mum. 'Connie's got to go in now, Sita,' she says to Mental Sita in a strange sweet voice, as if she's talking to the baby Jesus, not a serial nutjob who killed ten cats with her bare hands. They both nod in response. I wish I had my mother to nod with. Then the three of us watch as Mental Sita leaps off the bench and runs towards the trees for a gambol in the leaves. I wonder whether her mother knows what a voracious onanist her daughter is.

Not long after, all of us, my new motley crew and I, head back inside.

Chapter 15

Do you feel like a god, Dr R? Healing the sick, easing the pain, dispensing your medicines with a scrawl of your pen? Or do you just feel like a glorified drug dealer (with a shitter car)?

They both promised it was over. Ness sent me pleading texts which I ignored. *It'll never happen again. Please forgive me. I can't bear it.* I didn't respond. I wanted her to suffer. Actually, I tell a lie, I sent her one text: *Fuck off, cunt.* I was so angry. In some ways I found the Weasel easier to understand than her. I felt partly culpable for his behaviour. It had been a joint decision (or had it?) to go off the beaten track in our marriage; I was responsible in some way for his needing to feel attractive and due to the fact that he was fundamentally lazy, he had barely looked further than his own front door. But *Ness*? No, she'd known how things were, she'd milked my weaknesses; she'd manipulated events to her own advantage.

There were dark hours where I was eaten up with angst, sifting through memories, catching the lies, like the time she told me she was at the theatre and that same night Karl told me he was playing football and I had thought it odd that he'd left his kit behind. A drumming panic would take hold. But what could I actually *do* about it? What choices did I have? She and I were too far immersed in each other's lives, not just school and the community but our families. By cutting her off I would be creating a trauma for everyone – we'd have to move house, upheave our family, all because I couldn't hack something that I had brought about. Besides, there was no possibility of *not* seeing her so I had to find a way of dealing with it: I even flirted with the idea of polyamory. Could the three of us share love? To be honest, Dr R, I was slightly hurt that neither of them had presented that as an opportunity before starting their own club without me. I'd have thought it might have flitted through the mind of Karl and his cock. Was I just jealous of the fact she had chosen Karl over me?

I tried to find positives in the situation – to enjoy the fact that my husband was attractive enough for the beautiful Ness to have desired him. I was looking for ways to exist without the pain, you see, trying to trick my feelings. But I was much more conventional than I had hoped I'd be. I had two choices: either I grinned and bore it or I made life very difficult for everyone. *Karl and my reckless stupid adult decisions must not affect the kids.* I had to accept it. The warfare continued but after a couple of weeks I let Karl back into the bedroom.

I changed quite rapidly. My joy had upped and gone and I couldn't find it. I was cynical and suspicious with everyone – including myself. How could I have been so wrong about these people closest to me? If they were not who I thought they were then therefore neither was *I*.

In private, I spent hours looking out of the window, finding relief in alcohol or sleep, the children's needs and demands drifting over me. I had absolutely no interest in writing my book any more. I'd lost all perspective; it seemed ridiculous to be fabricating stories when my own world was replete with such hideous dramatics – I'd found myself living in a bona fide cliché: husband and best friend. Zero out of ten for originality. Home now felt hazardous, a minefield to be negotiated. I could see her house from the back window; every time I went upstairs my eyes glanced over at the goings-on there.

In public, I was developing a peculiar jolting laugh that had nothing to do with what I was saying or feeling. And what I was *saying* had nothing to do with what I was *feeling*. I was ghostly, wearing this strange brave face: at the school gates, in Sainsbury's, on football sidelines, on the street. But any small rudeness was enough to let them see. I was floored by a stranger's car horn, an unfriendly look, a passing comment or a mistimed jostle on the pavement; the tears would spring to my eyes. I had never felt this fragile; my edges were bone china-thin.

Usually I would have had my mother to run to, to shelter me, to put my pain in perspective with her wonderful words and unflinching love: *this is just a chapter in the novel of your life, darling, adding depth and intrigue, challenges to be overcome*, etc. But confiding in my mother was out of the question now, the Alzheimer's made her a liability in front of the children. I missed her so much, Dr R, my mother from before. The sad thing is, when you are most vulnerable, most in need of friendship and contact, you are in the weakest place to ask for it. I couldn't confide in anyone. It was too close to home; there was too much at stake. The possibility that the children might overhear a careless comment, a fragment of gossip that could crush their world, was too much to entertain. My silence was vital.

Then Grace, my oldest friend, rang me, expressing concern at a photo I'd been tagged in on Facebook: I was scrawny and had dark bags under my eyes. She lived in Norfolk and had nothing to do with this tiny world so I walked along the river talking to her on the phone, breathing in the fresh, home-free air, and dared to explain what was happening. But I retracted like a spider when I sensed her reaction to my 'arrangement' with Karl. I could hear it in her voice: *well, if you will play with fire you're bound to get burnt*. I shut up and came off the phone feeling more isolated than ever. She was *right*: I had only myself to blame. I was responsible for this mess. I didn't deserve the self-indulgence of victimhood. I couldn't eat. I didn't sleep. Night after night I'd wake with a thumping heart in those eternal pre-dawn hours, feeling myself slipping into the dark abyss, clinging on to the sides until the sun hauled itself up and the day offered the small respite of routine. Josh asked me what was wrong: *Are you going to divorce?* When I said *I don't know* he slammed the door. *Everything will be all right*, I'd said to the door. My other work was suffering; I missed a deadline and lost a job. And worst of all, the Lofepramine was having no effect whatsoever – it couldn't deal with a *real* crisis, just an imagined one.

'Hello,' Dr Rhys Evans said as I came in, her eyes upping and downing me, her lips pursed, her rigor mortis grin matching my own. I detected a glint of glee at the sight of my appearance; you see, she saw me as part of the cool club and it's always pleasurable, isn't it, Dr R, to see the mighty fallen?

'Good to see you,' she said, swivelling in her chair, crossing one expensively booted leg over the other. 'Hey, are you going to the quiz tonight?'

I'd been dreading the school quiz night. We'd had a table booked before any of this started; the usual gang, our two families – even Leah was coming. (Everyone was always congratulating Leah and Ness on having developed a perfectly amicable relationship.) The quiz was an annual highlight for the kids and was impossible to get out of. I owed them a semblance of normality.

'Yes,' I said. I just wanted her to up my antidepressants and to get the hell out of there.

'How's Ness?' she asked chirpily.

I smiled and nodded gamely but couldn't speak.

'I saw her the other day. Blimey! She's too bloody beautiful, that woman! She was put on this earth to make the rest of us feel like crap!'

I grinned some more. *Give me the fucking prescription.*

'And your mother?'

'Same really . . .'

I would have to be upfront. She was not the sort of person who was sensitive to atmospheres or subtext. 'I'm wondering about the Lofepramine . . .'

'Right,' she said, eyes feasting on my stomach. She looked pained. 'My gosh, you're always so slim,' she said. 'How the hell do you do it? Skinny cow!'

I was temporarily stumped. *Oh, you know, the Cuckold Diet, works a treat.* I couldn't speak for fear of crying.

'Anyway, how's it going, any side effects?'

'I'm pretty anxious,' I said. 'I'm not sleeping.'

'Oh?' I didn't like her tone. 'Anything in particular keeping you awake?'

I shook my head. 'I'm just stressed.'

She stared at me for a bit. 'What about your periods? How are they?'

'No, it's not that . . .'

'Peri-menopausal hormones can make us a bit doolally.'

I cannot live with this pain inside me. You have to help me. 'It's more anxiety,' I said. 'I'm having these panic attacks . . .'

'I tell you, HRT is the way forward.'

'My therapist said I should see you about my prescription . . .'

That was a lie, of course. I don't have a therapist. I'm not against therapy but I've always assumed I'd never find one I respected. If I'm going to look for advice, I want it from someone I can truly look up to, preferably someone perfect, like a guru or a saint. At least someone who lives an exemplary life themselves, not someone like you with your Si Hubby problems and your calorie bars in your bag. No offence.

'Anxiety and insomnia . . .' she said, sucking on her pen in a strangely suggestive fashion. I got the uncomfortable feeling she was trying to impress me.

'She thinks you should up the dosage,' I lied. She didn't like being told that, I could see. She raised one of her ventriloquist-dummy eyebrows and tapped something into the computer.

Then she turned to me, all swivel and secrets. 'I might have just the thing . . .'

She knew she had me hooked now and there was nothing Dr Rhys Evans liked more in the world than having people hooked; it happened so little outside her surgery. 'Look,' she said conspiratorially. 'Not to name names, but all the celebrities we get in here are on these little beauties. Between you and me, I gave Leah some and she said they were just amazing.'

I want them.

With hindsight, she was unbelievable, that woman; she had both name-dropped and broken the ethical code in one sentence. 'What are they?' I asked, too desperately, like a drowning woman grabbing on to a twig.

'They chill you out, like Valium or Zanax. They're the same family, benzodiazepines. Take as and when needed, if you know what I mean. I'm only allowed to give you fourteen at a time.'

We both listened as the printer wheezed my hopes asthmatically into life.

'Just promise you won't sue me in ten years' time!' she laughed, which you must admit is quite an odd thing for a doctor to say.

I snatched the prescription out of her fingers.

'As and when needed' turned out to be that evening, when the prospect of the quiz with its conspiratorial huddles, imparting of whispered secrets, the whole charade that it would entail, became too much. I popped my first pill just before I left the house. I locked the door and Annie ran off to catch up with Polly. Josh sweetly pretended he wanted to talk to me for a while but was quickening his pace and soon all eight of us were walking together, just as we had every year for the last six.

Everything was exactly how it always was, except that I was dying inside. Josh and Evie were holding hands, Josh trying to include me in their conversation. I'd noticed how he'd sensed my vulnerability recently, how he'd changed his behaviour towards me; he was kind and gentle around me. He'd even been tidying his room regularly. I loved him so fiercely right then.

Annie and Polly had run ahead to draw chalk circles around dog craps. I came across the first: *Truly delitefull*, Annie had scrawled. *Delishous* by the next. She was really mastering sarcasm. Leah was checking her phone, half present as usual, oblivious to the antics of her ex-wife. And then there were the traitors. I watched them: I hated them both. Ness had the grace to look a bit twitchy and couldn't meet my eye but Karl was laughing, striding ahead, appearing wholly unwrecked by his deeds. Was there no price to be paid for betrayal? I wondered how the hell I would get through the evening without punching them. Only a miracle could save me now.

Lo and behold, you know what? A miracle *did* save me, Dr R! I began to feel different almost the moment we got there. It was extraordinary. I could actually feel the tension in my body begin to disperse. It was magical, as if the hand of God had been placed on my shoulder; I could feel His big strong world-crushing fingers gently untangling those knots in my back, digging into my neck, massaging away all that stress. By the time we'd been handed a glass of wine and were chatting at the doors, my body felt warm and malleable. Then when I sat down at our table, I noticed something beautiful happening inside my head: I can only describe it as my brain being

placed in a warm bath for a long soak. I sat there grinning. I don't think I had ever felt this good in my life
before: 100 per cent good. So complete! So peaceful! My
troubles were risible. Why had I been so worried about
everything when *this* was how life could be? There was
nothing to fear, it was so obvious to me now: life was a
gift. I waved at Dr Rhys Evans and that lovely idiot of a
husband of hers. I waved at everyone. I loved everyone. I
loved the school. I loved Karl. I loved Ness. I *was* love.

OK, perhaps I got a touch overenthusiastic during the
quiz, possibly a little too competitive with the maths
teacher's table – maybe I shouted too loudly, laughed too
raucously, and yes, I saw the way the headmaster was
looking at me. I definitely shouldn't have danced like
that or fallen over and given myself an egg-head and, all
right, crashing out in the kids' toilet by the bog brush
was not the best idea – *but*, never in my life had I felt such
peace and compassion for the human race.

Yes, Dr R, heaven is a 1 mg pill called Lorazepam.

*

The next day my head was not as bad as you might
imagine and the egg had subsided considerably, along
with my feelings of overpowering love. Ness begged me
by text to go for a walk with her and I deigned to agree.
I sent a curt reply: *4.30. Outside yours*. I didn't bother
with verbs and nouns – she didn't deserve them. I turned
up late, just to demonstrate that I was calling the shots. I
didn't want to go through the gate and knock on the
door – things I had done thousands of times before were

now impossible, so I loitered in the street, but unfortunately I was spotted by Evie, who came to open the door. I hovered and smiled and made banal comments like *Make Josh do some work, will you?* Then Ness came out.

'How's your head? Do you think it's going to rain?' she said, like this was just a normal day. I was pleased when the sky spat at her. She looked pretty awful, which was good. She *should* look awful. It surprised me to see that she was shaking; her hands trembled as she straightened out her jumper (actually *my* jumper – I'd given it to her), those dark eyes flashing nervously, settling nowhere, and it struck me with some satisfaction that she was *scared* of me. Her body was shaking beside mine. She *should* be afraid. She *should* tremble. She *should* be ashamed.

I walked in silence. She could do the talking; I had nothing to say to her. We crossed the main road and headed to the river, neither of us needing to agree on a route; we had walked this walk hundreds of times. 'Con,' she said as we came down the steps, 'I just want you to know that I really thought I knew myself better than this . . . I'm really shocked.'

And I bet she was. She was such a *sensible* person, you see, Dr R, she was so *straight* – she was wearing her blue cagoule, for Christ's sake. She was Ness – the big sister, the responsible one, the efficient, sensible Mrs Jones, the moralizer, the put-on-another-jumper preacher, the sock-puller-upper. Adultery and betrayal *was* out of character and I could imagine her surprise at what she was capable of. Her fingers shook as she tried to unzip her pocket to get out a tissue. I would draw the line if she started crying. If anyone was going to cry it should be *me*. Fortunately she just blew her nose. 'I let myself get too close to him.'

'You can say that again,' I said. We were now in the open space of the towpath. It was muddy and I was wearing the wrong shoes. The tide had come and gone, litter clung to branches, the water was indeterminable from the sky – the whole scene was drenched in drabness.

She touched my arm.

'Don't touch me,' I said, stopping in my tracks. I know, very melodramatic – but I couldn't bear her to touch me; she had sacrificed such intimacies with her actions. There had to be some sort of payback, karma, whatever. 'How long has it been going on?' I asked, using the present tense despite their promises. But of course they'd got their stories straight: it was only the second time it had happened. Suspiciously unlucky to have been caught on the second time, wouldn't you say?

Just then another mother from school, Alison, and her dog passed by and the three of us stopped to chat. Now here's an interesting and bizarre thing, Dr R: we laughed and chatted as if nothing in the world had happened. We told amusing children/school/doggy stories; I don't remember precisely which, but there was no mention of the fact that my best friend, the woman at my side, the *lesbian*, was a husband-fucking harlot. Were Alison to know the truth of the situation – say if in two minutes' time I were to have stuck a branch deep into Ness's throat and Alison were to give a police statement – she would never in a million years have believed such a thing possible. Aren't we strange beings? It was almost as if Ness and I were playing roles in a theatre play and this was an interlude. After Alison left and we carried on walking it would have been the most natural thing in the world for me to take Ness's arm – I nearly did; I had to stop myself and remember how things were. We waved Alison off and promptly returned to Act Two: wronged wife and remorseful slut.

'Can I please ask you not to tell anyone?' Ness said.

I stared at her. 'No. That's not up to you,' I said. Blimey, give her an inch. Besides, did she seriously think I would be broadcasting my own humiliation? I looked her up and down. She looked like shit. If she'd still been my friend I would have been appalled to see her in such a state; as it was, I was just curious. 'Aren't you even going to apologize, Ness?' I said.

She looked flustered. 'I thought an apology would sound trite.'

'Well, you might have tried!'

'Of course I'm sorry, Connie.'

'No, you're right. It does sound trite.' I was aware that I was being cruel, but again, it felt like I was *playing* at being cruel, as if the whole situation were constructed – the mud, the miserable day just set-dressing. Another day it might be sunny and we might swap roles. Does that sound mad?

'It's not going to happen again, I promise,' she said, touching me one more time and letting go quickly. And suddenly we weren't play-acting. It was serious. We stood there in the pouring rain and I felt indescribably sad.

'How could you?' I said, genuinely flummoxed.

The rain dripped off her nose. 'I've been trying to work it out. I think I've been terribly lonely after Leah left and Karl's just been . . . there . . . so easy to talk to . . . he just, he was so kind . . . and we crossed a line, I got too close with him.'

'Are you in love with him, Ness?'

'It was a mistake. It's finished.'

'How am I ever meant to trust you?' I asked her. 'You knew *everything*, all my secrets, and you used them against me . . .'

She shook her head. 'No, that's not how it was . . .'

Well, there's no arguing with the different stories we tell ourselves, is there, Dr R? I looked over her shoulder at the steady flow of greyness moving away to somewhere else, leaving only more greyness in its place.

'I miss you so much,' she said. I was pleased by this stage to see the tears. She'd earned them. Besides, this is exactly what you want to hear when you've been left out of the club, isn't it? *The club is rubbish without you. We miss you. We made a mistake. We need you. You're a core member.*

'I'm so sorry . . .'

'You fucking should be.'

What could I do? What would *you* do, Dr R? Suppose Si Hubby *is* shagging someone in the orchestra; would you forgive him? I reckon you would. None of us are perfect, not even you. And *I* missed *her*, you see. So much. I was lost without her. Especially during this nightmare, she would have been the person I turned to. Do you think people deserve a second chance, Dr R? I do. We can all fuck up. What are we if we don't show forgiveness? After all, how do we know that we are no better? How do we ever know that we, given the right conditions, wouldn't shit on our own doorsteps too? Oh, we *hope* we are better, we like to think we are better than that, we would take our dumps elsewhere – bury them perhaps, but how do we *know*? I had to give her a chance. I too would want forgiveness.

Ness read me well and cautiously reached out her fingers to take mine. I responded in an infinitesimal way and she clutched my fingers and twisted them in her own. Then she shuffled forwards and hung her head. I let her crumple into my chest. I appreciated how she played the part of Humble Wretch so I could play the Great Consoler. I stroked her frizzy hair and told her it was all right, everything was going to be all right.

Chapter 16

The Squeak is late on her rounds today. Dr Robinson has already arrived and thus gets to watch the loony taking her pills. She seems slightly embarrassed to watch her own handiwork in play and keeps getting up and down to open the unopenable windows; it's become a sort of nervous tic. The weather has turned cold again, freezing cold – it is Christmas time after all. The sky is low and white. That glimmer of hope the sun brought with it a few days ago was all a trick. Pan's a sham. The Squeak and I both watch Dr R struggle with the locks but neither of us says anything. The Squeak hands me my antidepressant; I swallow it. The Squeak hands me my anti-anxiety pill and my mood stabilizer. 'Yum yum,' I say, and wink at Dr R who is coming over to sit down again. I swallow them. And lastly I'm handed my anti-psychotic meds. I amusingly cross my eyes at her in an impression of a true psychopath.

'It's a wonder you don't rattle,' says the Squeak, joining in on my larks uninvited.

'Off you go,' I say to her, and dismiss her with a flick of my hand before turning my full attention to Dr R who, I suddenly see as she bends down to zip her bag shut, is wearing a fluorescent elastic sporty bra beneath the subdued hues of her professional garb. It's difficult to imagine her running or getting down and dirty in a boot camp on a dingy green in north London amongst the dog mess; she doesn't strike me as the sporty type at all. I rather suspect she's one of those people who wear elasticated clothing around the house, sitting on the sofa eating chocolates *feeling* sporty, hoping by fabric osmosis to lose the weight.

We both wait for the Squeak to shuffle out, which she duly does. 'Thank you, Mrs Ibrahim,' says Dr R, and the Squeak nods and flashes her shark teeth as she exits.

'Have a lovely day, Mrs Ibrahim,' I add, and watch her disappear into the merry glow of the sunshine yellow hall. I turn back to Dr R, who has a file on her lap and has now covered her fluorescent strap.

'It says in your notes that you went back to Dr Rhys Evans within the month for some more Lorazepam.'

'I certainly did. And I topped myself up with Valium that I got elsewhere. But you know what? I don't think I was completely bozoed out until I was in that Milton House drowning in Clonazepam.'

'Where did you get them from? The Valiums?'

'A mother at school.'

'Was she a dealer?' Dr Robinson said.

'A dealer, yes. Just like you but without the medical degree.'

I make her smile and I feel good about that.

'Tell me about what happened the day of the Harvest Festival.'

I sigh. 'Do you dealers try your wares?' I ask her. 'Have you ever popped the odd Valium, Dr Frankenstein? Diazepam? Lorazepam? Peterpam?'

That faint blush always betrays her. Of course she has.

'Lorazepams are crazy, aren't they? I mean, I never got that beautiful brain-soaking feeling quite the same way again but I got hysterical and frequently passed out. I remember one night playing Scrabble with the kids –' I know, I was trying to make up for all the chaos, attempting to emulate a 'Goodnight, John-Boy' kind of home (had John-Boy been on Snapchat and Mrs Walton been on crack) '– and Annie put the word *anii* down on the board which she said was the plural of anus and I started laughing. I couldn't stop and I smashed my head against the mantelpiece and then apparently I just crashed out asleep, snoring on a triple word score . . .'

Sometimes I'd like us to walk out of here, share Lorazepam stories, go and have cake and tea somewhere; to play different roles than the ones we have been allotted in this room.

'And how was the anxiety?' she asks.

'Well, very quickly I needed more than 1 mg to have an effect and then I'd rebound to worse anxiety than before, so I had to take more pills just to feel normal. They are *completely* addictive, which star-fucker doctor failed to mention, and not just psychologically but *physically*. My body lost its own ability to calm down. Presumably you know the legal guidelines in *Safety of Medicines* say that no one should take benzodiazepines for more than one month. And they should only be taken for *acute* anxiety. Tell me, how do you define *acute*?'

'Tell me about the day of the Harvest Festival, Connie.' She's like a dog with a bone. I bet she drives Si Hubby

bloody mad. *Have you taken the rubbish out? – In a minute. –*
Have you taken the rubbish out?! – In a minute!

'You tell me about *you*. You know what it's like to be
on your knees, Dr R,' I say. I'm taunting her. I can be so
mean, but I don't like her like this, the snooty
superiority.

'We're not here to talk about me. Come on, help me
out here.'

'No. *You* help *me* out. Ask Karl to bring Josh and Annie
to see me.'

She cocks her head, arms folded, furrow-browed. She
looks like she's about to say something. But she's tired;
she might just get up and go. I don't want that. I look out
of the window. The sky seems to be up to something, a
smothering white dankness infusing everything, a pillow pressing down on London. I can feel it permeating
through the panes of glass, a wall of suffocating chill
right next to us.

'Oh, look!' I say, getting up. 'I think it's starting to
snow!' She turns suddenly and we both stare. It *is* snow-
ing. She joins me by the window. It's beautiful! Big fat
flakes start swirling silently past our noses; we're like
children, our eyes wide with wonder. We are no longer
psychiatrist and patient – we are just two people watching the snow falling.

When we sit back down, the atmosphere feels different. It's as if the snow has softened me; I stop being so
combative. I don't know why I'm so angry. I feel rootless
and scared sometimes in here. 'It's the context of the day
you have to understand,' I say.

'OK,' she says. She can be so gentle sometimes, so

motherly. What I really want to do is lie down with my head in her lap and go to sleep. 'Give me the context.'

I pause a moment and think back. 'I now need these pills just to feel normal, Dr R. On Wikipedia I find out that 1 mg of Lorazepam is the equivalent of 10 mg of Valium and some days I'm taking three or four. By this point, I'm a bona fide junkie and it's all pretty much legit.'

'Did your doctor know the quantities you were consuming?'

'My doctor snorts lines of cocaine in the children's toilet at the Christmas Fair, Dr R.'

'Did you confide in anyone?'

'I could hardly tell my parents. They're paid up members of the Bach Remedy Squad. I once snapped my shin as a child and my mother put me to bed and rubbed arnica on it.'

'And Karl? Did he know?'

'Yes, to a degree. But Karl was a great advocate of substance abuse; he was all for it. Besides, I think he preferred me dulled, less waspish, less *alert*. You see, my bone china edges had now become fuzzy and soft like cotton wool, cushioning life's little blows.'

'And how were those little blows? How were things between you and him?'

I sigh; I stretch out my stick-thin legs. I've got white leggings and white socks on and they look like two cotton buds. I have become something absurd.

'I'd forgiven him and Ness. Not for altruistic reasons, just because it was the only way in the end for everybody. This way, life could just carry on as normal. I wanted the kids to feel safe and I needed to reassure Josh that Karl and I were OK. I stopped giving Ness a hard time – she'd screwed up, she knew it, but it was *over*. Things were back to normal; if anything there was a deeper connection that forgiveness brings. She and the girls were at ours all the time as usual. Although . . .'

Talking about it now, something strikes me. 'Between you and me, it might have been nice to have seen a *little* more remorse from them. *Some* prolonged contrition wouldn't have gone amiss, or at least some hearty acknowledgement of my magnificent benevolence . . .'

She smiles and nods. I love it when I make her smile. 'But no, now they were absolved of their sins, they laughed and capered, seemingly impervious to any pain inflicted. So I licked my wounds in private with my sugary Lorazepamed tongue . . .'

'Admirable, Connie. Well done you.'

I flounder. Her empathy feels like small hands squeezing my throat, making my eyes water. I don't want to cry. Sometimes I worry that if I start to cry I'll never stop. 'The truth is I loved them, Dr R. And this way, I still had them in my life. I hadn't lost them.'

'I understand,' she says. She is smiling; she looks tired. I want to please her.

'Sorry, yes. *That* day. I woke up with these terrible period pains. You know the kind, that every-other-month ovary that's a killer. I was feeling really groggy and bleeding copiously. It had gone on the sheets, down my legs, on the carpet. Even after thirty-five years of menstruating, it still takes me by surprise every month. You have to understand, maybe you do, that even something as normal as a period demanded difficult decisions to be made – what order things should be done in – and my *medication* made me feel pretty numbed much of the time. I felt quite pleased with myself dealing with it all: sanitary wear, washing machine, carpet cleaner, ibuprofens, hot-water bottle down my granny pants.

'I could hear Annie downstairs practising her song. She'd been given a solo for the festival despite showing no musical ability whatsoever – presumably it was school policy that every loser was a winner. I listened to her downstairs singing lustily without hitting a note, a song about starving children and fruit salads, as far as I could make out. She was also to be dressed as a banana and hang out in a bunch with some boys behind the grapes. Polly was a dragon fruit, which Annie was a little jealous of – more tropical, more glamorous, I guess. Ness had been roped in to play the piano because the music teacher was ill, so she had been round practising with the girls on our piano. It was a big day in the Mortensen household. And I was going to rise to the challenge. I would go to great efforts to make my family happy. My parenting had been somewhat erratic recently but today I was going to make amends. Mum and Dad were coming to the service. Josh had training after school so would meet us there. Then everyone was going to come round to ours for supper, even Leah, and Poll was going to stay over. We would be one big happy family. All I had to do was make a lasagne.

'I took a Mother's Little Helper just to keep on top of things. I carried them around with me in my pockets these days: dressing gown, cardigan, coat, bag – I never knew when I might need one. Before Karl left the house, he made some dig about the state it was in and *how long was I going to go on playing the victim?* How *he* would cook and clean when he got back from a marathon day of meetings if I wasn't *up to it*. I saw the way he looked at me with a kind of general disappointment but I let it all bounce off my cotton-wool edges. "Great, I'll leave it for you," I said. Notice that I still had a little of the old spunk left, Dr R, a dirty residue of anger nestled deep in my colon to be gobbed out at Karl every now and then.

'The house was quiet. They'd all gone. I sat there on the bottom step, bemused by the chaos left in the wake of kid-departure, an ominous feeling that unutterable misery was lurking nearby. I stared at the mess unable to *do* anything about it. My phone rang. It was my mother in a panic because she couldn't find her handbag. She said, "Are you all right, darling, you sound a bit slurry?" It was unusual these days for her to notice me in that way. I was touched and told her I was fine and that she should keep looking for her handbag – I was going to clean the house and go shopping and I would see her later in the church. She asked if she could bring anything for supper but I knew she wasn't going to remember it so I said not to bother.

'But somehow I didn't get off that step for quite a few hours because I couldn't decide what order to do things in. I rang Ness for support but she must have been busy at the gallery. She rang me back a little while later – I was still on the step – and she suggested I didn't bother with cooking, to cheat and get a frozen one. She offered to pick something up after school. But no, I wanted to *do* this for my family. So, in an incredible display of togetherness, I ignored the filth, found the cookbook, made a list of ingredients and made my way up to Sainsbury's. Then on the way back I popped into the hardware shop, determined to give the house a proper clean, and bought all sorts of things, my coat pockets bulging as I made my way home: metal scourers and limescale remover for the showerhead, drain unblocker for that dodgy bathroom sink, Spirit of Salts for that yellow piss build-up in the toilet – I would not be outdone by my own house.

'In actual fact I didn't do any cleaning but I picked up things from the floor and ran the vacuum cleaner about the place. I concentrated my efforts on the lasagne and tried to consciously make it with love, but I found it almost impossible and couldn't keep count of the quantity of ingredients . . . it was going to be a disaster. Soon I was crying tears into the béchamel sauce – I don't know why I was so weepy: period? Pills? Deep sense of failure? – which I found strangely fascinating. I stirred them into the mix, popped another pill and told myself how stupid I was, how lucky I was to have what I had in my life: my beautiful children, my wonderful parents, a good husband despite everything.

'I covered the lasagne in tinfoil and left it on the side ready for the oven. I laid the table, which was not as easy as it sounds: I kept losing count of how many people would be there. I placed candles in the middle, waiting to be lit on our return. Then I had a bath, changed my clothes and made up my face for the concert. The prospect of actually leaving the house made me slightly anxious. I'd avoided social events, especially school occasions. So I crushed up a little diazepam to ease things along and grabbed my coat.

'I felt OK. It was raining and getting dark; I wanted to be late, I didn't want to have to chat to anyone, but I promised Josh I'd be there to meet him. Halfway there I realized I'd left my phone charging in the kitchen but I'd gone too far to turn back. The church looked beautiful, full of candles and flowers. It was warm and dry, filled to the brim, the chatter of a hundred voices, the buzz of excitement, keen parents who'd been there for hours to nab the best places at the front clutching cameras and phones ready to record their little fruity darlings. I said hi to various people, nodded at the grinning GP and the other drug-dealing mum. You know what? It was actually really great to be there, to be out in the world. And everyone was kind and funny and I felt *part* of it all again. I had a feeling that everything was going to be all right.

'I looked around for Karl and spotted my dad in a pew near the back reading a book. I made my way through the throng towards him. "Hi, Dad," I said, sitting down next to him beside Karl's folded leather jacket. My father looked up, momentarily surprised to see me, and seemingly surprised to find himself in a church at all. "Hello, darling," he said, and nodded towards Karl and my mother, who were both engaged in separate conversations by the pillar. Karl was talking to the vicar. "No Josh?" I asked, looking about the place. I could see the headmaster down at the front talking with Ness by the piano. She was laughing. I tried to catch her eye and wave. She was looking incredibly dashing, Dr R, I remember that. She was wearing a flowery dress, quite low cut, hair down. She looked fantastic. I wasn't the only one to notice her; a few fathers were hovering around the piano. I recognized that flirty air that I now knew she liked to create.

'Karl's jacket started buzzing next to me. I hoped it might be Josh trying to get through and I rummaged in the pocket and found the phone. It *was* Josh. He'd left a text. I tried Karl's usual code but it didn't work. I looked up; he was still over by the pillar charming the cassock off the vicar, his voice just that bit too loud, his laugh slightly over exuberant, being demonstrably entertaining company. I paused for a moment and tried the Sky code. Bullseye. I went to his texts: *Running late just missed bus. J.* I was about to put the phone straight back into Karl's pocket when I noticed that the previous text hadn't been read either. It was from X. I don't know why I looked. But I did. *You make me SOOO wet when you say things like that XX. Delete!!*

'I read it several times. I checked the number.

'Yes. It was her. It was Ness.

'It was as if my spirit rose out of my body. Up I went above the pews. I could see myself sitting there with Karl's phone in my hand, stock still, paused in a moment of time. I looked over at her at the piano by the pulpit, flicking her frizzy fucking hair, laughing a new *silvery* laugh, eyes flashing, in her element, surrounded by adoration, throwing a glance towards the pillar where Karl stood. They were parallel to each other, separate but connected, like they were dancing with each other, like they existed only for each other. I saw it all quite clearly.

'I stood up, back in my body with a thud, my blood

rampaging through my veins. I had to get out of there as quickly as possible. I shuffled past my father, not even taking my bag, past the people along the pew to the comparative safety of the aisle, heading for the exit. I felt sick. I heard someone call my name but didn't turn. I had one thought: I needed a Lorazepam *now*. I put my hand in my deep coat pocket but instead of the Lorazepams, my fingers found something else, something that might offer me far greater results. I stopped in my tracks. I turned around. I could see her. There she was, leaning against the piano, looking up, laughing, tossing her hair about, leaning forward, showing her cleavage.

'I *hated* her.

'Slowly I made my way towards her, like a steady but lethal missile. "Excuse me, excuse me," I said calmly, eyes focused on my target. I knew what I had to do. I stopped. I was no more than four feet from her. She was seated at the piano now, with her back to me, talking to someone – I have no idea who – I saw no one but her, the flowers on her dress, the moles on her neck, the necklace I had once given her. I fancied I could smell her, *my* Jo Malone perfume.

'I brought out the thick plastic bottle from my pocket and looked at it: *Spirit of Salts. Hydrochloric Acid. Hazardous.* I started to unscrew the lid. It had a child lock on it so I had to apply pressure with a twist.' I watched, quite mesmerized, as the acrid vapour swirled out of the bottle like a sick and dangerous genie.

' "Ness?" I said, my voice sounding faraway, even to me. She was smiling, beautiful. She turned round, her face dropping as she saw me. She knew I knew. And as I chucked the contents of that bottle straight at her, I felt this wonderful, almost perfect feeling of justice being done.'

Dr R has covered her mouth with her hand. And I realize she doesn't see it in quite the same way that I do.

'Don't worry,' I say to her. 'Some have-a-go hero leapt to the aid of the damsel in distress and I felt myself being jumped on, flung to the ground.'

I remember the fizz as the caustic liquid genie spilt himself upon *me*, on to my neck, down my own arm, on to my legs, denying me my wishes. I lay there on the floor with a stranger on top of me, acrid steam rising up from the tiles, getting up my nose, into my mouth, making me choke. And there she was: still beautiful, still treacherous, but acid-free, looking down at me while *my* skin sizzled and burnt itself raw.

Dr R listens carefully. Then she slowly takes her gaze out of the window and frowns. 'It wasn't premeditated then?' she asks.

'Not at all. It was divine opportunity.'

'Then what happened?'

I think back. I remember the searing pain on my leg, on my tummy, my arm. I remember people looking down at me on the tiles, their faces twisted with disbelief and confusion. Fear, actually. I saw fear. I was a *monster*. I was still holding the bottle and someone wrenched it from my grip as if I might be some sort of Spirit of Salts terrorist and liable to go rampaging around the church splashing all and sundry.

'I scrabbled to my feet. I had to get out of there. I ran out of the church by the little door on the side. It was dark outside. I kept on running, down the hill, across the road, over the railway until I got to the river. It was pitch black, raining and cold on the towpath but I was on fire, my skin was burning up, burning off my hands, my torso, my right thigh. I was crying out with the pain of it when in the darkness I saw this little flashing white light approaching. I thought it was a fairy, a spirit. But it was a woman on a bike. She screamed when she saw me. I remember thinking *why is everyone so scared of me?* Then I looked down at my body lit up by her flickering bicycle light. You couldn't see the burns but you could see the blood. I was covered from the waist down. Had someone stabbed me? Then it dawned on me that what with one thing and another, I'd forgotten to change my Tampax.'

But the blood was nothing compared to the pain. Holding my hand out in that winking white light I could see that the skin had burnt right off, as if the flesh itself was trying to breathe the air.

'I had to get into the water. I started ripping off my clothes. I slid down the bank as fast as I could, slipping in the mud, the woman still shouting at me . . .'

I remember the coldness of the river, squatting in the shallows, the filthy water soothing my fiery flesh. I remember wondering if I'd make it back in time for Annie's banana song. And what time I should try and get the lasagne in the oven. I needed to light the candles, put napkins on the table, decant the wine. But the next thing I knew, a policeman was dragging me out of the water along the shingle, scraping the skin off me. I felt like raw meat being scored. I was screaming, trying to stop him, fighting him off, but then more police came down to the water and there were more flashing lights. God, I needed some drugs.

*

Sep 30

I hate school. Phoebe B is a cow. Every time I went near her today she started holding her nose and waving her hand around and people started laughing. When we were waiting outside for cooking she said my mum was mentally insane. I said her mum was so fat it would take a space ship 3 years to circle her. She said that the harvest festival was delayed because my mum threw bleech over Pollys mum. Polly said it didnt get her. I said she didnt throw it it was an accident. She was cleaning and she tripped. Phoebe B said my mum was arrested for swimming in the river with no clothes on and they put her in a strait jacket and took her off to the mental home. We were outside room 6 so I pushed her down the stairs and she cried like a baby.

Miss G sent me to the headmaster. He told me to wait in his study with him so I sat there while he talked on the telephone and drank a coke. I told him coca cola had 8 spoonfuls of sugar in it. And he said yes it was very bad of him and asked me not to tell anybody. He told me I shouldnt have pushed Phoebe B down the stairs WHATEVER things she was saying. So I said what are you supposed to do when someone is saying nasty things about your mummy. You come and tell me, he said, which to be honest isnt very practical. He said there is a lady at school who is very helpful to talk to. Then he asked me how I was doing and he asked me if I had any questions. I couldnt think of any. Then I asked him if he knew what a strait jacket was. He said it was something to wear that stopped you hurting yourself. Like armer I suppose. We are studying knights. He kept looking at my school uniform. I couldnt find mine this morning so I was wearing one of Joshes shirts and I took my socks and skirt out of the washing machine but everything was wet and crinkled so I have been letting them dry on me. I tell you what, he said. Why dont we have a look in lost property and see what we find and then he took my hand and we went to look in the box. He kept saying I dont think anybody will be needing this and giving me clothes to put on. Strickly speaking he is a thief.

Oct 4

Me and Granny and Daddy and Josh went to see Mummy in the place where she is staying. Its a sort of hotel called Milton House where they give you pills and jelly. I ate Mummys jelly. I didnt like Milton House except for the vending machine with crisps and chocolates in it. Mummy was in a room with another lady who had a HUGE belly and was about to drop a baby out of her urethra. Mummy was wearing her tracksuit bottoms and her nighty at the same time sitting in a chair in a room watching an old episode of Tracy Beaker on telly. Mummy HATES Tracy Beaker but she didnt complain AT ALL. She was all sleepy and her voice was different like she was forign or something. She smelt funny. Granny told me and Josh to give Mummy a hug. To be honest I didnt want to give her a hug but I did and she wouldnt let go and my hair hurt and she had a bracelet on with her name on it. WHY would she need that? Afterwards I asked Josh if he thought that she really was our mummy. He told me to stop being a retard.

Daddy told me to give her my card which I drew of me wearing new clothes pushing Phoebe B down the stairs and she stared at it for a long time but didnt ask me what it was about. First she was smiling but tears came out of her eyes without her crying from her mouth. I said whats wrong but she kept looking at the card. Then I started crying too and Granny took my hand and we went and got some lucosade sport from the vending machine. Granny was very rude to a lady saying theyd turned Mummy into a BLOODY ZOMBIE and what the hell was going on and she wanted to see the manajer. When we went back to say goodbye Josh had changed the channel to football and they were all watching the telly apart from Mummy who had gone to sleep and it was only 3 oclock. In the car on the way home Granny was crying. She had a headache. I dont like it how things are at all any more. Maybe Mummy is a zombie which means shes dead. I want to go to Nesses.

Chapter 17

The sun was shining and the snow had turned to a dirty sludge as Emma made her way down the high street. She was feeling excited, slightly nervous; Si had no idea she was coming. She had a lot of making up to do with him. They had both been neglectful of their relationship and let things slip. Her plan was to turn up after practice and take him out for supper; she had booked a table at their local Italian and afterwards a late showing at the old picture house. She was unusually early; orchestra didn't finish until five and it was only twenty to. She decided to wait for him in the pub across the road from where she would see the crypt doors.

She went in. It was like stepping into a time warp. A few grey heads turned to stare before slowly returning to their pale ales, old addled white men glued to their stools, lined up like babies in high chairs supping from their beakers. There was still a stigma in pubs like this, a woman coming in on her own; their stares made her self-conscious but it was too late to walk out. She would never have had the nerve to come into a place like this as a younger woman; she had always felt threatened by it. At least age brought with it a certain confidence in this respect, a safety. She thought of Connie's confidence; her sense of self had somehow remained intact. Connie, who was never far from her mind, had become a kind of behavioural barometer for Emma's own dealings with the everyday and Emma was surprised by how fiercely protective of her patient she had become – in meetings, in her professional dealings, with the press, in social situations, in private. Despite her obvious vulnerability, Connie had a strength to her and some of that strength had rubbed off on Emma.

She approached the bar and ordered herself a gin and tonic from the pretty eastern European girl behind the counter. The girl failed to understand her so, with misguided intentions, one of the stool-dwellers repeated the order in a loud, patronizing voice with a conspiratorial wink at Emma, inviting her to team up with him against the dumb foreigner, who probably spoke more languages than the pints he'd had so far today. She felt their rheumy eyes on her hips as she took her drink over to a small table by the window where she could see the crypt doors; men like this were largely harmless but their insidious lechery was always disquieting. She leant over to pick up a red top paper that was lying on the bench, flicking a page for want of something to do, and there she was, faced with Minxy Mandy from Manchester and her unnatural attributes.

Emma put the paper down and got out her *Hotel du Lac*. She crossed her legs, registering the slinky feel of the silk of her knickers against the smoothness of her waxed skin. She felt a twinge of guilt. For *whom* had she suffered the agonies of hair removal? She might pretend it was for herself but she would be lying. And yet it *was* truly lovely to touch – she'd spent a long time running her hand over her own softness in the bath. But that wasn't the whole truth. She'd invited Si to come with her to the party, of course, hoping he'd say no, and when he *did* say no she'd felt a small disappointment, but was it only because she didn't like arriving on her own at occasions? *No, I understand*, she'd said when he'd dithered. *A reunion is always boring for partners.*

Sally Pea had looked exactly the same to Emma. Apart from the fact she now had blonde hair (with purple streaks) and they both used to have black hair. Plus she must be about four stone heavier than she used to be, which came as something of a relief – Emma had been half starving herself since Sally sent the invite. She'd somehow imagined everyone from her past being unravaged by time. But there was much that *hadn't* changed about Sally: her bright button eyes, her smile, her laugh, her warmth. She'd squealed with delight when she saw Emma approaching. They were both dressed entirely in black, perhaps subconsciously for old times' sake. And it seemed to Emma, who was filled with a powerful nostalgia, the craziest thing in the world that they had lost touch. How had that happened? How introverted and serious she herself had become with her small life and her big career. As they held each other at arm's length to examine the doings of time, Emma deeply regretted her self-inflicted isolation, all because of her inability to express her vulnerability. She had immersed herself in her work when perhaps it was friendship that got you up and down the snakes and ladders of life. Connection was all that really mattered.

'You won the lottery! I can't believe it!' she cried, clinking her glass against Sally's.

'I know! I'm a jammy bugger!' Sally hugged her tightly. She was already pretty plastered. Emma wasn't far behind – she'd knocked back a few Martinis on her own before coming.

'I can't believe you came! Mum! Mum!!' Sally called out behind her, beckoning wildly to a woman with identical hair. And there she was – Mrs Pea, ballooned and lined, but with those same bright eyes twinkling through the generations. They had always been a double act, Sally and her mother. Now they looked more alike than ever. Emma remembered how envious she had been of them as a teenager, the different atmosphere of their houses; the warmth in Sally's and the chilliness in her own. Sally wrapped her arm around her mother. 'Remember Emma, Mum? Clever Emma?' She was shouting loudly into her ear and turned to Emma with a grin. 'Deaf as a wombat.'

'Ooh! Lordy me! Emma Davis! I certainly do but I wouldn't have recognized you! You've lost a pound or two. What did you do, give it to Sally?'

Sally realigned a stray strand of her mother's hair. 'That's rich coming from you, Karen Carpenter.'

Mrs Pea wheezed a smoker's chuckle. 'What are you doing with yourself these days, Emma?' she asked. She meant marriage and kids, of course, the only female destination for her generation. 'You married?'

'She's only a frigging psychologist!' Sally yelled.

'A gynaecologist?' The unimaginable horrors of such a profession visibly passed across her features and Emma and Sally laughed.

'Not a gynaecologist, Mum. A *psychologist*.' Sally rolled her eyes at Emma. 'She doesn't know one end from the other . . .'

'*Psychiatrist*, I'll have you know, not psychologist,' Emma said, flicking back her hair, taking the mickey out of herself, so happy to be here. How on earth had she let the years slip by without Sally? She reached out and squeezed Sally's hand, overcome with fondness for the both of them.

'She's famous! She's doing that case in the papers, Mum.' Sally had bent forward to shout in her mum's ear again. 'You know The Yummy Monster? The acid attack woman?'

Emma flinched. *The Yummy Monster*. She *hated* that moniker. It had been splashed across the front page with two photographs of Connie. The 'Before': Connie at the school ball, a glamorous trendy yummy mummy. And the 'After': Connie looking dazed and confused in the psychiatric unit, her peculiar tufts of red hair sticking up on end, the grotesque scars on her neck and arms.

Although she smiled at Sally and her mother, she felt suddenly profoundly hurt for Connie, who would be sitting in that chair by the window with no idea that she was the subject of such careless gossip up and down the country.

'Oh, *her*? Albert's brother went to school with her brother!'

Why did everyone need a personal connection with tragedy? Sally turned to greet some late arrival with a whoop.

'Nasty piece of work,' Mrs Pea said to Emma. 'How's

your mother, Emma?' And Emma was glad she had moved on so quickly.

'Oh, she died a good few years back, actually.'

'She died? I'm sorry to hear that. I always thought, if you don't mind me saying, dear, that she was a bit *hard* on you. It seemed to me that nothing you ever did was quite good enough for her. And you were such a good girl.'

Emma felt a jab at those words. A jab of validation. 'Well, thank you for saying that,' she said. 'That was exactly how it felt.' A passing waiter filled up her glass as she had hoped he would.

'And you not having any siblings to take a bit of the flak . . . I always thought how lonely that must have been. You got kids?'

Emma took a long swig. 'Nope,' she said.

'Ah, what a shame.'

'Hey, listen to that!' Sally shrieked, necking back her glass, cupping her ear theatrically and then grabbing Emma's hand to pull her over towards the disco end of the room, where a silver ball spun slowly in a purple light. A couple of slightly younger women were enjoying themselves on the dance floor, exuding a physical self-confidence that normally would have left Emma feeling depleted – they were rock-chicky, slinky and sexy, blonde hair with dark roots, clothes slipping off smooth shoulders, tiny tattoos in erogenous places, oozing ease as they moved to the music.

But she had no choice: Sally was whispering to the DJ and soon their teenage years were beckoning. She laughed. 'Billericay Dickie'. She remembered the days spent in Sally's room working out dance routines to Ian Dury songs (before they embraced Gothdom and stopped moving altogether, and instead clung to dark walls in dark venues). It was amazing what the body could recall. The younger cooler women stepped aside, fans of Sally Pea, enjoying these old-timers and the snatches of remembered routines. Emma couldn't remember the last time she had danced. Let alone like this; she shed the years like skin from a snake. She was no longer old, square and past it, she was herself again. She and Sally strutted stupidly for song after song. And Sally's DJ just kept those old classics coming – Siouxsie, the Cure, the Clash – and they danced with all the exuberance of seventeen-year-olds and all the limitations of forty-seven-year-old bodies.

Then she spotted him, standing at the bar. He was watching her. Strangely confident with this new Emma reclaimed, she stopped dancing and went over to greet him. She was sweating, shining, happy.

'Hello there, Mr Thompson.'

'Nice moves,' he said, kissing her cheeks.

'I was wondering when you were going to turn up,' she said.

'Is your husband here?' he asked.

She shook her head. 'Is your wife?'

'Ex-wife. Yeah.' He nodded towards the rock chicks. Ah, of course he would have married a woman like that; he was Dougie Thompson, after all.

She was feeling fantastically drunk, unusually reckless. 'Thanks for giving Sally my number, Dougie. It's great to be here.'

'I'm glad you could come. Other side of London. Baby-sitter and all that.'

She shook her head. 'Actually, something's been bothering me since I bumped into you. I lied to you and I don't know why. Well, I do know why. My daughter . . . I told you my daughter was nine. I told you Abigail was nine. She's not. Sometimes I just say she is . . .' She was floundering, but she didn't want his pity, she just wanted to explain. 'Abigail died six years ago. She would have been nine, now.'

His face dropped. 'Oh, I'm so sorry, Emma. I had no idea.'

'Of course not. Why would you? You just kind of caught me at a moment . . . I don't—Oh my God! Is that James Storm?!'

He looked around. 'Yes, it is!'

A large bald man was approaching them. 'Hey, Dougie! How goes?'

'Jim! Look who it isn't!' Dougie said, putting his arm protectively around Emma's shoulder.

'Oh my God! No! Emma Davis!' James said. 'Wow! You look . . . great!' It was the weight loss, he meant.

'Hi, James,' she said. 'Actually, I was just remembering the other day a party at your dad's house . . . we'd all finished our mocks or something. Do you remember it?'

'I certainly do. So does my dad: Mickey Gray puked in his bed.'

She laughed.

'I remember that party,' Dougie said. And she found that she couldn't quite look at him.

'I saw your name in the papers. You're on that case,

aren't you?' James was looking at her excitedly. 'The Yummy Monster. Is that right?'

'Yup, that's right,' she said.

'Fucked up!' he said. He was glowing.

Emma nodded. 'Do you know, I'm pretty sick of that name . . . just because she's white and *middle-class* . . . .' There was an awkward silence and Emma felt obliged to fill it. 'What do you do these days, James?'

'Oh,' he said. 'I'm an estate agent.'

'Fucked up!' she said, and Dougie laughed, caught a passing waiter and handed her a glass of bubbly, a gesture befitting a partner. She took it without thanks, like a partner might.

'I'm just going outside for a quick smoke,' Emma said, getting out her cigarettes. 'I'll be back in a minute.'

It was really cold outside and strangely silent because the snow had settled; at least, it had in this garden – not much, but enough to quieten the city by a decibel or two. In fact, she could see a few snowflakes, or perhaps they were just ash, swirling up in the warm yellow glow emanating from the Christmas bulbs in the tree. They were in Battersea somewhere, a warehouse in a back street. There were other people outside smoking and she went a little way off and sat at a table beneath the tree under a little awning. Her tights were thin and the metal bench was icy against her soft, hairless thighs. She shivered.

She felt exposed in all senses: the cold, the Yummy Monster, Abigail. She *never* talked about Abigail. Only twice had she ever spoken of her death in detail – once with Si and once with her psychiatrist in the months that followed. It was in the past now. She couldn't help thinking of Connie sitting there in her room being *forced* to remember, and how generous she was with her honesty.

'You OK?'

She looked up and smiled. Dougie sat down beside her and she offered him her cigarette.

'I don't smoke,' he said, and took it from her fingers.

She laughed. 'That's right. You're action man, aren't you?'

'I am a bit,' he said, taking a drag and passing it back.

'You were always sporty.'

'I liked sport. Still do.'

'You were so clever, Dougie. Why are you working in boring old IT?'

He laughed. 'It's not that boring. Not as exciting as *your* work, no doubt. So you're fed up with everyone asking you about that case?'

'Could you tell? Was I rude?'

'It's bloody freezing,' he said. 'Here, have my jacket.' She let him put it around her shoulders. Were her generation the last that were allowed to enjoy such gentlemanly gestures?

'Can you keep a secret?' she said.

'Sure.'

'She's a great woman.'

'Who?'

'Constance Mortensen.'

'Is she?' He sounded surprised.

She sighed. 'I like her.'

'Are you allowed to feel attached to your patients?' he asked.

She shrugged.

'She doesn't remember it, you know, driving the kids into the river.'

'Luckily for her.'

'No. She's disassociated herself from her actions.'

He shivered and she pushed her body into his a little to warm him up. It was dangerous, flirtatious, but she owed him some of the warmth of his jacket.

'Don't you think we're all capable of anything, given the right triggers and the wrong medications?' she asked him.

'Not *anything*,' he said. And she realized she didn't know anything about him at all really.

'Maybe we're all just ticking bombs . . .' she said softly, looking up.

The lights seemed to be spinning above them; she was really pretty drunk. He took the glass out of her hand and put his other hand under his jacket, around her back. She felt the danger, the thrill. She *was* the ticking bomb.

'You're lovely, Emma Davis,' he said. 'I always thought that.'

This was it, the moment she had fantasized about, the moment she had *manipulated*. She felt her body responding to his words, to his touch, her heart dropping with a thud to the base of her womb somewhere, her body suddenly pounding with anticipation from her Brazilian bikini line to the tip of her tongue. Her mouth was moist, ready. She thought of Connie, she thought of Karl and Ness, of the fantastic search to feel *alive*, to feel truly present, that tangible thumping wonder of being human, his breath on her face, those dark familiar eyes.

And then she thought of Si.

'What is it?' he whispered, his lips close to hers.

'I'd like to kiss you, Dougie, more than anything in the world. I wanted to kiss you thirty years ago on that grubby brown sofa. And how my seventeen-year-old self would hate me now because I'm *not* going to kiss you . . .'

'You're not?' he said, not really believing her.

'No.'

'It's just a kiss,' he said. 'That's all.'

'No . . . But thank you.'

He nodded and smiled, moving imperceptibly away from her, his eyes still shining. 'Sensible Emma Davis.' He sounded a bit annoyed and she was intensely glad she'd stopped this before it began. *That's right*, she remembered now, *he was always used to getting what he wanted.*

'I don't know who he is but he's a lucky guy,' he said, handing back her glass.

So here she was on a Saturday afternoon waiting for her lucky guy to come out of his orchestra practice. A stream of musicians filed out of the church and then she saw him. He looked different to her, there amongst his 'people', in his element, sharing a joke with someone at the door, holding it open for others. He was an average middle-aged man, she could see that; ostensibly there was nothing remarkable about him at all and yet everything about him spoke of reassurance, dependability – he was that person you might go to in a crisis. She watched as he let the door go and then tripped on a paving stone. She was momentarily embarrassed for him, the buffoon with a bassoon. But he was *her* buffoon with a bassoon and she loved him. She downed the remains of her gin and tonic and left the pub, smiling at the Polish girl behind the bar, throwing a cursory nod at the addled old men.

Outside the pub in the sludge, just before she drew Si's attention with her arm poised for a wave, she saw a small dark woman come to greet him. It took a moment before she recognized her: it was Savannah, Adrian's new girl-friend. They kissed each other's cheeks and then hovered, looking left and right as if deciding where to go, totally oblivious to Emma on the other side of the road.

She watched curiously as they ambled towards the junction. Then slowly she followed them, parallel, slightly behind. They turned right. She crossed the road and could see them enter a cosy-looking gastropub with a log fire inside. Through the glass she could observe them approach the bar where they were taken to a table with no concern for anything but each other. She went into a bike shop from where she could still see them, hid-ing herself behind a frisbee which turned out to be a wheel. She needn't have bothered hiding; they were entirely wrapped up with each other, not looking out for Adrian as she had half hoped. And the longer Adrian didn't turn up, the greater the sinking feeling in her stomach became.

Emma got a bus straight home, opened the door, turned up the heating and sat at the kitchen table with a bottle of Rioja. After a while she took her glass upstairs and ran herself a bath. The towels were damp and smelt faintly of mould so she put them in the laundry basket and went to get clean ones. She paused at the linen cup-board. At the bottom lay the wooden framework of the cot. They kept it under the pretence that someone with a baby might stay. It was easier that way. She rested her head against the cupboard and stayed like that for a long time, pressing the soft cotton of the clean towel to her nose.

After her bath she tried to get on with some work on her laptop back at the kitchen table, some unfinished Crown Court consultation work, risk assessment and management, but she soon found herself staring out into the garden. Then she stopped bothering trying to work and pulled her chair up to the glass garden door, and sat there by the radiator in the hazy sunshine, her feet up on another chair, her smooth legs extended, a glass of wine in one hand and a cigarette in the other, the ashtray on her lap, looking out at the remnants of dirty snow, awaiting his return.

'Hi,' he called when he eventually arrived. She turned and watched him hanging up his coat in the hall. 'I thought you'd be out,' he said as he came through, putting his bassoon case on the kitchen table. He was in good spirits.

'Hi,' she said, smiling coolly, pouring out the last of the bottle into her glass. 'How was orchestra?'

'Great. Did my solo. Want to hear it?'

'Sure,' she said, taking her legs off the other chair and crossing them slowly, leaning over to pick up her cigarettes.

He took off his jumper and chucked it over a chair, and then he opened up his case and got out the bassoon as she lit up, pulling the glass door ajar to let the smoke out into the garden. She watched him then as he fixed the mouthpiece. His mouth was so familiar to her; that mouth that *she* never kissed but now someone else did; how nice for him to be wanted. Then when he began to play she turned away to watch a plump pigeon land in the cherry tree, peck at a few old berries and fly off again. She couldn't ignore the music; it was haunting and tender and she did her best to remain untouched by it. As he finished, she turned to look at him again to find that he was evidently expecting some kind of response from her.

'Very nice,' she said.

He didn't move. 'What's the matter?' he asked, noting the empty bottle, slowly lowering the bassoon.

She held his eye. 'Do you feel rejected by me, Si?'

'What?'

'Have I pushed you away?'

'What are you talking about?' He yanked the mouthpiece out and started putting the bassoon back in its case.

'Just answer the question.'

'I don't understand the question,' he said, snapping the bassoon case shut. She looked back out into the garden and inhaled slowly on her cigarette.

'What's going on?' he asked, moving round the table to her side, pausing, perching himself on it, folding his arms.

'I wonder,' she said, watching him carefully, his studied cross-examination pose. 'You tell me. What *is* going on, Si?'

'You're talking in riddles.'

She turned her body to face his. 'I understand, you know. You can still have children. I'm holding you back.'

'I'm sorry?'

'And you need to feel needed.'

'Is that right?'

'And you don't get that from me.'

'You can stop now, Emma, you're not at work. I'm not one of your bloody patients.'

'Am I wrong?'

'That I need to feel needed? Of course I need to feel needed. Everyone needs to feel needed, even you, Emma. Except you just don't like to *show* any neediness because you think making yourself vulnerable means you're weak or something, and God forbid you shouldn't be able to *cope* with everything.'

She blew the smoke out of her mouth slowly in a steady stream. 'Wow, that was quite an outburst,' she said, stubbing out the cigarette, twisting it firmly in the ashtray which rested on her past-its-sell-by womb.

'For example,' he carried on, 'whatever idea you've got in your head right now, you can't *say* it, you can't show that you *care*, you have to turn it into some kind of Gestapo inquisition.'

She angled her head and gazed at him. 'You have so much anger towards me.'

'Stop it! Stop twisting everything.'

'Said the lawyer. How's Sahara, Savannah, whatever the hell she's called?' She winced at herself; she hadn't meant it to come out like this.

'What?'

'You heard me.'

He laughed, took a few steps away from the table and ran a hand through his hair. 'Have you been following me?' He sounded really annoyed.

'I came to meet you but discovered you were otherwise engaged.'

He looked at her, aghast. 'What do you take me for? She's my best friend's girlfriend, for Christ's sake.'

'Ha! That old chestnut.' She bent down and picked up her glass.

'What? Go on then! Ask me the question! Oh, you can't because it might make you look too *needy*.'

'Well, are you?' she said, tapping out another cigarette.

'Am I *what*?'

She lit up and inhaled as if she had all the time in the world. 'Are you screwing her?'

He shook his head with disbelief. 'No, I am not screwing her. She came to meet me because we're planning a surprise party for Adrian's birthday. OK?'

Emma chuckled and then laughed out loud.

'Is that so funny?'

'A surprise party! How original, your honour.'

'You drink too much, you know that?'

She looked at him. 'You hate me, Si. Underneath it all, you *hate* me. Just admit it.'

'What?'

'You'll never forgive me.'

'Don't, Emma,' he said. 'Don't start this now. You're drunk.'

'We don't even *talk* about her any more. We don't even say her name.'

He was silent, head bowed, eyes on his feet.

'Say it!' she said.

'No, I'm not doing this.'

'Say it!'

'No.'

She stood up; she was angry now. 'Just fucking say it, Si! Say that you blame *me*! Say that it was *my* fault!'

He looked up then. His bottom lip was trembling but his voice was steady. 'Maybe *you're* the one who needs to say it.'

Then he turned and walked out of the room.

Chapter 18

Dr R is distracted today; she's flushed and her mascara has smudged a little beneath her left eye. She's all in black, no glimpses of a neon strap, and I'm very surprised to notice that her earrings are two tiny skulls; beneath her rectangular veneer there is a wannabe rebel. She tucks her hair and cocks her head to focus on me but the notebook on her lap is upside down, negating any semblance of togetherness. I wait for the Squeak to shift her bulk before I say anything.

'Had a fight?' I ask. Dr R is not wearing her wedding ring. She sees me looking at her finger and covers it up.

'Don't tell me it's that girl from the orchestra.'

She crosses her legs and does a good job of ignoring me.

'We need to talk about Milton House today,' she says, noticing that her pad is upside down and trying to turn it around without drawing my attention to it.

'Tell me she's not twenty-three,' I say.

'Not today, Connie,' she says quietly, tucking her hair behind her ear again, and I think about backing off, but I can't.

'Is he having sexual intercourse with her?' I ask in what I consider a doctorly fashion. 'Are they copulating?'

'Apparently not,' she says in a clipped voice. I'm stunned

255

that she includes me in this way, in her very private world. I look for signs that she regrets it but I don't see any. She's not blushing; she's not even fidgeting. Her eyes are a little bloodshot and I wonder whether she's been crying.

'Did he say it was just sex? Or is he *in love*?'

She waves a hand, gesturing for me not to ask any more, but she's not quick enough today to divert me. I won't stop now. 'You know, I once asked Karl, "Do you love Ness?" And he said, "I don't know." Can you believe it? *I don't know!* I'm still outraged by that conversation. I needed to hear him say *yes*. If he said yes I could get my head around it. I could understand that. But why would he take all these risks with his family if he didn't even love her? Would a man do all that just for his cock?'

'Love . . . what is love?' Dr R says dismissively. She is very negative today. I'm not sure psychiatrists should be so doom-laden. I press on.

'So I said to him, "All right then, Karl, let me ask the same question in a different way: Have you told *her* that you love her?" And he said, "Oh yes, of course I have!"'

Dr R sniggers. I love making her laugh. She has a wonderful smile. She rolls her eyes, shakes her head. I really haven't seen her like this before. She looks exhausted, weak, run down, past caring. I must milk it.

'At least *she* had the grace to later send me a text saying she just couldn't help herself – she was *madly in love* with him. Which is bullshit, by the way: there's always a choice down the line somewhere.'

'There is a choice! I totally agree!' Dr R says, perking up, raising a righteous finger. I'm surprised by her vehemence. She puts down the notepad altogether – she never managed to turn it the right way up – and stretches her legs. She stands up in that leisurely way she has and starts strolling around the room with some inner purpose that's lost on me. But I like watching her in this new dark attire with those skull studs in her ears. Then as she passes me, I catch a whiff of her: she's been drinking again. It's only the middle of the day but I'm pretty sure she's been drinking.

'Tell me about Milton House,' she says, leaning against the windowsill, raising one eyebrow.

'Nothing to tell. Do you know it?' I ask.

'No. I knew someone who worked there once.' Again, this is unlike her; she never proffers personal information.

'Why did they move me *here*?' I ask.

She stares at me for a long moment and then says, 'Milton House, Connie . . .'

'I don't really remember it.'

'You were there for six weeks, you must remember it.'

'What do you want to know?'

She folds her arms. 'I want to know everything. But in particular I want you to tell me about the night you escaped.'

'I don't remember that,' I say.

'Well, try.'

I've said it before but she should really watch that school ma'am side; she does herself no favours. Si Hubby has probably had quite enough of that; I bet the twenty-three-year-old doesn't give him that attitude. I bet she thinks the sun shines out of his proverbial. We all thrive on adoration.

'I don't remember much. They had me drugged up to the eyeballs.'

That's not completely true; I do remember snippets of it: arriving there and a leery man in a white coat telling me he had to keep the door open so that he could come in and look at me – he was a perv who liked watching me get undressed; queuing up for drugs like something out of *One Flew Over the Cuckoo's Nest*; being watched swallowing pills; being jabbed in the arse if I refused; being in this hypersensitive state most of the time and therefore like a magnet for the insane – I felt like the Pied Piper of Mentalists; the colour of the doors – a sickly green; the lights in the corridor that came on when you stepped on the lino and went off behind you, giving the peculiar sensation of being both in control and paranoid at the same time; knowing that I was in a *forgotten* place, that I'd slipped through the net to somewhere deep and dark where no one was looking out for me; and other stranger things that don't need remembering.

'How did you feel in there?'

Ha. 'I *didn't* feel. That was the point.'

'I need to know what you remember.'

How can I explain to her with words? I was in a kind of fugue state where things were too complex to express. All I could say was *This isn't right*. I remember Karl coming to see me, sitting there grim and tight-lipped, me trying to explain, saying that perhaps I was just an unusual sort of person. *No,* he'd said, *you're not unusual at all.*

'Do you remember being told of your mother's death?'

I look down at my wrist cuts and pick at a scab. 'Yes.' I pull off the scab. 'One of the doctors came into my room;

he said my mother had *passed away*. I hate that bullshit language. You'd hope a doctor could use the correct term: dead.'

On the way out he'd popped a lozenge into his mouth and I'd heard him outside saying my door should remain open, that I should be on suicide watch. Which initially sounded ridiculous; for starters, I didn't believe him about my mother. I trusted no one any more, I knew that people were liars and deceivers and I became convinced that they were *trying* to drive me mad, all of them, even Karl – he was in league with them. He came to see me later without the children – the children were *scared* of me, apparently. He was crying when he said Julia had taken an overdose. And I wondered for the first time whether it was true. I waited for her every day but she didn't come and neither did the children. I grew anxious; what was my life without my children and my mother? What was I doing in a place like this? Yes! *Suicide watch* because suicide was a *good* idea.

I'd made a friend of sorts, this hugely pregnant Chinese woman, who was in there for trying to cut out her baby, but other than that she seemed pretty sane to me. I kept telling her I wanted to die and one day she'd had enough and asked me why I didn't just get on with it. So I mentioned swallowing washing powder or somehow jumping off the roof. And she said *What's stopping you?* I had to think about that. And you know what? It was just cowardice.

'It seems unfair not to be allowed to kill yourself humanely, don't you think, Dr R? Why does it have to be so painful?'

'Were you feeling suicidal when you phoned home on

November 2nd? It's important that you try and remember. Annie answered the phone . . . do you remember that?'

She's looking at me intently, leaning forward, blinking a lot. I feel like I'm in a cop movie. Everything is hanging on my answer. 'No,' I said.

'You rang the house phone. Annie answered. Try and remember.'

'I *don't* remember.'

But I do try. And I *do* remember being in the hall in the telephone queue. I wanted to talk to my children, to tell them that I loved them, that they needn't be afraid of me. I remember some rude cow behind me in the queue told me that I stank, which was true. I was refusing to wash; it seemed about the only thing I could control. I hadn't washed for weeks. If I put my nose down into my nightie I could smell that sweet soft seaside smell of dirty vagina and sticky skin.

'Did you ring to say goodbye to them?'

I think I did. I nod.

'Were you going to kill yourself, Connie?'

I nod again. Yes. 'I missed my mum. I was saving up my medication.'

Then I remember: she was right, Annie picked up the phone. Annie and Polly used to answer the house phone in silly voices, trying to annoy the cold callers, pretending they'd been kidnapped or that they were aliens, that sort of thing. *Hellooo*, she said in a rather poor Scottish accent. *I like eating poo poo*. And I could hear Polly sniggering behind her. And I was happy she was well and getting on with things . . . I tried to answer her but my voice was so incredibly small that I couldn't locate it. *Annie*, I mouthed because no sound came out. *I love you.* But I don't think she heard me. And yet after a moment she said, *Mummy?* And I was floored by it, by my name, the only name that meant anything to me now . . .

My eyes fill with tears. I don't want to remember all this. Dr R is staring at me; she looks frustrated, cross. It's not working.

'Tell me, what did Annie say . . . ?'

'I heard a woman's voice in the background – "Annie, who is it?" I knew that voice very well; it was Ness. Then she took *my* phone in *my* house and asked me, "Who is this? We don't want to buy anything." *We*, she said. In *my* house, she said *we*.'

'And how did that make you feel?'

'Livid.'

'So what did you do?'

'I don't remember.'

She sighs; she's annoyed with me. 'Yes, you do remember.' She looks up now, her cheeks a burning red. 'You *do* remember.'

I shake my head. 'I don't.'

'What did you do after this? Was this what set you off?'

'I don't remember.' I want her to shut up, to stop asking me questions, to stop fishing in my brain.

'You must remember!' She sounds really annoyed with me. 'What happened in the weeks after the phone call?'

'I don't remember! I really don't remember!'

'What happened, Connie?' She's gone puce. I've never seen her like this. 'Connie, you have *got* to remember! None of us want to remember these things but we have to!'

'Why?' I'm shouting back at her.

'Because we have to *own* ourselves! We have to own our actions! We have to take responsibility!' She is really furious with me; I am quite alarmed.

And then something awful happens. Dr R turns her back on me and I can tell from the movement of her shoulders that she is crying. She is standing there at the window looking out and crying, really sobbing. I don't move. I am silent. What did I say? I have no idea why she is in this state but I am glad it's her, not me. I leave her to cry for a bit and then I get up to bring her some loo paper and I join her by the window. Her head has dropped and her shoulders are heaving now; she's in floods of tears. She takes the loo paper from my open palm. She blows her nose and stares out at the tree, hiccupping, blotchy-faced, mascara running down her cheeks. Gradually she calms down but she appears to be in some kind of trance looking out of that window.

Then she says, 'That bloody leaf won't let go, will it?' as if that is why she is crying. She's talking about *my* leaf. I too watch it waving about all alone on the tree now. I'm happy to share it with her. It can be *our* leaf now.

'I'm sure the Squeak will make you some tea if we ask . . .' I say, which is highly debatable – she's unfathomably lazy – but I need to say something reassuring.

'No, I'd rather no one saw me like this,' she says, glancing at me, and I'm flattered that she doesn't count me as anyone. Her eyes are the most beautiful turquoise blue – the tears have made them luminescent, her sadness lighting her from within.

'Sit down!' I say, pulling up two chairs to the window,

and she does as she is told. I get her a plastic cup full of water and she takes it. She sips at it, still dabbing her eyes. I sit down next to her and look out at the naked tree and we sit like that for ages.

'Can I tell you a story, Connie?' she says, just when I think it might be the end of the session. Her voice is calm now. She's finished crying.

'Sure.'

'OK.' She blows her nose again and is quiet for so long that I think she must have changed her mind. But then she begins the story in a quiet, detached voice, like she's giving a police statement.

'So, there's this young man and this young woman. They meet and fall in love. They are both materially successful people, they have always worked hard and they have good careers. They own their own flats and are used to a certain kind of lifestyle; they take good holidays and buy fancy things. They can indulge their whims. And then comes the time for settling down. They sell their flats and buy a house further out and have a small but tasteful wedding. For a long time they are very busy with their important careers and they are no longer quite so young when they decide that it is the right time to start a family. But life has other plans and it turns out that she's got a problem with her tubes – his sperm is fine – and that conceiving will not be easy. They start to obsess about it. Well, she does, he doesn't, because let's face it, he's OK and he's got all the time in the world, but her clock is running out. She really wants this baby and will do anything to get pregnant, from headstands to two rounds of IVF. It's expensive and unpleasant. She injects herself daily and gets fat, something she hates, something she really hates. And then bingo! The white stick says *Yes, You're a normal woman now!* She's pregnant. They're elated; she cannot believe it.

'But she is terrified something will go wrong during the pregnancy. She knows all the risks, she cuts down on her workload, she eats all the right food, takes all the right supplements, and she grows this baby as if it were a pearl inside her. But they don't buy any clothes or paint the nursery room because they're so scared that they'll jinx it somehow. The birth is utterly awful but it turns out that they are the luckiest couple in the world and they leave the hospital with this beautiful baby girl in their arms. She's perfect. She's exactly what they dreamed of. She's just beautiful . . .'

Dr R pauses, licks her lips and takes another sip of the water from the plastic cup. 'Even the woman's mother can find no fault with this baby. And they're so happy. The woman is already exhausted, of course, because she barely slept for the last few months of the pregnancy, which was then followed by a forty-eight-hour labour, an emergency caesarean and chronic mastitis. But the woman is on a high and she daren't complain because most of womankind has gone through this before her and because this is exactly what she *wanted*.

'As the months go by the woman becomes more and more exhausted. She has to take more time off work because she can't focus any more. The baby doesn't sleep – well, never for more than an hour and a half in a row and never, not once, does the baby sleep through the night. She becomes so tired that she cannot sleep.

She has one night of respite when she takes a Temaze-
pam having breast-pumped her milk out like a cow so
her husband can feed the baby. But she feels guilty, stupidly worried that the baby may suffer. She becomes
depressed, which she feels deeply ashamed about because
she has everything that she ever wanted. This is a woman
who can usually solve problems: she has patience, she
can manage other people, fix her own computer, she can
assemble flat-pack furniture, she can change a tyre, she
can cook for ten, but there is no instruction pamphlet
that came with this baby and she feels a total failure that
she cannot cope.

'And the baby becomes a toddler and still doesn't sleep.
She is like any toddler: adorable but a handful, sweetness
and tantrums. The mother is in this strange new endless
exhausting hamster-wheel cycle of washing, cleaning,
feeding and crying. She doesn't know how to deal with
these tantrums – the child is a ball of fury and rage – and
any of her usual strategies and logic fall on deaf ears. Her
threats are hollow because she simply does not have the
energy to carry them out. She is on medication now,
belatedly self-diagnosed with post-natal depression. She
is angry with the father because he sleeps soundly in the
spare room, because his work is somehow more important than hers, because his body has not been sucked,
stretched and mauled beyond recognition. Anyway,
thank God for play-dates and mothers' clubs and friends
in the park, because otherwise this mother, who is truly
grateful for the blessing of her daughter, would be driven
round the bend . . .'

She pauses here again and takes another sip of her

water and wipes her nose. She turns her chair a little, so she is talking to the tree.

'Then one day, the mother and the toddler are meeting friends in the play area of the local park. She's pushing the pushchair up the crescent, the swings and slides visible through the railings and the bushes. She can feel the stretch in the back of her legs, the fumes from the traffic; the toddler is kicking her legs with excitement, her little red wellies going up and down, because she too can see the swings and slides, better from her height because she only has the trunks of the bushes to see through – she can probably see her little pals already playing.

'But just as they get to the entrance gate, the mother bumps into an acquaintance, another doctor, who is leaving the park. They stop at the gate to chat about the bad nights. This other doctor has been trying a new herbal remedy that seems to be working and she starts looking up the name of it to share when the toddler – who is justifiably furious with her mother for stopping *right here* to chat, so tantalizingly close to their destination – starts whining and trying to get out of her seat, but she can't because she's strapped in. The mother tells the toddler that she will just have to wait. Well, the toddler *won't* wait, she is a toddler after all, and she wants to go on the swings. She starts to scream now and the mother, who has had enough of this and, who knows, is perhaps eager to demonstrate that she has *some* authority over this crazy screaming miniature human being, tells her child with a firmness she has no energy for to *Stop it!* But the toddler kicks off – she goes purple in the face and screams like a demon. She is now having a full-blown tantrum and the mother, beside herself with exhaustion and some embarrassment now at her own utterly useless parenting, loses it completely. "Shut up! I've had enough of this, Abigail!" And she manhandles the pushchair, roughly swivelling it one hundred and eighty degrees to face the opposite direction so that the toddler can no longer see the playground. And then the mother turns her back on the child, pointedly ignoring her, teaching her a lesson that she will *not* always get her own way by screaming.

'It seems to work. She's aware, as she chats with the doctor, that the tantrum is subsiding. They talk about one of the families in the playground whose children sleep through the night. But what neither the mother nor the doctor notice is that the pavement is on a gentle slope and the pushchair is moving, and right at that moment a lorry is speeding round the crescent. And when the brakes screech and the mother turns around it is too late. It takes for ever for the lorry to stop, dragging the push-chair in its front wheel as it spins across the road. And when it does eventually come to a halt maybe fifty yards away, the pushchair is tipped forwards and there is no movement at all. There are no more tantrums.'

I stare at Dr R. She's gazing out of the window without looking at anything, eyes glazed, tears all shed.

'You didn't put the brake on?' I say.

Dr R turns to me and very slowly she shakes her head. 'No. I didn't put the brake on.'

Chapter 19

Tom, Tatchwell's clinical director, had left a message on Emma's phone asking that she come straight to his office before she visited Connie that day. He'd sounded pre-occupied, worried about something, inordinately formal. When she got to his door she sensed his secretary was being cagey with her, and she worried that it was bad news about the girls.

'Ah, come in, come in, Emma!' Tom said, holding his office door open for her and shutting it gently behind her. His office was a mess but he seemed unaware of it. He bowed his head and was rubbing his beard thoughtfully.

'Are the girls all right? Annie and Polly?' she asked.

'I haven't heard otherwise . . .' he said, making a perfunctory effort to tidy up his desk.

'Right,' she said, waiting for him to elaborate, but he didn't.

'Do sit down,' he said, gesturing to an uncomfortable-looking plastic chair.

'Is something wrong?' she asked.

He smiled using only his bottom lip and neck muscles before taking his place behind his desk. 'How are you, Emma?'

'Well,' she said, taking the proffered seat and putting her bag down. 'I think we're getting somewhere.
Both her verbal and non-verbal behaviour indicate no
positive malingering. I'm undecided about her fitness
to stand trial at the moment. The amnesia seems to
have had a sudden onset and is blurry around the
edges, which is to be expected, according to what
I've read, in these rare cases of family annihilation. The
psychotic episode seems to have been triggered by a
number of events. In fact, there are serious questions
to be raised concerning the benzodiazepine prescrip-
tions from her GP and particularly the Clonazepam at
Milton House—'

'Um,' he interrupted. 'That's not really want I meant.'

'Oh?'

He looked like he'd rather be anywhere else on earth.
'Emma, I was never made aware of your situation before
assigning you to this case.'

'My situation?'

'This was always going to be a very sensitive case. I
wasn't aware of your . . . personal bereavement.'

Emma felt herself harden up inside; it wasn't appropriate to hear him talk of Abigail. It wasn't in his remit. She
smoothed her skirt and looked him straight in the face.
He shifted his glance.

'My personal situation has nothing to do with this
case,' she said.

'Right, no,' he said, backtracking. 'Except I don't know
if that is entirely true. Had I known—'

'Had you known I had lost a child you wouldn't have
given me the case?'

'Emma, there have been formal complaints made about you,' he said, changing tack.

She looked puzzled. 'I'm sorry? From who?'

'Two members of staff have complained about you.'

'Complained about me? In what way?'

'There is going to have to be a formal review.'

'What are you talking about?'

'They say you've been turning up to see Constance Mortensen, a very vulnerable patient . . .' He paused and licked his lips. 'Under the influence.'

Emma was speechless.

' "Reeking of alcohol," ' he added, making patronizing quote marks with his plump fingers.

She didn't move a muscle but a deep blush rushed through her.

'May I ask *who* complained?'

'You see how this doesn't look good . . . ?' he said, ignoring her, fiddling about on his laptop. 'I was prepared to let one incident slip by but they sent me this.'

He turned his computer screen around so that Emma could appreciate the full impact of herself in muted colour lurching across Connie's room and throwing up in the toilet while Connie, *the very vulnerable patient*, held back her hair and rubbed her back, and then took her over to the sink and cleaned her up before lying her down on the bed, taking off her shoes and stroking her hair. He had the grace to fast-forward through Emma falling asleep and Connie clearing up the vomit. He slowed it down again as Connie put on Emma's jacket, shoes and bag and then, bizarrely, performed a little tap routine, all tits, teeth and jazz hands. Connie then tired of this, sat down and began rootling through Emma's bag, checking her phone, going on her iPad and finally sitting by the bedside until Emma woke up.

It was truly shocking; there was no denying it.

'I see,' she said. 'I apologize profusely. I came to . . .' She petered out. There was no excuse.

'I'm afraid, Emma, I'm going to have to take you off the case.'

Emma panicked. 'Please, Tom. I'm so nearly there with her. She won't talk to the social workers or the other doctors. If you take me off, she'll have to start all over again. I know I can get there.'

'No, Emma, I just can't.'

'*Please*. She needs me, Tom. I'm all she has right now.'

'I'm so sorry.'

'Yup.'

She thought of him playing *Call of Duty*, lying here with his duvet in the office. *What sort of a profession is this, are we supposed to be superhuman?* 'I understand,' she said. She would have done the same in his position.

'Perhaps you should consider a well-earned sabbatical . . . ?' he said, sounding cheerfully relieved that it had all gone in a reasonably painless fashion.

'Yup.' She just wanted out of there. She felt utterly humiliated; up until now hers had been a faultless career. The repercussions of this were too enormous to take in. She stood up and smiled at him. 'Can we talk another time?' she said briskly.

'Of course. Although one more thing – I will need your pass,' he said, 'before you go.'

'Right. I'll hand it over. I just have something I have to do. I'll return it later today.'

'I think it's best you give it to me now,' he said.

Her insides clenched like a fist and her voice pierced straight through the room like a rod of steel. 'I *said* I'll hand it in, Tom.'

He let it go. She was older than him. That should count for something in this world. Next he'd be telling her she ought to get some professional fucking help.

*

'Feel the weight of your eyelids. Be aware of the rhythm of your breath, in and out. Listen to the birds out there . . . the faint sound of cars in the distance somewhere, that siren a long way off, the aeroplane way up there in the sky, just a hum . . . listen until you can hear it no longer. Try and empty your mind of any thoughts that might be going round. Let them go; they are not important. Just focus on what you can hear outside . . . then come back into this room . . .'

Emma was surprised at the power of her own voice, at her own conviction. She was going to get Connie to the end of this. Connie was sitting in the chair with her eyes shut, her hands loose on her lap. Because it was so warm in this place she was wearing only a T-shirt and some boxer shorts, and it was the first time Emma had seen the burns on her upper leg. They covered her entire right thigh and the inside of her left and were now a dark maroon, scabby in patches, a few areas still an angry red where she'd picked at the scabs, the skin around them taut and thin, peeling in places. Emma had grown used to the deep dark gashes striping Connie's left wrist and the acid burn marks up the inside of her right arm, but she hadn't had the opportunity to stare before. What a wrecked thing she was.

'You are feeling alert but relaxed now, Connie, and all you have to do is listen to the sound of my voice. You are in a safe, calm place and nothing bad is going to happen to you. If you want to stop you just say so. Nod if you understand . . .'

Connie nodded.

'I'm going to take you back to Milton House . . . I'm going to count down from ten and when I get to one you will be in a deep state of relaxation. All right . . . ten . . . nine . . . eight . . .'

Connie was surprisingly receptive for such a combative spirit; she'd been wary of doing this and only agreed when Emma had insinuated that their time was *extremely* limited.

'Three . . . two . . . one . . . I want you to tell me what happened at Milton House when you started taking yourself off the Clonazepam . . . What's it like there? How are you feeling?'

Connie sighed heavily and shifted herself. She bit her bottom lip and frowned.

'They've just put a tree up in the reception area although Christmas isn't for ages. It's really naff; it's from Poundland by the look of it but we're all staring at it like it's the Taj fucking Mahal. I can stare for hours at the lights. They have all sorts of different settings, flash flash gap flash flash gap, which they have to change because

one of them sets off the epileptics. But this is not a normal Christmas, is it . . .'

'Do you still feel like dying?'

'No.'

'What's changed?'

'It's not right.'

'What's not right? What's not right, Connie?'

'*Her* in my house with my babies. I need to get home
where I belong . . . that's what my mother says.'

'But your mother is dead.'

'She speaks to me . . . I can hear her.'

'What does she tell you?'

'The first thing I have to do is think straight and I can't
do that on my meds. I know I have to stop taking them.
So at med-time I queue up with all the others, swallow
them then regurgitate them in the toilet. Lin says Clonazepam is twenty times the strength of diazepam. Is that
right?'

'Yes.'

'She used to be a doctor in China.'

'What's the withdrawal like?'

Connie shook her head and paused. 'Not good . . .'

'Tell me.'

Connie continued to shake her head back and forth.
She was getting agitated and Emma leant forward.
'Observe yourself, Connie. Stay calm and focused on the
question in hand . . .'

'OK,' she said, nodding. 'It's frightening . . .'

'Why is it frightening?'

'*He* comes to me. No one else can see him.'

'Who comes to you?'

'Him . . .' She was shaking.

'Who is *he*, Connie?'

She whispers, 'The Devil.'

'The Devil? But the Devil's not real.'

'He's real to me. He's been waiting for me, he says. Waiting in the darkness; he appears on the wall in the shadows.'

'And what about your mother?'

Connie shook her head as if she didn't have an explanation.

'Why's he come to you, Connie?'

'He's come to get me,' she said, as if it was obvious. 'I've been bad.'

'What does he look like, the Devil?'

'Like in the picture books. Exactly the same: red eyes, horns, a goatee, cloven hooves.'

'But he's not real, is he?'

'I don't know.'

'What does he do?'

She was still whispering. 'He moves about the room at lightning pace. I never know where he's going. He wants to get into my bed with me . . .'

'What does he want from you?'

She crumpled up her face, as if about to cry. 'He wants to drag me to hell . . .'

'Why would he want to do that?'

'Because I'm evil, because my children are scared of me, because I'm rotten to the core.'

'Does he come only at night?'

Connie nodded; she was scared. 'Mostly. He comes for three nights in a row . . . I'm so frightened I defecate in the bed . . . I wake up drenched in sweat with the stench of shit . . . I call for my mamma . . .'

'It's all right Connie, the Devil *isn't* real.'

'I close my eyes tightly and just keep repeating *I'm in heaven, I'm in heaven*. I find a staple on the floor and scratch it into the glass of the window, convinced that will stop him coming. *I'm in heaven.*'

Connie was breathing rapidly.

'It's all right, Connie. You're past that now. You are safe. Tell me what happens on the day you escape . . .'

Connie sighed again and frowned and slowly rocked herself back and forth.

'It's pouring with rain outside and a group of us are watching the downpour through the window in the canteen. It's like Armageddon out there and I wonder if it really is the end of the world. It sets a lot of people off; they're dancing on the tables. Not me. I'm standing there with Lin, watching it, but I have this ache in my chest, in my heart – a real pain and it won't go away. I can't stop thinking of my children . . .'

'And what happens?'

'Suddenly there's a loud crash from the reception area and raised voices and the whole herd of us rush over to the door to see what's going on, myself and Lin included. Two men in boiler suits are freaking out. One of them is holding up the end of a pipe which has just burst and is now hanging from the ceiling, water gushing down on to the lino. The Christmas tree lights flash like crazy for a bit and then go out completely. We stand there in a huddle watching the gushing water fill the hall; it's fantastic, it's exciting, it's sheer chaos. The security guy on the door is shouting at us, swearing, telling us all to leave the area, but it's impossible, people are already paddling in the water and one plucky old bird, she has to be about eighty, she's trying to swim . . .'

Connie began to smile, to laugh. 'It's mayhem. Several staff rush down the corridor and are trying to get people back to their rooms and the plumbers are trying to stop the water from going into the main block. Lin and I have moved over to watch the proceedings through the internal window in the canteen where some of us have been told to wait. Lin sees the opportunity: just for a moment there is no one on the door. The security door is open and the guard has abandoned his booth to talk to the plumbers outside while they get their kit from the van.

' "Go now!" Lin says. I turn to her: "Come with me." But she doesn't want to, she's just about to burst herself. She promises to put some pillows down my bed later and she gives me her slippers and her cardigan . . .'

Connie paused, lost in a reverie.

'So you just walk right out of there?' Emma asked, her voice low, urging her on.

'I never thanked her. I don't even know if she had a boy or a girl.'

For a moment, she looks as though she's finished talking.

'Then what happened, Connie?'

'I just race out of there into the rain in the clothes I have on and dart into the bushes towards the gate. I have no idea where I am, the outskirts of the city somewhere, in this forgotten place that no one wants to go to. I have no memory of even arriving there. I start to run, heading down side streets until I feel far enough away to stop. No one's following me so I stop running and just follow the sound of the traffic until I come to another main road where people seem to be going about their rushed businesses in the rain. Nobody pays me any attention at all.

'I feel good. I'm free; I can't believe it. But it's getting dark and I'm cold and wet so I decide to catch a bus. The first bus that pulls up says it terminates at Sloane Square. I know I can get the 22 home from there. I wait with a group of people under the shelter and the bus pulls up. I slip on at the getting-off doors behind a couple of young girls. The girls are giggling and I wonder whether they are laughing at me and my patches of hair and Lin's slippers. I suppose I look a right sight. I climb to the top deck and sit at the back and soon warm up. A man in front of me has glasses on and I'm pretty sure he is spying on me, filming me; they are special spy glasses. Then he gets off, pretending to ignore me. The journey takes for ever but I don't care; I look out of the window at the wet streets and people have started to put Christmas decorations in the shops, in the houses. I start to get excited. I think of the kids. I think of all the Christmas shopping I need to do, stocking fillers and presents. There's so much to get on with. It seems like hours before I change buses and get back to Putney . . .'

Connie's eyes were still closed but she paused; she was thinking, lost in remembering.

'And what happened when you got there?'

'I walk down the short cut, cross the little bridge and pass the cemetery. I feel as if I'm in a different reality, like a ghost, indomitable. I walk down Ness's street and slow down as I approach her house. I stand outside looking in. She has a tree in the window, flashing tasteful white lights, delicate baubles – Evie has probably decorated it. It feels strange to be here where absolutely nothing has changed except me. There's a light on in the kitchen at the back but I know no one is in – she always leaves it that way if she's going out. I keep staring at the house, the bright yellow front door behind which lie so many of my memories: happy times of bringing up our children, playing games, all of us watching Saturday night TV, the kids enacting their tangos or their waltzes, the adults marking out of ten, the kids racing around the house, the adults sitting round the table drinking wine and putting the world to rights, back to the days of Leah dishing the dirt on the entertainment business, New Year's Eves, birthdays, kids' parties, adult parties ... happy days indeed. And now here it is, the same bricks and mortar, but all broken and riddled with invisible cracks. I slowly walk around the side of the house to the back.

'Nobody's in the kitchen. I take the back door key from under the flowerpot where she always leaves it. I open the French windows and let myself in, closing the doors behind me. The smell is as familiar as my own house; hers is fruity and sweet, silent save for the buzzing of the fridge. Ness is messier than me; there's washing-up in the sink and kids' work all over the table, a pile of dirty clothes in the laundry basket, clean clothes hanging up everywhere, over radiators and off the backs of chairs.

'I step in, taking off my wet clothes and putting some

of her dry ones on. I feel much better now. I go to the fridge and notice a photo on the door of us all at the school ball, laughing, oblivious to the misfortunes that lie ahead. I take it off to see it better but it makes me nostalgic, homesick for something that's long gone. It actually hurts to look at it. So I open the kitchen drawer, pull out her big scissors and snip straight through her head between the eyes, and straight through his between his lips, and I feel the pain subside. The pieces fall to the floor.

'I hook the scissors on my thumb and open the fridge. I eat a piece of leftover apple tart before moving through to the hall, where I open the coat cupboard and see that one of Karl's jackets is hanging up inside. I press my nose into it. I can smell him on it. Next to it is Ness's leather jacket – one of mine actually, a brown leather jacket that I'd bought for myself but gave to her because she looked better in it. These scissors are very sharp – it's easy to slice clean through the leather, it's . . . satisfying. I cut both jackets clean in two before closing the cupboard and heading onwards, running my hand along the wall, deliberately knocking the photos off kilter, my damp fingers leaving a mark on the blue paint – chosen by me in happier times; my shoes squelching on the floorboards that I had helped her nail down.

'I go up the stairs, dragging the scissors along the wall, noticing the dirt on the carpet. I stop outside the bathroom; she's painted it an insipid pale yellow – or maybe he has; these things are new to me. I go to her bedroom and turn on her bedside light. I look around; I remember lying in this bed with her after Leah had left, comforting her as she cried, reading out loud to her from *Seeing Stars* to stop her sobbing and holding her tightly when she couldn't, bringing her tea when she couldn't sleep – this bleak future truly unimaginable then. *Everything will be all right*, I'd told her, quite sure of it. But it hasn't turned out that way . . .'

Connie moved her head this way and that as if she were standing in Ness's room, smelling that sweet fruity smell.

'I notice that *he* is in this room as well: a pile of loose change by the bed – his trademark night-time deposit. I pull back the duvet for more night-time deposits. I lean over and sniff their fuckdom; it's a familiar smell, musty and sweet, enticing and repulsive. I snip across the sheet in messy jagged lines. Then I look in the laundry basket for more evidence. Yes, there's some of his underwear, stains and all. I go over to the wardrobe and open it wide. I give myself a fright. In the reflection of the mirror is a monster with peculiar tufts of hair and ripples of burn scars down its neck. Its mauled arm reaches up to touch its patchy bald head. I turn back to the job in hand and bunch all her clothes together and smoothly chop the entire lot in half.

'I pause in my scissor-play when I hear a key in the door downstairs. It's too late to turn the bedroom light off so I swiftly move into Evie's room next door and hide in the alcove where the sink is, above which is a mirror where I can see both the door and the bed. I can hear a man's voice. I listen carefully – Evie is laughing. Then I realize that it isn't a man at all, it's Josh. Josh and Evie are coming up the stairs, chatting, giggling. I crouch down as they come into the room, pressing myself deep into the alcove, the scissors still in my hand. I watch him in the mirror, my boy, my man-boy. He doesn't see me for he has eyes only for Evie. He takes her in his arms and kisses her, like a man might. They lie down on the bed and I wait until they are lost in each other's bodies before I leave the room. I walk straight past them and leave them to their love. I go back down the stairs and exit the house the same way I came in, spinning the scissors in my hand like John Wayne might his gun.

'It has stopped raining now but everything is wet and gleaming in the street light. I look up. From outside Ness's house I can see the back of my own. What a beautiful house it is. We had it re-pointed and painted a very pale blue a few years ago, a lifetime ago. The lights are all on and smoke is coming out of the chimney, dark grey against the orange sky – Karl must have a fire going. The house radiates *home*, it's all warmth and security. I let out a little gasp of joy as I see small figures running up and down the stairs in a chase, shadows bouncing off the walls. I know they're Annie and Polly. I have to see them better. At the back of our house is a narrow overgrown alley that the neighbourhood cats crap in. I go down it, reach my hand over the wooden door and unlock our garden gate.'

Connie paused as if she were waiting for the time it took her to open the gate, her fingers twitching. 'I close the gate behind me. From the back of the garden, I can see people downstairs in my kitchen. I know perfectly well that they can never see me. You can go right up to that window and still not be visible because of the lights inside. I hear sporadic muted laughter but I can't make out the conversation. I walk down the garden path, past a pile of wilting footballs. Had Josh's obsession ceased now that he was having sex? Ah, there's Karl. He's *entertaining*. I haven't imagined him entertaining without me but there he is at the table, the jovial host, pouring out the wine, cracking the jokes. I stop.

'Oh.

'There *she* is, the jovial hostess, in my place, drinking from my glass, eating from my plate, lapping up my life. I wonder whether I ever existed at all. She is glowing, dressed in a T-shirt, hair tied back, radiant and unscathed as ever. I bend a little to see who the other adults are: the Stevensons and a woman I don't know. The Stevenson kids must be upstairs hogging the Play-Station. They are the worst guests; it's always the kids whose parents don't let them play who make the dullest play-dates, glued to a screen of any sort. They are more Ness's friends than ours. Karl and I don't know them well at all, only in a social media sense where they seem rather earnest, saving-the-world type people, posting dull photos of unappetizing health drinks and sugar counts, running moonlit marathons, permanently outraged by the fascist regime yet furious if someone disagrees with them. Karl and I, we used to take the piss. Not any more, obviously. Where had *we* gone, he and I, the *thing* that we were?

'The other woman is a stranger, possibly there as a stooge to distract from Ness and Karl's adultery, to stop the table feeling too *coupley*. But there they all are, having a *smashing* time, getting on famously, forging new friendships now that the old regime had been ousted, drinking organic wine and munching on their thrice-baked arse-beans or whatever they're eating, the remnants of which litter the table . . . *this isn't right . . . this isn't right . . .'*

Connie began to drum her fist into her palm and started mumbling something incoherently and Emma leant towards her. 'Just say what you see, Connie . . .'

Connie nodded and angled her head upwards as if she were looking up to the window above the kitchen.

'Upstairs, little people are still running all over the place – they're probably playing sardines or water-bombs. I even find myself thinking about the mess I'll have to clear up later on . . . You see, what I can't get my head around is how everything is exactly how it *always* is except I'm not there. I am superfluous. I have been replaced. I am just a ghost on the outside looking in. And, ghost-like, I shrink into the wet bushes at the side of the window to crouch and watch proceedings. I can't be more than twelve inches from the sink, not six feet from the table. In a way I am with them. I watch Karl get up, a gag on his lips, more laughter. I see the way his hand touches Ness's back as he goes past her – it might have looked casual to any observer but I see the way her body responds, their own intimate language, the validation she gives him. Is that all we're looking for in a lover? I hate him with his simple needs and his treacherous hands. He goes to the fridge and takes out another bottle of wine. I can see directly inside the fridge. It's full. I see things I would never have bought: cans of Coke, pork pies, cheap sausages, expensive wine. I look for signs of me in there but there aren't any. How has all trace of me disappeared so quickly? Then he shuts the fridge door and a school form wafts up into the air, revealing a photograph of me underneath: smiling, safe, sane. But the visit to the Horniman Museum, or wherever, flaps over my face like a veil.

'I sit there for hours, scissors in hand, the point digging into my palm every time I see some intimacy between them. I don't have a plan. I just want to be home. I get up to see better when Josh and Evie come back to the house, under the guise of having bought some lollies for the younger kids, but in reality they were fresh from the sheets; I can see their wonder, the wholly self-consuming appetite of first love. Annie, Polly and the younger kids come thundering down the stairs for lollies. I press my nose to the pane to see my little love. If anyone looks this way they might see the strange sight that is me, but no one does.

'Annie is in her giraffe suit that she's starting to outgrow; the legs come up to her knees. She's cut herself a fringe and it rises jauntily across her forehead. No one has tidied it up. Josh hands the lollies out and the Stevenson brats squabble about flavours – so much sugar deprivation has made them whiny and Andrea Stevenson duly reprimands them. Annie is on her knees following Karl about the kitchen, hands in a prayer position, and Polly is doing the same to Ness. I know what they are up to: begging for a sleepover. And a pathetic part of me feels even more forgotten. Negotiations will have to begin. I suppose it must be a Saturday. Handsome Josh will have a match tomorrow. There he is, so grown up, so satiated; he lifts Annie up from the floor and holds her under his arm like a handbag and starts play-fighting with her on the sofa. My eyes well up. I yearn for them, just to hold them, to touch them. Children need their mother. Or do they? Or is it just *me* who needs *them*? Didn't Karl say that they were scared of me? I think the Devil told me that too.

'I retreat into the shadows as Ness moves to the sink, *my* sink, to commence the mountain of washing-up. Andrea Stevenson joins her. The men do fuck all. My loyalty wavers. I move to the side a little to see better, to get closer to her, sure that the fairy lights within make it impossible for her to see me. I could tap on the glass now, give her a fright. As she turns her head to reach for a dirty pan, I notice that she has a few red burn marks on her neck and I feel good about that, the fact that she too is scarred. I hate her. I hate him. I hate the way they're all coping so well without me. I miss them all.

'I wait. I am happy to wait all night. I follow their movements. I stand at the back door looking in when the Stevensons leave – no doubt with hopes and promises of future good times together. The other woman goes with them and I can't see which kids are left behind but I can hear the boiler going on upstairs; someone is running a bath. Karl and Ness come back through to the kitchen, pausing right near me, his hand resting on her back, turning her around; they kiss each other hungrily as if they've been starved, wishing those Stevensons had gone hours ago. I see their passion. I watch as she pushes her body into his, moulding into his shape. They look wrong together, he's far too tall for her. She's too beautiful. I am mesmerized as they devour each other's faces like slimy feasting sea creatures.

'I see the way they leap apart when they hear footsteps upstairs, like thieves caught in the act. So they *do* feel guilt. They *do* feel what they are doing is wrong. Aha! They *do* have shame.

'I move back to the window to watch them tidy up; I observe the way she leans over to blow out the candles, *my* candles; the way he creeps up and down the stairs checking on the kids. I see her go over to her coat to get out her cigarettes and I move quickly then; she's coming outside. I spin the scissors in my fingers like I'm ready for the shoot-out and slip back into the bushes behind the bench as she unlocks the back door. She stands there to light up, like she has done a hundred times before. She's humming. She's happy. She probably never gives the monster in the psychiatric unit a thought. She steps out on to the gravel and wanders towards me, looking up into the night where the lights from a plane flicker in the foggy orange London sky. She stops a couple of feet in front of me and sits on the bench, back to me, and smokes with the nonchalance of a film star. She is true class, even alone. She is so close I can smell her; I can see the curls of hair at the back of her neck. I miss her, I want to reach out and touch her. Or ram the scissors into the softness of that skin.

'I do neither. She goes back inside and I know she is going to sleep in my bed.

'I wait for hours. I wait until the house is dark, all lights turned off, all doors locked, all boilers stopped, all embers dying. Even the distant traffic has ceased;

London is at last asleep. Then I open the shed door and find the back door key in the jar and let myself into my own house. I'm not thinking anything. I just want to be in my own home and pretend for a moment that nothing has changed.

'I leave Lin's slippers outside the back door, carefully open it and step over the squeaky floorboard. I shut the door behind me and listen to the stillness of the house. I go through the kitchen, down towards the sitting room, and step inside. Ah! There is the Christmas tree, of course. It's horribly decorated, naff silver baubles and coloured lights. The kids have been allowed to do it – always fatal. I stand in front of the fire and prod the embers with the poker; they glow an orange syrupy smile at me, welcoming me back. There are some cards on the mantelpiece; I've missed someone's birthday: Karl's. I read all the cards including one from Ness: *Happy birthday you wonderful man.* I John Wayne flip the scissors and cut it into small pieces over the embers and watch as the flames light up the room, making shadows on the wall. Briefly I think I see him there, the Devil watching me.

'I leave the sitting room and stand in the hall. The counter is littered with various unopened letters, car keys, shin pads, the usual stuff. I look up the stairs towards the bedrooms. Everything is silent. I move towards the staircase and cautiously start to climb it, placing my feet with precision; every inch of this house is in my body's recall, every creak is known from endless nights spent crawling out of the kids' rooms, praying for sleep. I stand on the landing, looking left and right: all doors are shut. I'm home at last. I feel inexplicably tired.

'I push open my bedroom door. And sure enough, there they are, there *she* is, sleeping in *my* great big bed, on *my* side, in *my* room, by *my* husband. Karl is on his side, sound asleep, facing her, his hand reaching out towards her. I walk round to where she's lying and I look down at her: she's on her back, lips parted, not a care in the world, her long frizzy hair splayed across my pillow, one breast exposed, the duvet pulled up to her ribcage. I can see the rise and fall of her chest, the exact place where her heart pumps beneath the skin.

'Her iPhone is lying beside her. I pick it up and look at the screen. She has set the timer for two hours' time, presumably so she can sneak out of the house and pretend to be a decent human being to her children. I turn the phone off.

'I sit down on the end of the bed for a while to think. I wonder about getting into the bed with them; us all being together again. But it's never going to work. So instead I pull up my sleeve and slice my wrist open.

'I feel no pain. The blood oozes out in a satisfying way, black in the dimness of the room. As it spills on to the white duvet, I cut again. The blood pours out this time, down my arm, down my hand, on to the bed and on to the carpet. But still I feel absolutely nothing.

'And then it occurs to me that perhaps I *am* a ghost, I am already dead. That is why no one saw me – not Josh, not Evie, not anyone on the bus, in the street. This is some other reality in the future that I have stepped into. I keep hacking at my wrist as if to prove it. Nothing! I can feel no pain at all because I am already dead. What a relief! What a marvellous relief! I cannot die again. The

Devil didn't get me! I tricked the Devil! I just keep slicing and the blood gushes out and I keep being a ghost.

'I have to tell the children that I am safe, I am in heaven. *Josh and Annie, my lovely children.* I quickly leave the room and race up to Josh's room, no longer caring about squeaking floorboards; I am made of light. I am weightless. I push open his door. It smells bad – of socks and teenager. But he isn't there. Does he openly sleep with Evie? Was I never to be consulted again in decisions of this nature? Of course not, I was dead! I made my way back down the stairs and pushed open Annie's door.

'Polly and Annie are both in the lower bunk, sound asleep. Annie is taking up all the room, sleeping with her arms and legs akimbo like a starfish, still in her giraffe suit, poor Poll squashed up against the wall. I put the bloodied scissors down beside the bed and I bend down and kiss her warm cheek. I bury my face in her sticky neck. She doesn't even stir.

' "My darling," I whisper. It's like coming home. My love for her is all-consuming. "I'm dead, I'm in heaven."

'And it feels so good and so safe. I must protect her. I must keep her from the Devil. I know then, as I breathe her in, what I have to do. I can save her now. I *have* to save her. Poor Annie, she has my genes, there is no hope for her, far better that she come with me now, where I can protect her and shelter her from him, because he'll want her too, to get his revenge on me. It's too late to save Josh, he is a man now, but Annie, she needs me.

' "Come with me, my little treasure," I whisper, scooping up her sleeping body into my arms. She barely stirs; she's so used to being carried in and out of various houses to and from cars and beds. She wraps her arms tightly around me and for a moment she knows it's me; she nestles her nose into my skin and breathes a puppy-dog sigh. I stand there feeling the love between us, her face against my neck. She is all mine.

'I take her down the stairs and pick up Karl's keys from the counter. I open the front door and carry her out into the cool night air. She shifts in my arms but the giraffe suit is furry; she isn't cold. I carry her down the steps. The night is dead. I look around for the car, our beaten-up old RAV4. I see it across the street and go towards it. I open the door and lay Annie down on the back seat, covering her with the old oily blanket from the boot. She stirs a little and asks me, "Mummy? Where are we going?" I tell her we're going on a drive. "Can Polly come? Get Polly, Mummy." "No," I say. And then I think *Polly? Why not?* Yes, perhaps she's right. Polly must be saved too – she's already tainted by her proximity to us. Her suffering will be great; the Devil will take her too. If there were more children in the house I would take them all.

'So I go back for Polly, following the dark splashes of blood, a Hansel and Gretel trail across the road, up the steps, into the house, along the hall and up the stairs. Polly is sound asleep and rolls into my arms without a fuss, vaguely waking for a moment, seemingly unsurprised to see me. "Where are we going?" she asks. I take her hand. She brings the duvet with her. Annie is sound asleep now on the back seat. Polly climbs in and sleepily leans against Annie. I cover them with the duvet.

'I close the back door and get in the driver's seat. I can see Polly's eyes closing. For a moment I sit quite still before turning on the engine. I look down at my flesh hanging open on my wrist, pull the seat forward and turn the keys. The radio comes on. How perfect: a choir of angels begin to sing. It's beautiful; I've no idea what it is. Hundreds of voices tearing at the heart, welcoming us home, letting the Devil know he can't get us now – because I'm taking them to heaven with me. I smile, peaceful in my certitude of what has to be done.

'Polly isn't properly asleep; she keeps sitting up to listen to the angels singing, so I drive around the neighbourhood until she lies back down. I begin to notice all the flowers people have laid out for us: wreaths on doors, decorated lampposts, twinkling lights. When I am sure that they are both sound asleep I turn left near the bridge and drive down towards the river. I can see that the tide is high. I stop the car at the top of the road. I reach back to take Annie's little black-nailed hand. I squeeze it tightly: "Here we go, my darlings, Granny will be waiting for us." I wrap the seat belt around my neck once, just to be sure the Devil can't drag me out. I take a deep breath. Then I put my foot down on the pedal and rev the engine, feeling the wheels spin on the tarmac. We lurch forward and begin to speed towards the edge of the walkway, my foot pressed to the ground. And the next thing I know the wheels are in the air, we are flying. Then the bullet-hard thud as we hit the water. We float for a moment. The temperature drops acutely and the river spins the car around and I can see the shore, the twinkling lights of life. The water begins to swallow us up, the car tilts on to its side and the singing angels stop their singing . . . no . . . no . . .'

Emma had not moved a muscle during the telling of this. Connie had been speaking quietly, unemotionally, her eyes closed throughout. Now she opened them wide and looked at Emma with a terror that Emma knew and recognized.

'They've woken up! They've woken up!' she cried. 'They're screaming!'

Emma reached out to hold Connie's arms.

But Connie wasn't aware of Emma; she could only hear their screaming. The blood was draining from her face, her body had gone rigid, the muscles in her scarred neck stood out; she was about to fit.

Emma got down on her knees and grabbed her firmly. 'Listen to me! Annie's OK. Both of them! They're OK! They're alive!'

But Connie could not hear her. 'Get them out! Do something!' She was screaming now, her whole body rigid as a plank of wood. 'Help us!' Then she let out a wail so inhuman, so visceral, so horribly private, that a chill went through Emma. She had heard that sound before; out of her own mouth a long time ago.

'Connie!' she cried, and slapped her hard across the face, and something in Connie shifted.

'They're out, Connie! Two men were returning from night shift at the cement factory . . . They saw your car go into the water, the force of the current dragging it. They went in, Connie. They got you all out. Annie's OK. She's OK. Polly's OK . . .'

Connie stared at Emma, her lips trembling, tears on her cheeks. 'Why did they save *me*?' she cried. 'They shouldn't have saved me.'

Chapter 20

I don't seem to be coping so well since she left. I don't know *why* she left. She was my link, my lifeline. And now she's gone. I still talk to her. *Dr Robinson,* I say, *that's a nice dress you're wearing. What did Si Hubby make for dinner last night?* Or if I'm feeling cheeky, like in the old times, I'll say, *Did Si Hubby get lucky last night, Dr R?* But she doesn't hear me because she's only in my head, I know that. But I imagine the way her hair will slip forward and how she'll blush and look a bit flustered. Or she'll smile and how great that will make me feel. But I didn't make her smile in the end. No, she gave up on me; I did something too awful to forgive. I have lost everyone now.

I think Karl has visited me once or twice. I don't remember seeing *him* but I have seen a Twix by my bedside and a crap magazine. I do not eat it and I do not read them. I do not wish or deserve to be alive any more, yet still my body carries on. And I wonder *why*; I don't use it, I don't feed it and I don't want it. All it does is lie on the bed; I have a tube that feeds me, pumping in the nourishment, and another one that pumps out the waste. Sometimes people turn me this way or that or wash me and I suppose time passes, but I have lost all concept of that because time is perspective and too much perspective is a terrible thing. Perhaps the Devil got me in the end and I am in hell and hell is here in this room.

The ceiling has fifty-seven panels on it; the paint is peeling off two of them. *Is this hell, Dr Robinson? Please tell me. Are you at home, Dr R, with Si Hubby, Netflix and chilling? Do you ever give me a thought? I miss you and your endless silly questions.* I imagine her getting on with her busy professional life, visiting other patients, sitting there with her notepad upside down, vomiting in their toilets, and I'm jealous. I thought we had something. I look back to then as the good old days; sometimes I go through every session we had in my head, everything she said, all the secrets she told me. I imagine I am her, pushing that pushchair, hungover with tiredness, that screaming child . . . I never offered her comfort. I wish I had. Oh so many things I wish I had done differently.

'Connie?' The voice is so familiar; these days I cannot tell what is inside my head and what isn't. I don't bother opening my eyes.

'Connie?'

'Yes,' I say.

'It's me,' she says.

'Hello me,' I say.

'I'm here,' she says. And then I begin to think that perhaps this voice is not in my head and with great effort I open my eyes and focus on the ceiling. There's daylight. The panels look grey not white in this light. There are three peeling, not two.

I feel a hand take mine; it's cool and clammy. I try to turn my head. I see someone sitting there at my bedside, a bag on their lap. I don't recognize her at first: she's sideways to my horizontal world and she looks different. But I know that fragrance. Yes, there she is, sitting on the chair, full of the glow of outside people from that other reality I am no longer a part of. I think perhaps I am imagining her.

'Ness?' I say, but my voice has gone now, there's been no call for it. She smiles. She is so familiar to me. She's cut her hair and she looks older but she is just as beautiful. Her dark eyes are full of a sweet sadness that I do not recognize.

'Oh, Connie,' she says, and for some reason she starts to cry; silently, just tears spilling down her cheeks.

I wonder if something has happened. I try to squeeze her hand but I'm so weak I don't know if she can feel it. She leans forwards and rests her head on my hand. I look down at her, confused, and then I notice my wrist; the scars are pink now so some more time must have passed by, weeks I suppose. Months? What does time matter? Slowly I raise my other hand and touch her frizzy bob and we stay like this for a while.

It's so lovely to have her here, even if she is only in my imagination. I have that peculiar feeling again that we are playing parts in a play, that we are old souls, battling through eternity together. This time I am an invalid and she is a nurse. We say nothing; we have no need for words because they are inadequate. But I feel her love.

The moment is crudely interrupted by the door opening. It's the Squeak, my only constant. 'OK Connie, sit up for your visitor,' she says, and I know then that Ness is real. I stare at her as the Squeak walks round to the side of the bed and talks to me like the simpleton I have become. She leans over, presses a button and makes my bed move into a semi-upright position, and Ness spins round accordingly.

'Would you like some water?' the Squeak asks, not expecting a reply. 'Come on, Connie,' she adds admonishingly. 'She's being a very silly girl,' she says to Ness before leaving the room.

I try to say something but it comes out as a whisper and Ness leans in to hear better.

'She's a right cow,' I say. Ness smiles. I feel only love for her; I become aware of my heart beating and momentarily feel connected to my body.

I wriggle my fingers and she takes my hand again. I close my eyes. This is not hell. This is the first piece of peace I have felt for a long time. I feel her touch on my skin and I wonder what she is doing, why she is tickling me. Then I realize she is running her finger along my suicide scars, the hackings I made on the bed while she slept. She is running her finger up and down each one, feeling every bump and shine as if she wants to feel my pain. I feel the shame of myself. What a *silly girl*.

I open my eyes and she is looking at me with those sad brown eyes and takes a deep tremulous breath. 'I'm so sorry,' she says, and I am truly puzzled. I shake my head. I don't know what to say. I don't know what I can *ever* say to her.

She takes something out of her bag, I cannot see what. But I see her unscrew a lid and tip something into her hand. Then with her fingertip she gently rubs some oil on to my wrist. I can smell lavender. It feels lovely, her touch on my skin; no one has touched me in this way for so long, no one has caressed my ugliness. I sigh, stretch out a little. She doesn't stop at my wrist; she quietly moves round the bed and picks up my other wrist, examining my hand. I feel the shame again, those scars that were meant for her. I try to withdraw my hand but she doesn't let me. She kisses my scars. Then she carefully places my hand back on the bed.

'Let me . . .'

And I do let her. I close my eyes. I hear the glug and slap of the oil in her hands as she rubs them together, before gently picking up my hand and lightly massaging my skin, the base of my palm, between my fingers, up over my wrist, along my arm, following the macabre patterns of the acid scars. It feels so wonderful, her touch on my neglected skin, the slippery smoothness of the oil, the warmth of her hands, the love she is giving me. I feel myself relax as those pliant fingers seem to place me in my body again. She doesn't miss a single scar, from my fingers to my toes, via my arms, my neck, my chest, my breast, my stomach, my groin, my thigh, my knee, my foot; each damaged place she gives her full attention. She is giving me my body back; I am reclaiming this flesh.

When she has finished, I cannot move. I lie there in a blissful state breathing in the lavender aroma of the room. When I open my eyes she is still there waiting for me, watching me. She smiles.

'I brought you something,' she says, and she passes me a white envelope on which she's written *For Connie*. I try to sit up; I reach out with my rejuvenated hand and slowly take the envelope from her. I study the familiar handwriting. I love her handwriting; it is practical, masculine. I carefully open the envelope and pull out several photographs.

She helps me. The first one is a shot of Josh and Evie. It takes my breath away. They look so bright and young, so happy, so in love; Evie is leaning against Josh's chest, he has his arm around her. I run my finger over his changing face – his nose is bigger, his jaw more pronounced.

I look at it for so long that Ness says, 'There are more.' And she helps me go to the next one. It's Annie, smiling at the camera. Her two front teeth have fallen out and she has a huge gap that she is clearly proud of. I am overwhelmed; my eyes begin to sting. The next photo is of Polly and Annie, all skinny and knobbly-kneed doing hula hoops in the garden. I feel my body begin to fill up, a tidal wave of emotion spreading through me. I look up at Ness.

'They're fine,' she says.

I nod.

'Everyone's fine,' she says. 'We're going to get you out of here, Con.'

And as I begin to cry I feel alive again. And Ness leans forwards and rests her forehead against my own and holds me. I don't deserve this. When I finish crying, she takes the photographs from my hands and goes through them all, showing them to me, reinforcing her words: the children are fine. *The children are fine.* And I begin to think maybe, *just maybe*, I am going to get out of here.

4 April

Dearest Connie,

I am sorry that it has been so long since you have heard from me. Please forgive me. I also offer my profuse apologies for my behaviour and for letting you down. It was deeply unprofessional of me. I hope my absence was explained to you by Dr Johnson. The truth of it is – and I know what a stickler you are for the truth – that several complaints had been made about me (there was also CCTV footage) and I was taken off your case abruptly by my boss and was denied contact with you. It is not how I wanted to end things.

I want you to know that I have been deeply impressed by you, not just in regards to the work we did but as regards the work you do on yourself as a human being. You and your indomitable spirit have been an inspiration to me.

I was delighted to be informed, as no doubt you have been by now, that the Domestic Court has given you visitation rights twice a month. This is really very good news and I am sure your relationship with your children will thrive and that your life will take a strong turn for the better. Be sure that you keep taking the medication, which at last seems to be sorted. I am actually writing an article for the BMI regarding the misuse of benzodiazepines. Your story has deeply concerned me.

My news is that I am taking a year's sabbatical. Si Hubby and I have decided to make a change in our lives. We are selling the house, putting things to rest and finally moving on. We have found a place in Sussex away from the dirt and grime of city life. I am looking forward to a new start, although I shall always return to Enfield to visit Abigail's grave.

I wish you only the best with your journey. Look after yourself, dear Constance. It has been a blessing getting to know you. And I want to thank you for your boldness, your wit and your incisiveness, and for making me see the world a little differently.

Yours,
Emma Robinson

Hey, Dr R. It was so good to get your letter. How I love snail mail; it feels so fantastically old-fashioned. I keep it by my bed and read it often. I'm sorry I've been so slow in responding (it seems that somehow spring has arrived) but until very recently, writing has felt like an impossibility and besides, I really didn't have an awful lot to say.

It was the Squeak who ratted on you. What an unforgiveable sweat patch of a woman she is. And yet I have grown so accustomed to her that she is now just part of my life – like haemorrhoids (my body has begun to protest about all this lying down and rubbish food). I suspect that she is also the person leaking things to the press. I do hope she doesn't mention you but I wouldn't put anything past her. Oh, and the other ratter was Dr Twat, I've no idea what his real name is – Johnson, perhaps, as you say. I don't think he has ever said two words to me but he swoops about the place brandishing his sword of mediocrity.

By the way, I hope you don't mind but I wrote to your idiot boss, Tom Warner, to complain about the way you were treated. I've written a glowing report, signed off 'The Yummy Monster' (Jesus, who comes up with this shit?).

I have two things to tell you; three, actually. Firstly, thank you for your kind words. I was very touched and surprised by them. I wanted to thank *you* for everything. Without you I wouldn't be where I am now – on the mend. You have made me radically change my views about your profession. Although I'm not too impressed with your replacement; not only does she have arrest-worthy sartorial taste but she suffers from a particularly deadly variety of halitosis. I'd say absolutely anything at all to get her out of the room, which seems to be a technique that works a treat for us both.

I got the wonderful visitation news from the social worker! I am over the moon! It's actually once a month initially and as long as I continue to take my medication and accept my condition – bipolar psycho fuckwit – it will increase to twice a month.

The second thing is that something extraordinary happened yesterday. I know you'll be interested – you lot are, in essence, just nosy parkers. Now that the weather seems to have picked up a bit – there are apple trees at the back of the garden, by the way, and the blossom has come out; they are truly lovely – I spend as much time as I can outside. Oh! And our leaf is still clinging on! I check on it daily; can you believe such perseverance? Anyway, I was humouring Mental Sita on the lawn – she wanted to play doggies (actually she wanted to play *dogging* but I drew the line, although God knows I miss the human touch) – when the Squeak told me I had visitors. Plural: *visitors*. I beckoned to her grandly that she may bring 'said visitors' to the garden – I've become even more dismissive of her now that I know what a genuine

scumbag she is. I was expecting it to be Karl and my
father (who, incidentally, told me last visit that an excep-
tionally kind psychiatrist had visited him but he couldn't
remember anything about her – was that you?). Wrong
again. Guess who?

Yes, Dr R, my children came to see me! Josh and Annie
were standing there by the back door staring at me with
a social worker hovering nearby. I felt this extraordinary
love rise up within me; the umbilical cord of mother-
hood is never really cut. I know that you know that. My
eyes filled with tears. They looked so much bigger than I
remembered and a little apprehensive, which was not
surprising.

It was not the impression I would have ideally wanted
to give – I had Mental Sita on the leash, she was cocking
her leg against the litter bin, and I was so surprised to
see them standing there that I let go and she bounded
across the lawn towards them. Mental Sita can be disquieting at the best of times but now she was literally
barking.

'Tell her to get down!' I cried. 'She's pretending to be
a dog!'

The children just stared at her and then back at me. (I
don't look so freaky any more; my hair has grown back
thick and strong. I've got a slight tan from the recent sunshine. I look OK. But the fact of the matter was I had a
huge Indian woman on all fours on a leash.)

Annie, as ever, was game. 'Down! Bad dog!' she said,
and Mental Sita obediently sat on her haunches and
panted, ready to play. I caught up with her, picked up the
leash and tied Mental Sita to a tree.

In a way, it was quite a good ice-breaker. 'Hello, guys,' I said. And we stood there for a moment staring at each other. I held out my arms.

Even a mental mother is better than no mother at all, wouldn't you say, Dr R? We stood there hugging for a little while under the keen eye of the social worker, and then I took them down the lawn towards the brook, which turns out to be more of a puddle with an exit. (Don't think we ever made it that far?) These days I have no pills to pop, I have to make do with twiddling a leaf in my fingers.

However, in essence we were all the same as ever. Annie and I sat down in the sunshine and took our shoes off and put our feet in the water and started making daisy chains. Josh squatted underneath one of the apple trees nearby. And the social worker was now sitting on the bench not too far away, looking as awkward as we were all feeling.

Annie started asking me lots of questions about the place and I pointed out various rooms in the building. She asked if she could come and stay with me sometime and whether we could watch people dying in the electric chair. I don't know what she's been watching but I said I didn't think we had one.

'Don't have any more breaking downs, Mummy,' she said, apropos of nothing.

'No, I won't,' I said. 'I just want to say how sorry I am for everything I've put you through, and I want you to know that I love you more than anything in the world and I never meant to harm you.' I looked up at Josh; he was harder to read.

'Well, you mustn't do it again,' Annie said. But her attention was on Mental Sita; she kept looking back towards the tree, where Mental Sita was busy licking imaginary scrotums.

'I won't. I promise. And I'm going to be allowed to see you twice a month.'

'Will you have to live here?'

'For a while.'

'Do you think she wants to play sticks? The dog lady?' Annie asked.

'Go and ask her.'

Annie leapt up. I watched her little athletic frame run back up towards Mental Sita, the social worker momentarily dithering about who was the greater danger here.

'How are you, Josh?' I said.

He shrugged. 'Well, it's all a bit weird, isn't it?'

I nodded. And we both smiled.

I gestured for him to come and sit beside me. I put my arm around him and he leant against me a fraction. How I've missed him and our little chats; we had a special bond, he and I. I know you're not meant to say this but sometimes it felt like we were friends or siblings, not parent and child.

'I'm so sorry for the mess, for not being there, Joshy. It's not been fair on you two.'

'Are you better?' he asked, scratching his calf. I could see that his legs were hairier and I suddenly felt in awe of myself: it's quite a feat being a mother of a man.

'Yes. And I'm going to be well again,' I said, smiling at him, determined for it to be true. 'How's Evie?'

'They're outside in the car.'

'Oh,' I said, presuming he meant with Karl or Ness or both. I wondered how he felt about them but I didn't ask. It was strange how differently *I* felt about it all now; it seemed so unimportant, so trivial in the greater scheme of things. In fact, if I felt anything I felt grateful to her for being there when I hadn't been able to be.

'How's school?' I asked.

He shrugged. 'School's school.'

'I'm so sorry, my love.'

He shrugged again. He was distant.

'You have every right to hate me,' I said.

'It's nothing to do with you,' he said, sounding just slightly irritated with me. God, of course not *everything* was about me; this is the trouble with mental illness – we become so introverted, spinning in our own vortices. I had been so busy gazing at my own navel and the reality is: life just goes on, doesn't it? I knew better than to press him so said nothing. I glanced back at Annie, who was throwing Mental Sita a stick.

Josh picked up a blade of grass and stretched it between his thumbs – carefully, intently. Then he turned and looked at me. 'Mum, Evie's missed a period,' he said.

I held his gaze but my eyes widened; I really hadn't seen that coming at all. He carried on, 'The Boots early test thing said she wasn't pregnant but that was six days ago and she's convinced she is.'

Oh. My. God. 'She's probably fine,' I said. 'Does Ness know?'

He shook his head. Six days. She should take another test right now. I put my hand on his back and soothed him like I used to do when he was little. 'Don't worry, darling. Nothing is insurmountable . . .'

He nodded and went back to his blade of grass. 'Just to let you know . . . the thing is: if she *is* . . . we want to keep it.'

I stared at him. I was incredulous. When he looked at me I saw a steadfastness in his expression that was new to me; I saw a young man. A flurry of pink petals blew off the apple tree behind him, landing on us like confetti.

I suppose I was meant to say, *Don't be mad, you've got your whole life ahead of you: exams, university, career, plenty more fish in the sea* . . . But I didn't. I didn't feel that way; I was shocked, yes, but the truth was I felt *glad* for them in that moment. I felt emboldened by them.

I picked a petal off my lap and gently rubbed its smoothness against my upper lip. I thought of all the relationships that would be changed by a baby aside from his and hers – Ness and I would be for ever entwined, Karl and I, Karl and Ness, Ness and Leah, Leah and Karl – and my head began to spin. I reached out and took his hand in mine and lifted it to my lips. 'Everything will be all right, whatever you decide, Josh. You hear me?'

He smiled and put his arms around me and pulled me close. I rested my head against him and felt more peace right then than I can remember. Both of us were quiet, listening intently to the tinkle of the brook, interrupted sporadically by Annie's husky voice confidently bossing around Mental Sita: 'Fetch! Good dog!'

I suppose I'm not the same person as I was before, Dr R. I suppose middle-class sixteen-year-olds are not meant to keep babies in our society, are they? It's against our principles of focused achievement. Then again, middle-class women aren't meant to have breakdowns and become family annihilators, are they? Oh no, we leave such nastinesses to the *others*, to the uneducated, to the neglected, so we can get on with listening to *The Archers* and running the show; let the disenfranchised, the dispossessed conceive young! The disappointment for them is so much less when the show implodes because their lives were shitty to begin with. And what, after all, Dr R, is this show we are so eager to get up and running?

Another breath of wind rained pink petals down on us. For the first time I thought seriously about getting out of here, of finding somewhere to live, of getting better, of being a parent again, a grandparent if need be, of what else was waiting for me, getting myself back to work. A *future*.

'Hurry up and get the hell out of here, will you?' he said, as ever in tune with me. 'Ness told me to tell you that you can stay in her parents' cottage when you get out . . . down in Suffolk. They said it was fine.'

I was surprised by this. I thought about it. She hadn't mentioned this to me.

What do you think Ness wants from me, Dr R?

I think I know what it is. She wants what you want, Dr R. What *I* want. She wants *forgiveness*. And I thought of you and the way you could forgive me my actions, but you couldn't forgive your own. And the way I can forgive her but I can't forgive myself. And the way she can forgive me but can't forgive herself.

How *do* we forgive ourselves? Josh might say, *Guilt? What's the point of it – it's just you telling me you're a nice person*. But I disagree. What are we without a conscience? We're just animals, survivalists: eating, plundering and fucking. You were right to make me remember, to take me through it, to feel the pain of my actions, to feel the guilt. Because surely guilt means we are self-reflective and therefore able to change. Anyway, I'm not sure it's about self-forgiveness at all; I think it's more about self-acceptance. And I'm not there yet, that's for sure.

But maybe that's just me telling you I'm a nice person.

Acknowledgements

I would like to thank Matthew Hamilton for his laid back but relentless encouragement, his meticulous editing and his Captain-esque capacity to keep calm and carry on – all in all, for just being such a great agent. I must also thank Lesley Thorne for her constant support, her professionalism and her naughtiness. I am so lucky to have two such honest and fun agents. Thank you to all the foreign publishers who showed such enthusiasm so early in the writing, giving me much confidence. And, of course, to Darcy Nicholson, for picking up the baton here – I am very grateful.

I want to thank Mel Hudson from the bottom of my heart for her generosity in sharing information, specifically about the use of benzodiazepines – and for generally being an inspiration.

I cannot underestimate the value of my wonderful book-club for their early reading and unerring frankness, kindness and love: Nita Instrall, Becky Harris, Justine Vaughan, Susannah Doyle and Lori Shaul. They are my props.

On a familial note, thanks must go to my fabulous boys: Sydney and Noah for their love and support, my sister and brother, Natalie and Daniel, for their constant encouragement with this work and all things. It is lovely to know that my back is watched!